Windslash

The Last Elemental

By

Chris Bennett

Grosvenor House
Publishing Limited

This book is published by
Grosvenor House Publishing Ltd
Link House
140 The Broadway, Tolworth, Surrey, KT6 7HT.
www.grosvenorhousepublishing.co.uk

A CIP record for this book
is available from the British Library

Paperback ISBN 978-1-83615-280-4
Hardback ISBN 978-1-83615-281-1
eBook ISBN 978-1-83615-282-8

Preface, Acknowledgements, and Introduction

Since I was kid, I've been into Trading Card Games, and Mythology from around the world. It was many years ago whilst playing a Trading Card Game that I came up with the idea for this novel, and with Atlantis being my favourite myth I decided to use it as the setting for the story. Unfortunately, when I first started writing it, the laptop, I was using was damaged, and I was only able to salvage so much of it, which put me off writing it, and it got put aside for many years until last year when I decided to finish it.

I'd like to thank my friends who I used to play against in the Trading Card Game that gave me the initial inspiration for this story. I'd like to thank who convinced me to finish the book. I'd like to thank those who took the time to beta read the manuscript. I'd like to thank my hometown, who gave me inspiration for this story, and more to come.

I've started by creating a world that exists in Greek Mythology, but in a future story I'd like to bring the remainders of this world into the present day. I hope you find yourself captivated by this world, and as gripped as anyone else who has read it, and enjoy the journey within it as much as I've enjoyed creating it.

Chapter One
Legend of the Elementals

Long ago, when Atlantis thrived above the seas, the earth was calm, volcanoes lay dormant, and the winds were mere gentle breezes. Four great warriors lived during this time, each possessing the ability to control one of the four Elements: Water, Earth, Fire, and Wind. They resided on the legendary island filled with lush forests, surrounded by crystal-clear waters that made the inhabitants believe the ocean was bottomless. Peace reigned supreme until a power-hungry Archmage, convinced he was the true ruler of Atlantis, brought this era to an end.

For years, the Archmage served alongside the Atlantean King, using his Dark Magic to manipulate and poison the King's mind. His ultimate goal was to overthrow the King and take control of Atlantis. However, his treachery was uncovered by a young member of the Royal Guard. This brave guard severed the Archmage's staff with his sword, knocking it from his hand and neutralising the spell he had cast over the King. With his plan exposed, the Archmage was forced to flee the Royal City. Before his departure, he vowed that he would one day seek his revenge.

The Archmage went into hiding, gathering followers to seek revenge against the Atlantean Kingdom. Power-hungry as he was, the Archmage and his followers travelled through Atlantis for years; using the Dark Magic he taught them, they hunted down and exterminated those they deemed inferior. Their ultimate goal of overthrowing the Atlantean Kingdom led them to revive a great evil that had long been thought destroyed by Atlantis' ancestors: Leviathan. A sea serpent of darkness and malevolence that left chaos in its wake. Wherever it encountered peace, it left destruction. Leviathan brought nothing but devastation and misery to the legendary island, resulting in the loss of a significant portion of Atlantis' population.

All hope seemed lost for Atlantis until a miracle occurred. It wasn't until four exceptionally skilled warriors, each hailing from a different corner of Atlantis, stepped forward that the Atlanteans even realised they had a chance. Each warrior possessed the ability to control one of the four elements. Armed with their magical powers, they took it upon themselves to combat Leviathan in hopes of defeating the Sea Serpent.

Using their Element Magic, the four warriors fought back against the Sea Serpent. Despite Leviathan's might, it was unable to harm them. However, the warriors soon realised that, individually, their Element Magic was not enough to bring down the Sea Serpent, which was preparing to strike back with one final attack.

In a desperate last effort, the four warriors combined their powers into a single, powerful spell, merging the four elements into one formidable attack.

As the Sea Serpent launched its attack, the four warriors executed a coordinated counterattack, halting the creature in its tracks and temporarily stunning it. In that crucial moment, the Atlantean King seized a powerful weapon that had been locked away in the Royal Vault for generations—the Sword of Arcana. He charged forward, and the Sea Serpent barely had time to react before the sword struck it down.

What should have been the end turned out to be only the beginning; Leviathan survived. To prevent Leviathan from rising again and bringing more pain to Atlantis, the Atlantean King cast a powerful spell to seal Leviathan's power within four magical artefacts known as the Dragon Crests. These four Crests were infused with powerful Magic to help keep Leviathan's power contained, and they were entrusted to the four warriors for protection. The Dragon's Eye Crest was given to the Warrior of Wind, the Dragon's Fang Crest to the Warrior of Water, the Dragon's Claw Crest to the Warrior of Fire, and the Dragon's Horn Crest to the Warrior of Earth.

Leviathan was sealed away inside a Magic Urn for eternity, and the four warriors were tasked with guarding the Dragon Crests. Atlantis survived, and the four warriors were looked upon as heroes. Each warrior wore their corresponding Crest around their neck as a symbol of Leviathan's defeat. However, what initially seemed like a small price for victory, the truth was that they had no choice. It was the only way to ensure that the Archmage and his followers could not get their hands on the Dragon Crests.

The spell placed upon the Dragon Crests by the Atlantean King ensured that Leviathan's power could not be unleashed if the Crest was taken by force or stolen. Its power could only be released if the Crest was willingly handed over by its guardian or if the guardian was killed. However, the King vowed to relieve the four warriors of the Dragon Crests once the Archmage had been brought to justice. The four of them knew better but were proud to serve their kingdom.

As a final precaution ordered by the Atlantean King, the Magic Urn containing Leviathan was sealed in a deep area of the Royal Vault. Only a member of the Royal Family could unlock the Magic Seal. Additionally, the King ordered the destruction of the Sword of Arcana and any scrolls detailing how to forge the weapon. This measure ensured that such a powerful weapon would not fall into the wrong hands. The four warriors went on to serve as the protectors of Atlantis and the Atlantean Kingdom, keeping the lands safe and unharmed.

Due to their magical abilities, the people of Atlantis referred to the four warriors as the Element Warriors, while others called them the Elemental Knights. Ultimately, they became known collectively as The Elementals. While residing in Atlantis, The Elementals encountered others who, like them, possessed the power to control an element. Taking it upon themselves to protect the lands, The Elementals decided to train these young warriors.

The students learned how to harness and control their magical abilities, as well as how to synchronise their Magic with the weapons they wielded. Once trained to the point where they could defend themselves and others in battle, the students earned the title of an Elemental.

Wind Elementals wield twin short swords as their primary weapons. They are trained in both swordsmanship and the application of their Wind Magic in combat. With their magical abilities, Wind Elementals can create powerful gusts of wind, glide through the air using currents, and extract air from an area to generate tornadoes and blasts of wind as fierce as a storm. Their combat style is characterised by speed and devastation, as they can infuse their swords with Wind Magic, releasing it as a blade of energy capable of cutting through anything.

Wind Elementals reside in Eastern Atlantis, inhabited by the island's master weaponsmiths. Many of the most powerful weapons forged on the island come from Eastern Atlantis, including some that are used by the Royal Family themselves.

Water Elementals wield trident staves as their primary weapons. Their battle tactics are heavily reliant on water, thanks to their exceptional swimming skills. The Water Magic they possess enables them to breathe underwater and manipulate water at will. They can freeze water or turn it into mist for cover while engaging in battles on the surface. Additionally, these Elementals can use their powers to heal injuries and purify water.

Water Elementals reside in Western Atlantis, a region inhabited by magical practitioners known as Seers. Seers have the unique ability to foresee the future. While some individuals are naturally gifted with this ability, others cultivate it by drinking from an Enchanted Chalice. However, it is important to note that what the Seers perceive in their visions is not necessarily a definite future. The most crucial lesson for Seers practising foresight is to differentiate between what they see in their visions—what can happen—and what will actually happen.

Earth Elementals were formidable hand-to-hand fighters. Their Earth Magic made their skin as hard as stone, providing them with resistance to all forms of Element Magic, except for Water Magic. This Magic also granted them immense strength. In combat, Earth Elementals could manipulate sand, soil, and stone against their opponents. They had the ability to create earthquakes and fissures and even transform the ground beneath them into quicksand at will.

Earth Elementals resided in Southern Atlantis, where the inhabitants were skilled armorsmiths. They forged armour strong enough to withstand magical attacks. Some of this armour was as simple as an Enchanted Medallion.

Fire Elementals wielded broadswords in battle and were also skilled archers. With their Fire Magic, they could manipulate and create fire at will. They had the ability to ignite the blades of their swords, and when they were running low on arrows, they could create fire arrows using their Magic.

Fire Elementals resided in Northern Atlantis, a region known for its practice of various forms of Magic, including Magic Staves, Spell Books, Magic Items, Potions, and Wands. While Dark Magic was generally frowned upon, the Mages recognised the importance of studying it in order to understand the nature of it and combat its dangers.

Central Atlantis was the home of the Royal Family. It was part of a vast empire known for its magical qualities, which granted great power and extended the lives of its inhabitants. The Elementals collaborated with the Mages of North Atlantis, who supported them in combat by crafting magical items for battle. Additionally, the Mages were also skilled scientists, infusing Magic into the weapons produced in Eastern Atlantis and the armour made in Southern Atlantis. They also developed various utilities for the civilian population.

The magical items created by the Mages for The Elementals and those they trained for battle included several essential tools. These items consisted of Magic Dust, which could inflict various ailments on enemies. The most common type of dust induced sleep, allowing battles to end before they even began.

They also developed Magic Potions to treat injuries, especially in situations where a Water Elemental was either unavailable or when the injuries were too severe.

Additionally, there were Magic Gems that produced a small light to signal the user's location or emitted a blinding flash for either a pre-emptive strike or a quick escape.

Finally, they developed an item known as a Teleport Rune that enabled the user, along with several others, to magically teleport from one area to another, particularly when the destination was far from their current location, and reinforcements were needed.

By studying the Elementals and their student's abilities, the Mages of North Atlantis were able to create a powerful item known as the Element Stone. These stones were crafted from magical minerals found throughout the four corners of the Atlantean Empire and were forged in four distinct colours: Blue, Gold, Red, and Green. Element Stones bestowed unique abilities upon their users and enhanced their Element Magic. Obtaining an Element Stone represented the final trial for an Element Student before being promoted to an Elemental. Once a student was promoted, the Element Stone was worn as either a necklace or a bracelet.

These powerful substances were challenging to handle, requiring intensive training for their use. While an Element Stone could elevate a user's magical abilities to new heights, it also had the potential to backfire, resulting in dangerous and disastrous consequences. This could put not only the user at risk but also others around them, affecting them physically, mentally, or both. Consequently, although their training as students was complete, their journey as Elementals was only just beginning.

The effects of an Element Stone are temporary; once its powers are neutralised, it turns into a clear stone and becomes useless until its Magic recharges over time and it regains its colour.

Blue Element Stones were utilised by Water Elementals. A Blue Element Stone granted the Water Elemental, wearing it, the ability to walk on water, enabling them to engage in combat both above and below the surface. With advanced-level training, a Blue Element Stone could enhance a Water Elemental's Magic to the point where they could shapeshift into the bodies of water they were in contact with. This capability made Water Elementals excellent spies and provided them with significant opportunities for pre-emptive strikes, as they could still hear their surroundings while transformed into water. Additionally, they could co-exist within larger bodies of water.

With master-level training, a Blue Element Stone enhances a Water Elemental's Magic to a point where the user can shapeshift into water without needing to be in contact with it, all while maintaining their physical form. This ability also increases both offensive and defensive capabilities but comes with significant risks. If the user's body mass becomes dispersed while using this magical ability, only the Element Stone will remain. The stone will draw back the dispersed body mass, allowing the user to reform their body. However, if the Element Stone runs out of Magic or is destroyed before the user's body has fully reformed, it would cost the user their life.

Gold Element Stones were utilised by Earth Elementals. A Gold Element Stone enabled an Earth Elemental to become one with the earth itself, allowing them to transform into sand, soil, or even stone. With advanced-level training, a Gold Element Stone could significantly enhance an Earth Elemental's magic, granting them the ability to leave their opponents Earthbound by binding them to a source of earth. However, this power came at a cost: restraining their opponents required the users' concentration, leaving them vulnerable and unable to defend themselves.

With master-level training, a Gold Element Stone can enhance an Earth Elemental's Magic to a point where the user can render their opponents Earthbound without needing to concentrate on them. This allows the user to defend themselves and continue fighting. However, the power of the Element Stone depletes faster with each opponent made Earthbound. Once the Element Stone exhausts its Magic or the user's concentration wavers, any enemies that were made Earthbound will be released.

Red Element Stones were used by Fire Elementals. A Fire Elemental wearing a Red Element Stone became immune to fire. With advanced-level training, a Red Element Stone enhanced a Fire Elemental's Magic, allowing the user to increase their power when near multiple Red Element Stones. With master-level training, a Red Element Stone could elevate a Fire Elemental's Magic to the point where they could gain strength from being close to multiple Element Stones, regardless of their colour.

As their Magic grew stronger, Fire Elementals could not only transform their weapons into fire but could also turn themselves into fire. However, this high level of Magic is very dangerous. If the Element Stone runs out of Magic, the user loses their immunity to fire, making them vulnerable to their own flames. This could result in severe burns, which may be potentially life-threatening.

Green Element Stones were utilised by Wind Elementals. However, these stones could not allow their users to transform into wind itself due to its inherent instability. If a Wind Elemental attempted to become wind, their body would not be able to reform, leading to their demise. Instead, a Green Element Stone granted the Wind Elemental, wearing it, access to a form of Magic that enhanced their stamina in battle.

With advanced-level training, a Green Element Stone could elevate a Wind Elemental's Magic to the point where they became stronger even when their stamina was low. This meant that, despite feeling fatigued, they could still effectively fight back. Upon reaching master-level training, the Magic provided by a Green Element Stone enabled Wind Elementals to harness the power of thunder by manipulating electrical currents in the air. This ability allowed them to charge their weapons with thunder and generate strikes to attack their enemies.

This Magic could be so potent that it seemed as though the users were summoning thunder from the heavens to strike down upon their foes, potentially taking out most, if not all, of them, depending on the strength of the opponents they faced. However, utilising this powerful Magic would deplete the Element Stone's energy more quickly, resulting in the loss of the stamina boost once the stone's Magic was exhausted.

Despite years of searching, the Archmage was nowhere to be found, and his followers, known as the Acolytes, continued to torment the Atlantean Empire. An attack on Northern Atlantis brought the Acolytes before a group of Elementals, who fought back to prevent them from causing harm. However, one of the Acolytes destroyed several phials of Magic Dust, creating problems for both sides. Taking advantage of the chaos, this Acolyte stole a crucial item and presented it to the Archmage, who had been hiding in disguise among the Acolytes or his victims.

The item he presented was a Teleport Rune, which the Archmage needed to return to the Royal City. Gathering his strongest Acolytes, the Archmage used the Teleport Rune to infiltrate the Royal City, where they ambushed the Royal Guard. Their use of Dark Magic resulted in several casualties during the assault.

Using the cover of his magical disguises, the Archmage made his way to the throne room inside the Royal Court while his Acolytes engaged the Royal Guard and several Elementals. He planned to exact his long-promised revenge on the Atlantean King.

Upon entering the throne room, the Archmage was confronted by several members of the Royal Guard and Elementals, all of whom he subdued with his Dark Magic. The final obstacle in his path was the King's personal bodyguard, who happened to be the same young guard that had exposed the Archmage all those years ago.

Harbouring a grudge against the young warrior for thwarting his plans, the Archmage knocked him aside with his Dark Magic and began to torture him while simultaneously holding the King in place to deal with him later.

Despite the Archmage's immense power, the young warrior managed to resist his Magic, thanks to the armour he wore, which had been forged in Southern Atlantis. After knocking the King's bodyguard aside, the Archmage intended to take his revenge on the King. However, just then, a group of Elementals materialised in the throne room through a Teleport Rune. These Elementals were the same ones attacked by the Archmage's Acolytes in Northern Atlantis.

The Archmage used his Dark Magic to strike at the Elementals, and the King's bodyguard seized the opportunity and captured the Archmage. Using one of the Archmage's own creations—a pair of enchanted shackles designed for the Royal Guard—he was able to restrain him. These shackles were specifically made to capture and restrain magic users by neutralising their abilities, rendering the Archmage completely powerless.

The Archmage originally created the shackles to easily eliminate anyone who practised Magic and was deemed a threat to him. At the time, he still had influence over the Atlantean King, but due to his arrogance, he never considered that the shackles would one day be used against him. With the Archmage restrained and his Acolytes defeated, the King sentenced them all to imprisonment for the rest of their lives. They were confined to a secure prison built by Southern Atlantis, where their Magic would be rendered useless.

On their way to imprisonment, the Archmage caught sight of an Enchanted Chalice. While the guards were distracted by opening the door to the prison, the Archmage seized the opportunity. He grabbed it and took a drink but suddenly collapsed to the floor, overwhelmed by a vision triggered by the chalice.

A smile spread across the Archmage's face as he began to laugh menacingly. He proclaimed to those around him that this was not the end and that one day, Leviathan would rise again. Unfortunately, the strain on his body led to a fatal heart attack. Despite his life coming to an end, he lay there with a smile on his face.

Despite the Archmage's death, the Elementals refused to relinquish the Dragon Crests as long as there was anyone capable of restoring Leviathan and fulfilling the Archmage's prophecy. Vowing upon their honour and lives, the Elementals pledged to protect the Atlantean Empire and all its inhabitants. They committed themselves to safeguarding everyone from those who practised the Dark Arts, which were believed to have been eradicated when the Archmage died.

The first four Elementals who initially appeared could not train their students indefinitely. Eventually, they chose a single student as their heir and successor, tasked with becoming the next guardian of their Dragon Crest. This successor would continue training new students to become Elementals and help defend Atlantis after the predecessor passed on. When the time came for the Elementals to find an heir and successor, their Dragon Crest would begin to glow when a worthy candidate was found, signalling that this individual would be the one to take on the responsibility of guarding the Dragon Crest and training Atlantis' forces.

Generation after generation, four new Elementals were chosen to guard the Dragon Crests. Eventually, the Dragon's Fang Crest passed into the Royal Family with each new King of Atlantis, strengthening the bond between Central Atlantis and Western Atlantis. Over time, the Archmage's prophecy began to fade into legend; some believed it to be the mere ramblings of an old man on his deathbed. The Seers, who never witnessed the prophecy in their visions, dismissed it as something that could happen rather than something that would happen. However, the Elementals were unwilling to take any risks until they were certain that Leviathan could not be revived.

However, something was approaching that would cause the city of Atlantis to be lost to the seas forever...

"Now, my students," said a man dressed in an emerald green robe, "we will be practising our defensive skills today. Master Byrne has kindly brought his students, who will practice their offensive skills to provide balance." The man in the emerald green robe wore the Dragon's Eye Crest around his neck, while Master Byrne, in his crimson red hooded robe, displayed the Dragon's Claw Crest. The Wind Students were dressed in seafoam green garments, and the Fire Students wore tiger orange clothing.

"Thank you, Master Phaedo," said Master Byrne as he stepped forward, pulling down the hood of his robe. "Now!" he exclaimed in a strict tone. "Your training today is simple: each of my students will pair up with one of Master Phaedo's students. My students will attack with their Fire Magic, and Master Phaedo's students will defend with their Wind

Magic. Neither I nor Master Phaedo want to see any soft shit here today. One student will attack while the other defends; it's not going to be one student attacking while the other falls down. Now, I don't know what the fuck is going on around here, but if any of you students hope to become Wind Elementals or Fire Elementals anytime soon, you need to start pulling your shit together, especially you Wind Students. Me and the other masters have already found our successors to guard the Dragon Crests, so it's about time a successor was found to guard the Dragon's Eye Crest. Now, are you ready?!"

The students replied in a loud and frightened tone, "Yes, Master Byrne!"

After getting his message across, Master Byrne shouted, "Pair up and begin!" All the students paired up and scattered around the training arena except for one young boy. Master Phaedo and Master Byrne began to walk around the arena.

"I don't understand, Phaedo," said Master Byrne. "Why do you have to be so soft with your students and not stricter?"

Master Phaedo replied, "Because, Byrne, despite the emotions involved, Wind Magic requires a calm mind, which is what makes it difficult to master. One needs to maintain a calm mind in any given situation when using Wind Magic, unlike your fire students who are... shall we say, hotheads."

Master Byrne shook his head. "Hehehe," he chuckled. "Phaedo, you're so full of shit. I remember when you were a Wind Student; you were creating twisters by the time you were a teenager."

Master Phaedo sighed deeply. "I know," he replied. "But it wasn't until I achieved a calm mind that those twisters became tornadoes. Even my master was strict with me about that."

Master Byrne then stopped and turned toward his friend. "Exactly," he said, pointing across the training arena. "See young Hermocrates over there?" He gestured to a young girl in scarlet red robes, one of the fire students. "The Dragon's Claw Crest chose her as my successor two years ago, and she wouldn't be where she is today if I had been calm and soft with her. She's close to gaining her Element Stone."

Master Phaedo interrupted, "Alright, alright. You've made your point. However, if I boost the strictness, you'll need to cut down on the bragging."

Master Byrne placed a hand on Master Phaedo's shoulder, chuckling as he patted his friend. "Good man, Phaedo... good man." The two friends turned their attention back to their students. Unbeknownst to them, a young boy sat just a few meters away without a training partner. Meanwhile, the Dragon's Eye Crest around Master Phaedo's neck was slightly glowing.

Chapter Two
Hidden Power

Master Phaedo and Master Byrne continued to observe their students as they trained. Master Byrne was not impressed with what he saw. "Do you see what I mean, Phaedo?" he said in a disappointed tone, shaking his head from side to side. "If your students don't step up their game, all we're going to get are these shitty results. Despite using their Wind Magic to defend themselves, my students are still managing to knock them back."

Master Phaedo explained, "It's because their minds are not calm." Master Byrne looked at his friend with confusion. "They're scared of the Fire Magic being used by your students, which is preventing them from calming their minds." Unable to believe what he was hearing, Master Byrne let out a frustrated "Tch." Just then, he turned his head and noticed a young wind student who hadn't found a partner to train with.

"Hey!" Master Byrne shouted, startling the boy and making him jump to his feet. "Yes, Master Byrne," the young boy replied in a frightened tone. "What's your name, and why aren't you participating in this training exercise?" Master Byrne asked angrily. The young boy stood there trembling. "Master Byrne, my name is Timaeus," he responded. "I didn't have anyone to partner with, Master."

With a disappointed look on his face, Master Byrne raised his arm and pointed toward the other students. "Well, why didn't you work alongside one of your fellow students and take turns in the training exercise?" he inquired. Still trembling, Timaeus replied, "Because... the thought never occurred to me, Master Byrne."

Master Phaedo spoke up in Timaeus' defence. "Surely it was just a simple mistake, Byrne," he said.

Master Byrne turned to Master Phaedo with a stern expression. "Fucking slacking if you ask me, Phaedo. It seems to me that young Timaeus needs to learn the importance of keeping up with his training," he said firmly. He grabbed Timaeus by the arm and pulled him toward the other students.

"ATTENTION!" Master Byrne shouted, and the entire training arena fell silent. "It appears that Master Phaedo and I have encountered a little shit who thinks it's acceptable to slack off and neglect his training. As punishment, young Timaeus here will face my successor in combat."

Byrne's words sent chills down the spines of the other students; even Hermocrates looked surprised. Timaeus, however, was utterly petrified.

"Please, Byrne, I must object to this," Master Phaedo said, his voice filled with concern.

"Do not make Timaeus face Hermocrates; she has much more experience than he does, and we both know he's no match for her." Master Byrne turned to Master Phaedo and said, "Don't worry, Phaedo. Given that every other student here has been training hard, it wouldn't be fair to have Timaeus face any of them. He's at full strength due to his slacking, which would give him an unfair advantage. This sparring session is just to help Timaeus catch up. If he can outlast Hermocrates, I'll overlook his slacking. However, if he doesn't, he will face the consequences of being singed by Hermocrates."

Master Phaedo then asked, "Is that really necessary, Byrne?" In a firm tone, Master Byrne replied, "It's better than being singed by me. Plus, this is to ensure that slacking doesn't happen again. Now, Timaeus and Hermocrates, make your way to the centre of the training arena. The rest of you, go to the edges of the arena."

With an embarrassed expression on his face, Timaeus entered the arena, followed by Hermocrates, who maintained an emotionless demeanour. Once they reached the centre of the training arena, Timaeus spoke softly, "Hi, my name's Timaeus."

Hermocrates turned to him, her gaze intense. "Hi, my name's Hermocrates, but my friends call me Hermos," she replied. Timaeus extended his hand for a friendly handshake. "Pleased to meet you, Hermos," he said.

However, Hermos drew her sword and curtly responded, "I said, my friends." Timaeus felt hurt by her words.

"Timaeus!" Master Byrne shouted. "Draw your weapons. This isn't for making friends; this is punishment."

Timaeus quickly reached for his swords. "Yes, Master Byrne," he replied.

Master Byrne raised his hand. "Now!" he shouted. "If Timaeus can last five minutes against Hermocrates, he will be excused from slacking. However, if he is unable to last the full five minutes, he will be singed by Hermocrates for every minute he fails to endure." With that, Master Byrne lowered his hand and shouted, "BEGIN!"

Hermos made the first move, raising her sword and swinging it downward toward Timaeus. He raised both of his swords to defend himself, but when he tried to counterattack with his second sword, his lack of confidence held him back. This allowed Hermos to defend herself and knock Timaeus back.

A fierce sword duel began, with Timaeus using the advantage of his two swords to block Hermos' incoming attacks. However, he struggled to find an opening in her defence due to his lack of experience.

Despite the circumstances, the spectators were surprised at how well Timaeus was managing to defend himself. "Timaeus seems to be doing quite well," said Master Phaedo. Master Byrne turned his head towards him and replied, "He's performing much better than I anticipated," before turning back to the action. "However, so far, Hermos hasn't really tried. The little shit doesn't know what he's in for." This caused a worried expression to cross Master Phaedo's face.

Timaeus was still maintaining his defence when suddenly Hermos stopped her attack. "You do realize I've been holding back this entire time," she said. Timaeus looked back at her with a surprised expression. "Huff... huff... What?" he gasped, catching his breath. Hermos then glanced at a fire torch at the edge of the training arena. She raised her hand and said, "Éla Fotiá," summoning the fire from the torch into her palm.

Hermos positioned the flame to her sword and recited, "Anáflexi Lepídas," igniting the blade. Timaeus could hardly believe his eyes. "Now it's time we start getting serious," Hermos declared. She launched a renewed assault, making things increasingly challenging for Timaeus as the fire on her sword hampered his defence. The heat affected the metal of his swords and made it difficult for him to grip them securely.

"Éla Fotiá!" Hermos shouted, conjuring fire from another torch into her free hand. She then raised her hand toward Timaeus and yelled,

"Ékrixi Flógas," sending a blast of flame in his direction. In response, Timaeus called out, "Ánodos Anémou Fterón!" using his Wind Magic to defend himself. However, his defence was insufficient, and he was struck by Hermos' Magic, knocking him backwards onto the ground and causing him to drop his swords.

Timaeus brought himself to his knees but couldn't find the strength to get back up. "That's three minutes," said Master Byrne. "So Timaeus will be singed twice... Hermos, continue."

Hermos raised her sword and said, "Éla Fotiá," drawing flames from its blade. Then she shouted, "Ékrixi Flógas!" sending the fire toward Timaeus. "AAARGH!" Timaeus screamed as the flames struck his back. Hermos invoked the spell, "Éla Fotiá," again to draw out more fire from her sword. She stood ready to singe Timaeus a second time.

"Did you actually think you stood a chance against me?" Hermos asked. "You're always gonna remain the same pathetic piece of shit you are now." Unbeknownst to anyone in the training arena, Hermos' words fueled Timaeus with rage. "Ékrixi Flógas!" Hermos shouted, sending the flame from her hand towards Timaeus.

Just then, Timaeus grabbed his swords and sprang to his feet, much to everyone's amazement. In a fit of rage, he swung his swords around and shouted, "Anáflexi Lepídas!" causing the blades to ignite. The entire training arena couldn't believe their eyes.

Fueled by anger, Timaeus swung his right sword and shouted, "Lepída Flógas!" sending a blade of fire towards Hermos. She dodged the fiery attack, but Timaeus quickly swung his left sword, again shouting, "Lepída Flógas!" This time, the blade of fire struck Hermos, knocking her to the ground.

Master Byrne watched in awe, but he wasn't pleased that his successor-to-be had been taken down. "Hermos, get up!" he shouted.

"Don't let yourself be knocked over by that fucking little slacker..., finish him!" Master Phaedo shockingly reacted, "What the fuck are you doing, Byrne?" He asked. Master Byrne turned towards Master Phaedo and replied strictly, "After what we just saw..., I wanna see what this little shit is capable of."

Hermos stood up, giving Timaeus a harsh glare; she raised and pointed her sword towards him. "Don't think for one second that you've beaten me," she said angrily. Timaeus raised his swords and stood in a fighting position "Bring it," he replied.

The two ran towards each other, once in range of each other; Timaeus swung his swords to attack whilst Hermos raised her sword to defend herself. Once their swords connected, Timaeus shouted, "Ánodos Anémou!" Creating a rise of wind, which he used to jump over Hermos and half turn whilst, in mid-air, landing facing the back of her.

In creating an opening in Hermos' defence, Timaeus seized the opportunity and executed a side kick, causing Hermos to fall to the ground. However, Hermos was not finished yet; she quickly sprang back to her feet, angry and frustrated that she was struggling against an opponent who, moments ago, seemed to stand no chance.

Noticing the torches surrounding the training arena, Hermos raised her left arm above her head and shouted, "Éla Óli Fotiá!" She summoned fire from all the torches, forming a sphere of flame.

"Calm down, Hermos!" Master Byrne shouted, but she was too irritated to heed his warning. With a swift movement, Hermos pulled her arm back and then thrust it forward, yelling, "Apergía Meteoríti!" as she launched her attack. Master Byrne was about to intervene when he realised Timaeus was preparing to counterattack.

Timaeus swung his swords toward the sphere of fire and shouted, "Káfsi!" When his swords struck the sphere, the flames dispersed across the training arena. After halting Hermos' attack, Timaeus shouted, "Ánodos Anémou!" This created a gust of wind that lifted him into the air and propelled him toward Hermos.

While airborne, Timaeus extended his swords outward, then swung them downward, exclaiming, "Anemostróvilos!" This summoned a small tornado that surged toward Hermos, lifting her into the air. As Timaeus landed back on the ground, he quickly shouted, "Ánodos Anémou!" once more, summoning another gust of wind that lifted him skyward.

Taking advantage of the momentum, he half-turned while ascending, using the rising wind to lift his legs and execute a backward flip. As Hermos fell past him, Timaeus delivered a powerful kick, sending her crashing back to the ground.

As Timaeus fell back towards the ground, he half turned and landed standing above Hermos with both his swords above her throat. Timaeus knelt down on his right knee and said, "How do you like this pathetic piece of shit now?"

At Timaeus' mercy, Hermos caught a glimpse of some of the fire from her earlier attack and secretly started to charm it whilst turning towards Timaeus. "You're not pathetic I'll give you that," replied Hermos. "But a piece of shit all the same, Éla Óli Fotiá!" Hermos' spell then summoned all the fire she had secretly charmed towards her in the hopes of finishing Timaeus.

However, Timaeus swung his left sword towards it and shouted, "Anáflexi Lepídas!" Causing his blade to ignite. Timaeus held the flaming sword above Hermos' face. "That's enough!" Master Byrne shouted.

Heavily breathing and still filled with rage, Timaeus stood up and replied, "Yes, Master Byrne." He then turned and swung his left sword, shouting, "Lepída Flógas!" A blade of fire shot around the training arena, relighting all the torches as Hermos absorbed all the flames with her Fire Magic. Suddenly, the Dragon's Eye Crest began to glow. After witnessing this event, everyone was astonished by what they were seeing.

"I think you've just found your future successor, Phaedo," said Master Byrne. Master Phaedo turned toward Master Byrne, his expression one of shock. "No fucking shit," he replied, astounded by the unexpected turn of events. Curious to learn more, the atmosphere was thick with surprise, and Master Byrne declared, "All students are dismissed for today, except for you, Hermos."

With his mind filled with curiosity, Master Phaedo turned towards his students. "Thank you, my students, we are finished for today," he said. "You are dismissed... except for Timaeus." Master Phaedo and Master Byrne then focused their attention on Timaeus. "Young Timaeus, would you please come and join me and Master Phaedo?" asked Master Byrne. "You too, Hermos."

Hermos was still exhausted from her battle with Timaeus, but he offered his hand to help her up. Although reluctant at first, as she didn't want to appear weak or embarrassed by accepting help from the one who had just defeated her, Hermos eventually took Timaeus' hand, and he helped her to her feet. The two students then walked over to join their masters.

"I don't see how this is possible, Byrne," said Master Phaedo. "Timaeus has been my student since he was a young boy. How is it that a Wind Student is able to use Fire Magic?"

Master Byrne stood with a puzzled expression on his face. "I'm not sure, Phaedo," he replied, then turned his attention to Timaeus. "Young Timaeus, has anything like this ever happened before? Have you ever been able to use Fire Magic?"

Timaeus looked ashamed as he answered, "No, I haven't, Master Byrne.

"Hmmm?" Master Phaedo exclaimed. "If Timaeus can use Fire Magic, do you think it's possible for him to use all four forms of Element Magic?" A look of doubt crossed Master Byrne's face.

"As extraordinary as that would be, Phaedo, somehow I doubt it," he replied.

Meanwhile, Hermos, still exhausted, stood there, breathing heavily. "Huff... huff... Well, you could've fooled me," she said. "When you jumped and knocked me back to the floor, huff... huff... it felt like an Earth Elemental was hitting me."

Master Phaedo was shocked by the information. "Timaeus, what were your emotions before you used your Wind Magic to jump back into the air?" he asked. Timaeus paused, reflecting on the entire fight. "Anger and rage would be my best answer, Master Phaedo," he replied. This response piqued Master Phaedo's curiosity further. "Wind and Water Magic require calmer emotions," he explained. "On the other hand, Fire and Earth Magic demand fiercer emotions. So far, we have seen Wind and Fire Magic in use, and it seems Earth Magic was involved as well, but there was no water present during their battle to utilise Water Magic."

Just then, Master Byrne noticed something. "Why don't we test that theory?" he suggested, eliciting surprised reactions from the others. "There's a fountain just over there at the edge of the arena. Let's find out if you're right, Phaedo."

Master Byrne, Master Phaedo, Timaeus, and Hermos walked toward the fountain to investigate whether something previously thought impossible could actually happen.

"Now, young Timaeus," Master Byrne said, "let's see if Master Phaedo's theory about you is correct."

Hermos stood nearby, her expression filled with jealousy. "Tch. I've got to see this," she muttered.

Master Byrne turned to Hermos with an irritated look. "HERMOS! That's enough!" he snapped.

Hermos met his gaze with a hint of defiance. "Apologies, Master Byrne," she replied. "I just find this hard to believe. Up until recently, Timaeus could do fuck all against me; he was just a little Wind Student. Now, all of a sudden, he's using Fire Magic against me... and there's even a possibility he can master all four forms of Element Magic."

Master Byrne approached his student and placed a hand on her shoulder. "I know how you're feeling, Hermos," he said. "I'm finding this just as hard to believe as you are. That's why we're here—to see if it's true." Master Byrne then turned to the others and said, "Anyway, Phaedo, continue."

Master Phaedo and Timaeus stood by the fountain. "Now, Timaeus," said Master Phaedo, "let's put this theory to the test. Concentrate on the water in the fountain, calm your emotions, and let's see if you can use Water Magic."

Timaeus replied, "Yes, Master Phaedo." He stood at the fountain with his arms raised toward it, maintaining a calm demeanour. "Éla Neró," he said. Unfortunately, nothing happened.

"Well, it was a good theory while it lasted," Master Phaedo remarked.

Not wanting to disappoint his master, Timaeus asked, "Am I doing something wrong, Master Phaedo?" Master Byrne then spoke up, "It may have something to do with your emotions, young Timaeus." He continued, "Your emotions are undoubtedly calm at the moment, but they are as calm as the wind, which is required for Wind Magic. With Water Magic, your emotions need to be as calm as water. Refocus your emotions, young Timaeus, and try again."

Timaeus replied, "Yes, Master Byrne." He then closed his eyes to refocus his emotions. A moment later, Timaeus opened his eyes and raised his arms toward the fountain again. "Éla Neró," he said. After a few seconds of silence, the water in the fountain began to ripple. Master Phaedo, Master Byrne, and Hermos could hardly believe what they were witnessing.

"That's it, young Timaeus," said Master Byrne. "Calm as the water." Keeping his emotions in check, a small amount of water emerged from the fountain and moved toward Timaeus' hands. "Therapéfste To Neró," Timaeus instructed. The water he summoned enveloped his body, healing the injuries he had sustained in his earlier battle with Hermos. Master Phaedo, Master Byrne, and Hermos were left speechless.

"Well, Phaedo, old friend," Master Byrne said, breaking the silence. "It seems your theory was correct." Just then, the Dragon's Eye Crest began to glow again.

"Well, Phaedo," Master Byrne continued, "it seems the Dragon's Eye Crest wants young Timaeus to be its future guardian and has deemed him a worthy successor... You know what you must do now, old friend."

Master Phaedo approached Timaeus. "Kneel, Timaeus," he instructed.

Timaeus knelt on his right knee as Master Phaedo drew both of his swords. He placed his right sword on Timaeus' right shoulder and his left sword on Timaeus' left shoulder." Rise, Timaeus," said Master Phaedo. Timaeus stood up again.

Master Phaedo then asked, "Are you prepared to accept this responsibility, Timaeus?" With confidence, Timaeus placed his right hand on his chest and replied, "Yes, Master Phaedo, I am."

Master Phaedo then took Timaeus' right hand from his chest and placed it over the Dragon's Eye Crest that he held in his right hand. Clasping Timaeus' hand, he sealed the Dragon's Eye Crest between their right hands and spoke: "Desmevómaste Apó To Máti Tou Drákou." At that moment, both were engulfed in a green light.

"What just happened, Master Phaedo?" Timaeus asked, curiosity evident in his voice. Master Phaedo then released Timaeus' hand.

"That spell binds us to the Dragon's Eye Crest," he replied. "You are now officially the heir to the Dragon's Eye Crest and will be my eventual successor... When my life comes to an end, you will become the new guardian of the Dragon's Eye Crest." Timaeus was amazed by what had just happened. "What if something were to happen to me before that occurs?" he asked. A frown creased Master Phaedo's face. "If that were to happen," he replied, "then unfortunately, I would have to find a new successor." Timaeus looked shocked, but a smile soon returned to Master Phaedo's face. "However, based on what we've seen here today, I don't foresee that happening," said Master Phaedo. "Allow me to be the first to say congratulations."

Chapter Three
Phaedo's Successor

Master Byrne stepped forward and said, "And please allow me to be the second... congratulations, young Timaeus." He then turned to Master Phaedo and added, "And may I say congratulations to you too, Phaedo, my old friend." The two old friends shook hands and embraced in a hug. They then turned their attention back to Timaeus.

"We need to clarify what we're dealing with, Byrne," said Master Phaedo. Master Byrne nodded in agreement. "Yes, Phaedo... we do," he replied. Both Timaeus and Hermos looked at their Masters with confusion.

"Excuse me, Master Phaedo," Timaeus asked. "What do you mean by 'what we're dealing with'?" A concerned expression spread across Master Phaedo's face.

"Because, Timaeus," he replied, "as astonishing as it is that you can use all four forms of Element Magic, it's also... concerning."

Timaeus and Hermos were becoming increasingly confused by what they heard. "How so, Master Phaedo?" Timaeus asked. Master Byrne then stepped forward. "Magic always comes with a price, young Timaeus," he said in a serious tone. "Being able to use all four forms of Element Magic is one thing, but we still don't understand how this is possible or what it is truly capable of. For all we know, this Magic could pose a danger not only to you but to everyone in Atlantis." This expression brought a worried look to Timaeus' face. "How do you mean, Master Byrne?" he asked, his voice trembling with fear.

"To this day, the use of magic has always been uncertain," replied Master Byrne. "For centuries, the outcomes of Magic were unpredictable, unlike they are today. In your case, young Timaeus, being able to use all four forms of Element Magic could lead to many unpredictable outcomes. Today, you were simply switching between each form of Element Magic by changing your emotional state. However, if you were in a state of mixed emotions, it could have caused multiple forms of Element Magic to react unpredictably. Fortunately, that wasn't the case today."

As concerning as Master Byrne's words sounded, they brought a serious expression to Timaeus' face. "What are you saying, Master Byrne?" Timaeus asked. "Does this mean I'll have to learn how to use all four forms of Element Magic?"

Master Byrne turned to Timaeus and looked him straight in the eye. "It does seem that way, young Timaeus, yes," he replied. "But for now, we'll leave things as they are until Master Phaedo and I consult with the Master of Earth and the King of Atlantis."

Master Phaedo then stepped forward. "I agree, Byrne," he said. "Let us set this aside for now and continue our discussions tomorrow with Master Gorgias and His Highness, King Okeanos."

Timaeus and Hermos stood before Master Phaedo and Master Byrne, placing their right hands on their chests, and said, "Yes, Masters."

Timaeus then turned and noticed that Hermos still had injuries from their earlier battle. "Before we retire for the day, masters," he said, "there's something I need to take care of." With that, Timaeus headed toward the fountain, leaving Master Phaedo and Master Byrne wondering what he was up to.

He placed his hands in front of him and took a deep breath, exhaling slowly. "Calm as the water," he murmured before saying, "Éla Neró." Immediately, the water in the fountain began to ripple and flowed toward his hands. Timaeus walked back to Master Phaedo, Master Byrne, and Hermos, surprising them all as he held the levitating water between his hands.

Standing in front of Hermos, Timaeus declared, "Therapéfste To Neró." With those words, the water he carried soaked Hermos, effectively healing her injuries.

"It's the least I could do," said Timaeus as he offered Hermos a handshake. Hermos accepted the handshake with a smile. "Thanks, Timaeus," she replied, tightening her grip. "But don't think this is over... Once we've finished our training, there's going to be a rematch." Timaeus met Hermos' gaze squarely. "Oh, there will be," he said confidently.

Master Phaedo then cleared his throat. "I'm impressed, Timaeus," he remarked. "You're learning to refocus your emotions faster than I expected, especially with how well you just handled that Water Magic." A slight frown crossed Timaeus' face. "It wasn't as easy as it looked, Master

Phaedo," he replied. "Although it was a bit easier this time since I knew where my emotions needed to be, the difficult part was keeping them there."

Master Phaedo approached Timaeus and placed a reassuring hand on his shoulder.

"Yet you just managed to control a larger amount of water than before," he said. "You moved it from one place to another, and to top it off, you used it to heal Hermos. You should have more confidence in yourself, Timaeus." Timaeus' frown disappeared. "Yes, Master Phaedo," he replied. Master Phaedo then patted Timaeus on the shoulder. "Right then, let us retire for the day," said Master Phaedo. "Which reminds me, Timaeus, it would be a good idea for you to spend some time this evening practising with your emotions and the different forms of Element Magic." This caught Master Byrne's attention. "That's not a bad idea, young Timaeus," he said. "Use small items related to the four elements—a small torch, a handful of sand, and a small amphora of water." Master Phaedo responded positively. "Exactly!" he said. "Now, let's all retire for the day before we wither away. We'll meet again tomorrow at the consultation. Speaking of which, Byrne, you and I should go see Gorgias and Okeanos about this."

Master Byrne nodded in response. He and Master Phaedo then went to meet with Master Gorgias and King Okeanos, while Hermos and Timaeus went their separate ways. As Timaeus was making his way home, he was surprised by a fellow Wind Student who jumped out at him.

"Timaeus!" his fellow student shouted.

"Zephyr!" Timaeus replied in shock.

"What was that all about?" Zephyr asked. "One moment you're struggling against Hermocrates, and the next you're using her own abilities against her."

Timaeus placed his hand on Zephyr's shoulder. "If you think that's wild, wait until you hear what I have to tell you," Timaeus replied. He then proceeded to explain to Zephyr what happened after class was dismissed.

"Shit... What the fuck does this mean, Timaeus?" Zephyr asked, still confused. All Timaeus could respond with was, "I don't know."

Timaeus then said thoughtfully, "I'm not sure what it means. However, Master Phaedo and Master Byrne suggested that I use items related to each element to practice the different forms of each one." Zephyr, eager to help his friend, replied, "Let's head over to the courtyard. You can get your amphora of water from the fountain there." Timaeus looked up in agreement. "That's a great idea," he responded. "Come on, let's go!" The two Wind Students then made their way to the courtyard.

Chapter Four
Battle in the Courtyard

Once Timaeus and Zephyr arrived at the courtyard, they headed straight to the fountain that featured a statue of Poseidon, the God of the Seas. However, the two Wind Students were unaware that they were being watched.

"Hey, Timaeus," said Zephyr. "Do you think that amphora will do?"

Timaeus glanced at Zephyr and replied, "I don't see why not. It's not like I need all of the seas." Zephyr appreciated Timaeus' sense of humour. "Haha," he chuckled. "No, I suppose not."

Zephyr then pointed at the statue of Poseidon. "You don't want the God of the Seas coming after you to claim it back." The two friends laughed at Zephyr's joke.

Timaeus filled the amphora and set it on the side of the fountain when, suddenly, it shattered as if something had been thrown at it.

"What the...?" Timaeus exclaimed in shock.

"That amphora wasn't fragile enough to break that easily," Zephyr replied.

"AARGH!!!" he screamed. Something had struck Zephyr's left arm. Timaeus turned his head away from Zephyr's arm, and suddenly, something was fired at him. He managed to catch it before it could hit him. It was a small rock. "How the...?" a voice called from across the courtyard. "Show yourself," Timaeus demanded as he crushed the stone in his hand.

From the shadows of the archway across the courtyard, three young men stepped out—two wearing vivid yellow robes and one adorned in medallion yellow robes. "Earth Students," Zephyr said, clutching his arm. "*What are Earth Students doing in Eastern Atlantis?*" Timaeus wondered.

"I know you Wind Students are known for your speed," said the Earth Student in the medallion yellow robes, "but there's no way you should have been able to catch that."

Timaeus stood his ground confidently. "Lucky catch, I guess," he replied, a statement that annoyed the Earth Students. "Don't give me that shit," the Earth Student in the yellow medallion robes said, growing increasingly annoyed. As he and his fellow Earth Students approached Timaeus, Zephyr warned, "Timaeus, be careful." He had realised, "I thought these Earth Students looked familiar... That's Gorgas, the chosen successor of Master Gorgias. The other two must be his right-hand men, Roc and Ston."

The three of them stopped several feet away from Timaeus. "I see our reputation precedes us," Gorgas chuckled. "Hmph," Timaeus responded, which only served to anger Gorgas, Roc, and Ston further. "No Wind Student gets the best of my abilities," Gorgas declared, pointing his finger at Timaeus. "First time for everything," Timaeus shot back sarcastically. This response sent Gorgas over the edge; he launched his fist at Timaeus, but with quick reflexes, Timaeus jumped backwards, easily avoiding the attack.

"Don't confront them directly, Timaeus," Zephyr cautioned. Timaeus unsheathed his swords, ready to defend his friend against the three Earth Students. However, the Earth Students remained unfazed, standing their ground without feeling threatened by Timaeus.

"You're going down, Wind Student," said Gorgas, cracking his knuckles. "I wouldn't bet on it," replied Timaeus as circles of wind started to surround him. "Hehehe," chuckled Gorgas. "Bring it."

Timaeus held his swords in a reverse grip as he prepared to make his first move. The circles of wind started to intensify. Timaeus pulled his arms back, then threw them forward while shouting, "ANEMOSTRÓVILOS!" This created a twister that spiralled straight toward Gorgas. When the twister eventually dissipated, Timaeus was shocked to discover that it had no effect on Gorgas.

"Timaeus!" Zephyr shouted. "That's not going to work. Earth Magic is resistant to our Wind Magic." Hearing this, Timaeus had to rethink his strategy. "Right, thanks, Zephyr," he replied.

Suddenly, Gorgas rushed towards Timaeus and swung his fist, but Timaeus was too fast and avoided the attack. Timaeus attempted to counter with his swords, but Gorgas' Earth Magic made his skin too durable for the blades to have any effect. Roc and Ston tried to go after Timaeus as well, but like Gorgas, their efforts were in vain; they couldn't match his speed.

Despite the small wound he received from the Earth Students, Zephyr joined the fight. "Zephyr, are you alright to fight?" Timaeus asked.

"Yes," Zephyr replied as he got into a fighting stance. "It's just a small wound. I'll handle the lackeys; you focus on the main threat." This upset Roc and Ston, who both tried to take down Zephyr, but like Timaeus, he was too quick and avoided their attacks.

"Ston, sand distraction," said Roc. Ston grinned back at Roc when he heard the plan. "Leave it to me," he replied. Since Atlantis was an island, most areas were covered in sand. Ston clapped his hands together and moved them downwards beside him at a diagonal angle, saying, "Kálymma Ámmou." Instantly, the sand around him covered the courtyard as if it had fallen from the sky. Timaeus and the Earth Students were not affected, but the sudden cloud of sand forced Zephyr to shield his eyes, allowing Roc to set up a sneak attack. Unbeknownst to Gorgas, Timaeus remained unaffected by the sand, but he refrained from using his Wind Magic to clear it away, knowing that would only make things worse.

"What the? Let go of me!" shouted Zephyr.

"Ston, I've got him!" Roc called out. Taking advantage of the sand cover, Roc grabbed Zephyr from behind, leaving him defenceless.

Ston dropped the cover of sand and ran toward Zephyr, landing a punch in his gut. The Wind Student fell to his knees and started coughing up blood.

"Zephyr!" Timaeus shouted, his anger rising. Gorgas attempted to punch Timaeus, but at the last moment, Timaeus caught his fist, shocking Gorgas, Roc, and Ston. "FUCK OFF!!!" Cried Timaeus as he countered with his own punch, striking Gorgas in the face and knocking him to the ground. The Earth Students couldn't believe what they had just witnessed.

"Just a lucky shot," Gorgas muttered as he got back to his feet. "Speed equals power—that's all it is."

Timaeus ignored Gorgas' words, and his focus was now on Roc and Ston for what they had done to Zephyr.

"Roc, Ston, use the strategy you applied against his friend," Gorgas instructed. Roc and Ston grinned as they prepared to try to catch Timaeus in a cover of sand.

Like last time, Ston clapped his hands and moved them down beside him in a diagonal position, saying, "Kálymma Ámmou," which covered the courtyard with sand. Unbeknownst to the Earth Students, Timaeus did not need to shield his eyes from the sand. Roc attempted a sneak attack on Timaeus. "ARGH!!!" someone cried out. Thinking that was his signal, Ston lowered the sand cover and prepared to launch his attack, but he was shocked to see Timaeus elbowing Roc in the gut. Gorgas couldn't believe what he was witnessing.

Timaeus then grabbed Roc by his robes, threw him over his shoulder, and sent him crashing into Ston. After that, he went to tend to Zephyr. However, with his focus on his friend, Timaeus fails to notice Gorgas coming for him, allowing the Earth Student to finally land a punch on Timaeus, knocking him into the courtyard fountain.

"AT LAST!!!" Gorgas cried. "That'll teach that fucking little Wind Student to mess with the best of Southern Atlantis." He then turned toward Roc and Ston. As he walked toward them, Timaeus emerged from the waters of the fountain, completely unscathed. The Earth Students couldn't believe their eyes. "No, that's not possible," said Gorgas. "That little shit should be out cold."

The Earth Students prepared to launch one final attack on Timaeus. In that instant, Timaeus raised his arms and shouted, "Ánodos Neroú!" This caused the water from the fountain to rise dramatically. He then dropped his arms, and the water came crashing down on Gorgas, Roc, and Ston. Being vulnerable to Water Magic, the three of them found themselves lying on their backs, unable to defend themselves.

Timaeus stepped out of the fountain and said, "Elá Neró," summoning more water from the fountain.

He then turned towards Zephyr and spoke, "Therapéfste To Neró," causing the water he summoned to soak and heal Zephyr. Timaeus then walked towards Gorgas, Roc, and Ston, drawing his swords in the process. "Time for you and your fucking lackeys to get a taste of your own fucking medicine," said Timaeus.

As he raised his swords, a voice cried, "EPÍGEIA!!!" Timaeus found himself unable to move. "Stop, all of you," the voice commanded. Everyone turned towards the eastern entrance of the courtyard to see a man dressed in golden yellow robes adorned with the Dragon's Horn Crest.

"Ma... Master Gorgias," Gorgas said weakly. "Silence!" Master Gorgias shouted. "Gorgas, my successor, be silent." He then directed his attention to Timaeus. "Boy, put away your weapons," he ordered. "Or I will ensure that you cannot move again."

Hearing Master Gorgias' words, Timaeus sheathed his swords. Master Gorgias then nodded his head forward, and suddenly, Timaeus regained the ability to move. He placed his right hand across his left shoulder and said, "Thank you, Master Gorgias. My apologies."

Master Gorgias replied, "You have good manners, boy. I'll give you that. What's your name?"

Timaeus bowed his head and responded, "My name is Timaeus. If you'd allow me, I'd like to explain what happened, Master Gorgias."

However, Master Gorgias raised his hand in front of him. "There's no need for you to explain, Timaeus," he said. "I saw the whole thing. My successor-to-be and his two henchmen have a habit of picking fights with others, but this time, it seems they got more than they bargained for."

Timaeus and Master Gorgias both chuckled. "Thank you, Master Gorgias," Timaeus said, placing his hand across his chest once more.

Timaeus approached Gorgas, Roc, and Ston, who were still soaked from the battle. He raised his arms and said, "Therapéfste To Neró," causing the water on them to heal their wounds.

"So, you must be the Wind Student that Phaedo brought us here to tell us about," Master Gorgias remarked. "It's no wonder you were able to hold your own against all three of them. Phaedo has been telling us how you managed to withstand Byrne's successor."

Timaeus nodded and replied, "Yes, Master Gorgias. It was only by the narrowest of margins, though; with Hermos, it came down to emotions."

Master Gorgias began to reconsider what he had heard about the battle. "Hmm..." he mused. "From what Phaedo described, your emotions got the better of you when Hermos hurt you. Yet against Gorgas, you didn't need to rely on emotions because your speed was enough to evade his attacks."

Gorgas folded his arms and exclaimed, "Hmph." Master Gorgias raised his hand and said, "Epígeia." Gorgas found himself trapped and unable to move, just as Timaeus had been a few moments earlier.

"No need to be a sore loser, Gorgas," said Master Gorgias as he lowered his hand, setting Gorgas free. "In this case, you didn't begin using your emotions until your friend was injured."

Timaeus nodded in agreement and replied, "That's correct, Master Gorgias."

Master Gorgias then clapped his hands together. "Well then, I think I've heard all I need to hear," he said. "Phaedo and Byrne mentioned that they sent you to collect some resources to practice your magic."

Timaeus nodded again. "That's correct, Master Gorgias," he replied.

Master Gorgias then turned his attention to Gorgas, Roc, and Ston. "I assume that's when these three decided it would be funny to pick a fight?" he asked.

Timaeus stood his ground as Zephyr approached and positioned himself beside him. Both wore stern expressions as they looked at the Earth Students. "The three of them didn't appreciate their pranks being interrupted by a Wind Student," Zephyr remarked.

Glancing at his student with disappointment. "I understand," replied Master Gorgias. "Gorgas, Roc, Ston—return to Southern Atlantis; we will discuss this later. As for you, Timaeus, gather the resources you need and begin practising. I didn't see any Fire Magic being used; you'll need to be prepared if you want to impress the King."

Timaeus nodded and looked at the torches around the courtyard. He raised his hand toward one of them and declared, "Éla Fotiá," summoning fire to his palm, which left Master Gorgias and his students in shock.

"These battles you've faced have helped you with your emotions," Master Gorgias remarked. "However, you still have a long way to go if you wish to master all four forms of Element Magic."

Timaeus clenched his fist, extinguishing the flame in his hand, and then placed his hand on his shoulder. "Yes, Master Gorgias," he replied. "And Gorgas... Don't worry. Hermos wants a rematch, and you'll have one as well." Gorgas pointed a finger at Timaeus. "You bet I will, Timaeus," he responded. And with that, Master Gorgias and his students parted ways with the Wind Students.

Chapter Five
The Dark Elemental

As soon as Timaeus gathered the resources he needed, he and Zephyr parted ways to head home. Zephyr lived in the city of Eastern Atlantis, while Timaeus resided on the outskirts because he was an orphan—something known only to a few. Timaeus and several other orphaned children had taken shelter in an abandoned patch of farmland outside Eastern Atlantis. This farmland had been destroyed many years ago by Acolytes and had not been reclaimed since; however, the farmhouse remained intact, providing them with refuge.

Defending themselves was the most challenging aspect of their lives, as Timaeus was the only one among them with any combat training. When he returned home from training, the other orphans welcomed him, but one boy, in particular, was especially delighted to see him.

"Timaeus!" the boy shouted.

"Gale!" Timaeus shouted back.

Gale ran towards Timaeus, and the two friends embraced. "Why are you back so late tonight?" Gale asked. "And what's with all the supplies?" Gale was confused because, given their need to fend for themselves, the supplies Timaeus suggested acquiring for training could have easily been found on the abandoned farmland.

"Why don't we go down to the river and catch something for dinner?" replied Timaeus. "I'll explain everything on the way."

An excited smile spread across Gale's face. After Timaeus had dropped off the supplies at the abandoned farmhouse, grabbing two small fishing nets, he and Gale headed to the nearby river. Unbeknownst to them, something was hiding on the abandoned farmland.

"Wow!" Gale exclaimed. "So you have the power to control all four elements? That's amazing! Does this mean things will get better for us now?"

Timaeus knelt down and placed his hands on Gale's shoulders. "This won't make things better instantly, I'm afraid, little man. However, in due time, I promise you they will," he said. This brought tears of joy to Gale's eyes as he hugged his friend.

"But for now, let's catch something to eat," Timaeus continued. He then stood up and looked toward the river. He lowered his arms in front of him, turned his hands over, and raised his arms, saying, "Ánodos Neroú," causing the water from the river to rise. Timaeus then moved his arms sideways, separating the water he had lifted. Gale was shocked at what he was witnessing.

Next, Timaeus pulled his arms toward him, causing the water to fall onto the land along with anything caught in it. Gale closed his eyes in fear, but the water did not fall on him.

"Quickly, Gale!" Timaeus shouted. Gale opened his eyes to see Timaeus gathering up any fish that had landed on the shore.

"Catch as many of these fish as you can!" A smile spread across Gale's face as he marvelled at what he saw. He and Timaeus had gathered enough fish to fill their nets. "Wow, Timaeus," said Gale, excitement in his voice. "There's enough here to feed everyone tonight!" Timaeus smiled at his young friend and replied, "Let's get back then. I'm sure everyone's hungry." Gale nodded in agreement.

Suddenly, the two heard a strange noise. "What was that?" Gale asked, his eyes wide. Timaeus scanned the surroundings. "I'm not sure," he responded cautiously. "Stay where you are, Gale." Unbeknownst to them, they were being watched. Timaeus drew his swords as he began to investigate.

"ARGH!" a voice shouted. "Come on, Gale, we need to get back," Timaeus urged. He took hold of Gale's fishing net so they could return faster.

Timaeus and Gale rushed back to the abandoned farmhouse. Upon their arrival, they found the other orphans in distress; one of them was on the floor, writhing in excruciating pain. "What the fuck's going on?!" Timaeus yelled. One of the orphans turned to him and replied, "We were attacked by an Atlantean Viper. We managed to fend it off, but it's still out there. One of us got bitten and poisoned."

Timaeus looked down at the orphan who had been poisoned. "Shit!" he exclaimed. "All of you stay here. I have to find that thing before it harms anyone else." With that, Timaeus drew his swords and set out in search of the viper, knowing that it couldn't have gone far and would likely return to attack the orphans again.

Treading carefully, Timaeus searched a long patch of grassland on the abandoned farmland, knowing it would be the ideal hiding place for a snake. Suddenly, he heard a rustling in the grass and realised he was being watched. Standing his ground, Timaeus prepared himself, holding his swords down beside him as he waited.

Moments later, a viper lunged at him from the tall grass. Reacting quickly, Timaeus swung his right-handed sword and beheaded the serpent before it could reach him. With the viper now dead, he began to withdraw his swords. However, as he passed the lifeless snake, he noticed something unusual about its body. *"Oh no... This was no ordinary viper,"* he thought, alarmed.

With this unsettling discovery, Timaeus hurried back to the abandoned farmhouse to help the orphan who had been bitten.

On his way back, Timaeus could hear the orphan screaming in pain. When he finally arrived, the boy was in severe distress—vomiting and struggling to breathe. "Fuck!" Timaeus exclaimed. "He won't last much longer... The poison has almost done its job." The other orphans stood nearby in horror, realising they were about to lose their friend.

"Is there anything that can be done?" one of them asked. Timaeus turned back with a sad expression on his face and replied, "No."

Gale stepped forward, grabbing Timaeus by the shoulders. "Isn't there anything you can do, Timaeus?" he pleaded. Timaeus shook his head vigorously and replied, "No, Gale... I can't do anything to help him."

Frustrated, Gale shook Timaeus' shoulders and shouted, "FOR FUCK SAKE, TIMAEUS!!! You mean despite everything you've discovered about yourself today, you can't use any Element Magic to save him?!"

Timaeus grabbed Gale's wrists and shouted, "There's no time, Gale!" He released his wrists, his expression urgent. "I know what you're thinking, but the poison is too far spread... We don't have enough time to get him down." Suddenly, Timaeus recalled something from earlier, and a glimmer of hope appeared on his face. "Gale, quickly... There's still a chance," he urged. "Run inside and find the amphora I brought home today." Everyone looked confused. "Hurry, we don't have much time!" Timaeus yelled.

Gale dashed inside to fetch the amphora while Timaeus knelt beside the boy and examined his wound. Moments later, Gale ran outside with the amphora in hand. "Gale, pour the water from the amphora onto his wound," instructed Timaeus. Gale poured the water over the wound, and Timaeus raised his hand, chanting, "Therapéfste To Neró." But nothing happened.

"What's going on, Timaeus?" Gale asked, his voice filled with concern.

"I don't know, Gale," Timaeus replied. "I used this magic to heal others earlier, but for some reason, it's not working." Anxiety spread among the group as they realised the boy had only a couple of minutes left before the poison would take his life.

"Maybe it's because the poison has taken too much effect," Gale suggested. Timaeus shook his head in response.

"No, Gale. I think it's more likely that I'm not powerful enough to heal this type of injury."

Timaeus took the amphora from Gale and placed his hand over the boy's wound. They both noticed he was slipping away fast.

"Try one more time," Gale urged. "This time, make sure to have physical contact."

Timaeus kept his hand pressed against the boy's wound, poured the last of the water from the amphora, and began to chant, "Therapéfste To Neró."

At first, nothing happened for several seconds, but then, just as all hope seemed lost, a blue glow began to appear around Timaeus' hand. Everyone stared in disbelief at what they were witnessing. Moments later, the blue glow faded. Timaeus removed his hand from the boy's leg, and to everyone's amazement, the wound had vanished. Not only that, but the boy's health had significantly improved; he was fully recovered. Timaeus carefully sat the boy upright and helped him to his feet. He asked the boy if he was alright, and the boy nodded in response. The other orphans cheered, relieved that their friend had survived. However, suddenly, Timaeus collapsed to the ground.

"TIMAEUS!" Gale shouted. "What's happening?!"

Timaeus lay on the ground, groaning in pain and suffering the same symptoms the orphan boy had endured just moments ago.

"ARGH!" Timaeus yelled. "It seems that by healing our young friend... I now have to take on his pain."

Gale knelt down to assist his friend. "No, no, Timaeus! Have you been poisoned?!" he shouted, his concern evident. Timaeus lay on the ground, wracked with excruciating pain. "No!" he cried out. "I haven't been poisoned, Gale. I think it's because I healed the poison. Now I have to endure the rest of the pain, which should last just over a minute."

Despite knowing that his friend wasn't suffering from poison, Gale couldn't shake the worry over Timaeus' ordeal. As the pain reached its peak, Timaeus managed to push himself up to his knees, supporting himself with his arms on the ground. When the pain finally reached its climax, he coughed up blood and collapsed flat on the ground again.

"Timaeus... TIMAEUS!!!" Gale yelled, alarmed as his friend lay motionless, seemingly lifeless. A few moments later, Timaeus groaned and began to move again. Gale helped his friend to his feet. "What the hell happened, Timaeus?" he asked. "I thought Water Magic was supposed to heal, not cause pain." As Timaeus regained his strength, he began to clean the blood off his clothing and responded, "I don't know... I've never healed anything that severe before. The injuries I healed earlier today were from combat; they were just cuts, burn marks, and bruises. There wasn't any potent poison involved. All the different forms of Element Magic come with their costs."

Gale started to understand what had happened to Timaeus. "So, you knew what would happen if you healed our friend, but you didn't know how it would affect you," Gale said. "What I still don't understand is why you thought there was nothing you could do, why you believed there was no time left."

Timaeus looked at Gale and said, "The snake that attacked you earlier—none of you mentioned that its tail was missing." His words brought a look of confusion to Gale's face. "Gale, that was no Atlantean Viper," Timaeus continued. "That snake was a Chimera's tail, and their venom is stronger than any ordinary snake's venom. That's why the poison affected our friend so quickly. After I beheaded the serpent, I noticed it had no tail. I hurried back, but by the time I arrived, the poison had almost done its job. If it had been an Atlantean Viper, I would have had more time."

Gale struggled to believe what he was hearing. "How can that be?" Gale asked. "I thought Chimeras resided in Northern Atlantis." Timaeus was just as puzzled. "I'm not sure," he replied.

Gale was troubled by Timaeus' words. "It couldn't have migrated here because it's too far. Its tail wasn't cut off, so it was either brought here by someone or something else, or we could be facing an entirely different set of circumstances."

Despite their confusion, Timaeus said, "But we can worry about that when the time comes. Right now, we have our catch to cook and over a dozen hungry orphans to feed."

This thought brought a smile to Gale's face as he and Timaeus went to retrieve the fish they had caught earlier. A few small campfires were set up outside the abandoned farmhouse, but it was difficult to ignite them with only a small flint. Eventually, Timaeus managed to light one of the fires. Once the flames grew big enough, he extended his hands toward it and said, "Éla Fotiá," summoning the flames to his hands. He then pointed at the other two campfires and said, "Fotiá Anávei," causing them to ignite as well.

With the heat they needed, Timaeus, Gale, and the other orphans were able to cook and eat the fish they had caught earlier. Using some old situlas and terracotta pots from the abandoned farmhouse, the orphans gathered water from the river and stored it in several pithos that had been used on the farmland before it was destroyed. Timaeus also gave everyone a bonus by purifying the water with his Water Magic, ensuring they had safe drinking water. After dinner, everyone settled down for the night except for Timaeus. He stayed up a little later to keep watch and practice his magical abilities. Just as he was about to turn in for the night, Timaeus heard movement nearby. He heard it again and realised it couldn't be any of the other orphans, as none of them had come outside all evening.

"Who's there? Show yourself!" Timaeus called as he turned to scan his surroundings. When he turned back, a man in black robes stood a few meters away from him. The sight of the figure sent a chill of fear through Timaeus, but he held his ground for the sake of his friends. "Who are you? What do you want?" he demanded. The man remained silent, simply watching him. Then, raising his left hand toward the nearby campfire, he spoke in a chilling voice, "Éla Fotiá," conjuring flames into his palm. Concerned about what this man might be capable of, Timaeus drew his swords. "Please, I don't want any trouble. Just extinguish the flames and leave," he pleaded. However, the man continued to stand there, the fire flickering in his hand, and he said nothing.

Suddenly, he pointed his left hand towards the abandoned farmhouse and shouted, "KÓLASI!" He violently sent the flame in his hand towards the farmhouse, striking it and setting it ablaze. "GALE!" cried Timaeus. Without regard for his safety, Timaeus plunged his swords into the ground and raised his hands toward the fire, shouting, "Éla Fotiá!"

Concentrating all the fire he could summon into his hands, Timaeus turned to face the man in the black robes and shouted, "Apergía Meteoríti!" He sent the flames hurtling toward him. To Timaeus' disbelief, the man merely raised his right arm and halted the flames just before they reached him. Just as the man in black was about to send the flames back, Timaeus quickly raised his right hand and shouted, "Káfsi!" This caused the flames to explode.

"Timaeus, what's going on?!" Gale shouted. Timaeus turned around, relieved to see that his friend hadn't been harmed. "We're under attack," replied Timaeus. "Éla Fotiá!" he yelled, summoning the flames from the abandoned farmhouse into his hands. He then spoke, "Oi Flóges Svínoun," extinguishing the flames he held. Turning to Gale, he said, "I need you to get everyone out in case he sets the farmhouse on fire again."

Before Gale got to work, he asked, "Who or what are we dealing with, Timaeus?" Timaeus pulled his swords from the ground and replied, "I don't know, but he is trained in the art of Fire Magic. I'm going to try and buy you some time." Timaeus then turned away to face his attacker. The man in black robes had been knocked to the floor by Timaeus' sneak attack, but he rose again without any injuries.

Timaeus was about to gather the flames that had been unleashed when he suddenly saw a figure in black robes running toward him through the fire. Timaeus raised both his swords, ready to strike, but the figure in black caught Timaeus' wrists, halting him in his tracks. In a chilling voice, the man in black robes said, "Kafstikó Ángigma," and his touch seared Timaeus' wrists.

"ARGH!!!" Timaeus cried out, the pain forcing him to drop his swords and drop to his knees. The man in black smiled wickedly, revelling in Timaeus' suffering.

Determined not to give up, Timaeus clenched his fists and surprised his opponent by rising back to his feet. Unbeknownst to the man in black, Timaeus was using his Earth and Fire magic to withstand the pain. As Timaeus regained his footing, the man in black attempted to amplify the effects of his Magic, causing Timaeus to jerk his head back, screaming in agony.

Standing there silently, the man in black robes continued to let Timaeus suffer. To his surprise, Timaeus suddenly swung his head forward and headbutted his opponent in the face, causing the man to release his grip. Without hesitating, Timaeus threw a powerful punch to his opponent's abdomen, followed by a second punch to his face that sent him several meters away, landing on his back.

"Éla Fotiá," Timaeus said, gathering flames from his earlier attack before they began to spread. He then added, "Oi Flóges Svínoun," to extinguish them.

"Timaeus!" Gale shouted from behind him. "Everyone's out of the farmhouse. We heard what was going on... Who's attacking us?"

Timaeus picked up his swords, turned toward Gale, and replied, "I don't know, but whoever he is, his Fire Magic is unlike anything I've ever seen before."

A frightened look came to Gale's face. "T-Timaeus...," he said anxiously, pointing toward something in the distance. Timaeus turned around and was shocked by what he saw—it was the man in black robes.

"This is really bad, Timaeus," Gale said. "I don't know who he is, but I can tell you one thing: he's an Acolyte." Timaeus was taken aback by this revelation.

"An Acolyte?!" he exclaimed in disbelief. "I thought the Acolytes were wiped out centuries ago?"

An evil smile spread across the face of the man in black robes. "The Acolytes are long gone," he replied in a sinister voice. "You've yet to learn from your masters that the Acolytes you were familiar with have not been wiped out, as you believe."

Timaeus and Gale exchanged confused glances. "The Acolytes we once were are now known as the Dark Elementals," he stated ominously.

Timaeus was beginning to understand. "So that's how you're able to use Fire Magic," he said. "It also explains why its nature is different from any Fire Magic I've seen before—a Dark Fire Elemental." The Dark Fire Elemental simply stood there and laughed. "Dark Magic enhances Element Magic and makes us resistant to all forms of Element Magic," he explained.

"I think that's enough chit-chat for now. I'm here for the Element Students who are sheltering in this abandoned farmhouse. Bring me the Water Student I saw at the river earlier this evening and the Wind Student who beheaded my Chimera Tail." An angry expression crossed Timaeus' and Gale's faces as they glared at the culprit who had almost cost their friend his life. "The green robes and twin swords don't disguise the fact that you're the Fire Student; I just saw you using Fire Magic," said the Dark Fire Elemental.

"It wouldn't surprise me if you're also hiding an Earth Student in there as well—a full set to become Dark Elementals." The Dark Fire Elemental, unaware that the three individuals he was searching for were actually the same person, played right into Timaeus' hands. Holding his sword in front of Gale to prevent him from getting any closer, Timaeus quietly said, "Get everyone out of here, Gale. I'll hold him off while you lead everyone to safety." Despite still being injured from his earlier confrontation with the Dark Fire Elemental, Timaeus stepped forward, ready to face him.

"Hehe," the Dark Fire Elemental chuckled malevolently. "You know this is futile. I've already told you that the robes and swords won't hide the fact that you're the Fire Student." The Dark Elemental remained still, a sinister smile plastered on his face, showing no sign of concern.

Timaeus got into a fighting position, ready to face his opponent. "Who said I was hiding anything?" he replied, causing the Dark Fire Elemental to lose the smile on his face. Pulling his arms back and then thrusting them forward, Timaeus shouted, "ANEMOSTRÓVILOS!" A powerful twister formed, the same technique he had attempted to use against Gorgas earlier. Due to his arrogance, the Dark Fire Elemental barely had time to react and was swept into the air, giving Timaeus the opportunity he needed.

"Gale, get everyone out of here!" he shouted. "I'll provide the cover you need." Timaeus then ran toward the pithos, where the orphans had stored water earlier. He placed his hands in one of them and said, "Therapéfste To Neró," healing the wounds inflicted upon him by the Dark Fire Elemental.

After healing himself, Timaeus threw his arms upwards and exclaimed, "Ánodos Neroú," causing water to rise out of the pithos and into the air. He then commanded, "Kálymma Omíchlis," transforming the water into a cover of mist to hide his and the other's whereabouts.

"Gale, get everyone out of here. I'll keep him occupied," Timaeus instructed. "Get everyone to the city and find Master Phaedo." With that, Gale led the orphans away from the abandoned farmland while Timaeus stayed behind to prevent the Dark Fire Elemental from following them. He moved through the mist to confront his opponent.

"NRGH!" The Dark Fire Elemental groaned as he got up from Timaeus' attack. "How is this possible? How can this Element Student use multiple forms?" Before he could finish, Timaeus charged through the mist and landed a punch to the Dark Fire Elemental's face, causing him to stagger backwards.

"Little shit," he muttered as he prepared to attack Timaeus in retaliation. Fortunately, Timaeus used his speed to dodge the Dark Fire Elemental's strike and quickly launched a counterattack, hitting him in the abdomen. *"This strength—it feels familiar,"* thought the Dark Fire Elemental, recalling the force of Timaeus' earlier punch. Before the Dark Fire Elemental could recover from the blow, Timaeus cried, "AEROFOTOGRAFÍA!!!"

With a powerful blast of wind, Timaeus sent his opponent flying into the abandoned farmhouse. Using his Wind Magic, he cleared away the cover of mist surrounding them. He raised his hand and exclaimed, "Éla Óla Fotiá," gathering flames from all the campfires. Knowing that he and his friends would no longer be safe there, Timaeus cried, "APERGÍA METEORÍTI!!!" and launched the flames towards the abandoned farmhouse, setting it ablaze once more.

After destroying his home, Timaeus prepared to go find Gale and the other orphans. As he started to walk away, he heard someone clapping.

"So," said a creepy and familiar voice. "You can use all four forms of Element Magic."

Timaeus turned around, shocked to see that the Dark Fire Elemental was still alive.

"No... That's not possible," he said in a frightened tone. "Without a Red Element Stone, there's no way you could have survived that."

The Dark Fire Element stood with an evil grin and chuckled at Timaeus' words.

"Hmhmhm... Due to the Dark Magic I wield, I cannot use an Element Stone," he said. "However, as I explained to you earlier, Dark Magic enhances my own Element Magic and makes me resistant to all forms of Element Magic. This means I am immune to Fire Magic. Despite being only an Element Student, you are proving to be more trouble than you're worth, especially with all four forms of Element Magic at your disposal. So, it's time for things to get serious."

The Dark Fire Elemental raised his right hand to his left side, then moved his arm to the right and spoke, "Emfanízetai I Lepída." In response, a broadsword materialised in front of him, and he grasped the hilt with his right hand. Timaeus couldn't believe what he was witnessing while his opponent stood smirking ominously.

"Dark magic allows us to conceal our weapons in plain sight," the Dark Fire Elemental explained. "Normally, I wouldn't need to do this, but you're not leaving me much choice."

Despite the grim situation, Timaeus drew his blades, preparing to confront his opponent. The Dark Fire Elemental then raised his left hand and commanded, "Éla Fotiá," summoning flames from the burning house into his palm. He placed his left hand over the blade and declared, "Anáflexi Lepídas," igniting the sword.

With his blade ignited, the Dark Fire Elemental swung it horizontally toward Timaeus, who raised both of his swords to block the attack. However, the Dark Fire Elemental's strength made it difficult for him to hold his ground. While defending against the Dark Fire Elemental's blade, Timaeus left himself exposed to other attacks, allowing the Dark Fire Elemental to kick him to the ground.

The Dark Fire Elemental then swung his blade upward and shouted, "Kólasi Lepída!" A violent blade of fire erupted, burning through the ground and heading straight for Timaeus, who barely managed to avoid it. The Dark Fire Elemental shouted again, "Kólasi Lepída!" as he swung his blade downward, unleashing another fierce blade of fire.

This time, Timaeus decided to fight back. As the Dark Fire Elemental's attack rushed toward him, Timaeus raised his swords and shouted, "Anáflexi Lepídas!" in an attempt to ignite his blades with the Dark Fire Elemental's attack.

Unfortunately, due to the nature of the Dark Fire Elemental's Magic, Timaeus' strategy backfired, resulting in an explosion that sent him flying backwards across the abandoned farmland. He landed among the pithos storage, crashing into one and soaking himself with the water it contained. As he struggled to regain his composure, he uttered, "Therapéfste To Neró," healing the damage he sustained from the blast.

As Timaeus got back to his feet, he noticed a faint green glow at the spot where he had been standing before the explosion. However, he quickly dismissed it, focusing instead on the approaching Dark Fire Elemental. Without hesitation, Timaeus used his swords to shatter several pithos. He then raised his arms and shouted, "Ánodos Neroú!" This caused the water from the broken pithos to rise around him. With a determined thrust of his arms, he yelled, "Tsounámi!" Directing the gathered water toward his opponent in the form of a powerful wave.

The Dark Fire Elemental stood his ground, raising his blade as a powerful torrent of water struck him. Despite the force of the impact, he remained unharmed and firmly in place. "Fool!" he shouted. "Have you learned nothing? Thanks to my Dark Magic, I'm not vulnerable to Water Magic like an ordinary Fire Elemental would be."

Timaeus exited the storage area, prepared to face his opponent. He replied, "Actually, I've learned quite a lot... That's why that attack wasn't intended for you." The Dark Elemental looked slightly confused, but because of his arrogance, he had not considered that Timaeus' attack had extinguished the flame on his blade. Without hesitation, Timaeus charged at his opponent and slashed his arm with one of his swords, causing the Dark Fire Elemental to drop his weapon before he could ignite it again.

Timaeus followed up with a punch to the face that was as swift as the wind and as powerful as the earth, sending the Dark Fire Elemental flying into the distance. Not taking any chances after seeing his opponent survive the previous life-threatening attack, Timaeus stood his ground. He noticed the flames from the burning house beginning to flicker.

"Éla Fotiá!" the Dark Fire Elemental shouted from afar, drawing all the flames toward him. "KÓLASI VÉLOS VROCHÍ!!!" he cried, creating violent arrows of fire that rained down toward Timaeus. Realising he had no other option, Timaeus drew his swords and readied himself to counterattack.

Focusing his Wind Magic, Timaeus' blades began to glow. He threw his right sword downwards in a diagonal motion and shouted, "Lepída Anémou!" This unleashed a blade of energy from his sword toward the fire arrows. The energy blade struck several of the arrows, causing them to explode and take out some of the surrounding ones, but it wasn't enough to destroy them all.

With his emotions running high, Timaeus brought his left sword to his right shoulder and swung it horizontally to the left, shouting, "Lepída Anémou!" This unleashed a blade of energy from his sword, fuelled by the intensity of his emotions. The magical force cut through the winds, creating a powerful whirlwind that knocked the fire arrows off course. Unfortunately, despite being diverted, several fire arrows still reached Timaeus' location and exploded upon impact with the ground. Although his speed allowed him to dodge most of the arrows, the force of the explosions sent him crashing heavily to the ground. As he struggled to get back up, Timaeus noticed the green glow he had seen earlier. While seated on the ground, he realised that the Dark Fire Elemental had returned to reclaim his weapon.

Timaeus quickly turned onto his knees and shielded the green glow. "You fucking little shit," the Dark Fire Elemental said. "With all four elements at your disposal, your Element Magic is on another level. It's no surprise you've been such a fucking problem, even as a student. But this ends now. If your abilities were at a master level, Dark Elementals more powerful than I would be afraid of you."

He began to walk toward Timaeus, intent on killing the young warrior. With his life hanging in the balance and no options left, Timaeus understood what he had to do. The Dark Fire Elemental loomed over him and declared, "It's a shame, really... You would have been a powerful asset, but I can't take any chances with you anymore... You're dead."

He raised his blade, prepared to deliver the killing blow when Timaeus made his move. He turned toward his opponent, revealing a green glow in his right hand—a Green Element Stone. In one final attempt to stop his foe, Timaeus cried, "KALÓ TI VRONTÍ KÁTO APÓ TOUS OURANOÚS!!!" This invocation summoned a powerful bolt of lightning down from the heavens, striking the Dark Fire Elemental and knocking him down in his place.

Chapter Six
The Royal Court

Using such a powerful form of Magic left Timaeus exhausted. However, thanks to the stamina-increasing effects of the Green Element Stone in his hand, he was able to get back on his feet and pick up his weapons. The Dark Fire Elemental lay on the floor, heavily wounded by the Magic that Timaeus had unleashed upon him. With a distressed look on his face, Timaeus couldn't believe that the land he once called home was now gone. Suddenly, he heard a faint groan—"Argh..." It was the Dark Fire Elemental. "Nrgh..." he groaned as he struggled to get back on his feet. "You're fucking dead."

Timaeus was astonished that his opponent was able to stand and still fight back after enduring such a powerful magical attack. Despite the effects of the Green Element Stone, Timaeus felt too exhausted to defend himself. His opponent lifted his left arm and faintly spoke, "Kafstikó... Ángigma..."

He attempted to grab Timaeus by the neck and burn him with his touch when suddenly, a voice cried out, "AEROFOTOGRAFÍA!!!" This powerful blast of wind knocked the Dark Fire Elemental back to the ground. It was Master Phaedo who had come to Timaeus' aid, accompanied by several Wind Elementals.

The enemy was down, but he quickly got back to his feet. "Phaedo, you old fool," he said. "You may have won this battle, but you will lose the war when it comes." Master Phaedo stepped forward firmly. "Silence!" he shouted. "After what happened here tonight, I think it's safe to say that once my successor finishes his training, the war you speak of will be ended before it even begins."

Master Phaedo's words caused a worried expression to appear on the enemy's face. "Successor?!" he exclaimed, his tone filled with fear. "So... that fucking little brat who can wield all four forms of Element Magic is meant to inherit the Dragon's Eye Crest when you kick the bucket, Phaedo?"

The Dark Fire Elemental appeared as though he was ready to battle once more, prompting Master Phaedo and the other Wind Elementals to brace themselves. "I must warn my masters," the Dark Fire Elemental stated before shifting his focus to Timaeus. "But remember this, you fucking little shit: one day, I will return for you to finish what we started here today."

The Dark Fire Elemental reached into his pocket and threw a Magic Gem to the ground. "Ektyflotikó Fos!" he shouted. This caused the gem to emit a powerful blinding light, distracting his opponents and allowing him to make a quick escape. By the time the light faded, the Wind Elementals were unable to follow him.

Master Phaedo then turned his attention to Timaeus, who could barely stand after everything he had endured. "Come, Timaeus," he said. "Let's get you somewhere safe. Your friends are waiting for you in the city, eager to know that the one who risked his life for them is safe."

A small smile spread across Timaeus' face, but just as he was about to reply to Master Phaedo, he dropped the Green Element Stone he had been holding. Without its stamina-increasing Magic, he collapsed from his injuries. When Timaeus awoke, he found himself in an infirmary located in Eastern Atlantis. Master Phaedo sat beside him, relieved to see his successor awake.

"M-Master?" Timaeus said faintly. "How long have I been here?"

Master Phaedo stood up, poured a Magic elixir into a kantharos, and replied, "You've been unconscious for two days, Timaeus." He handed the kantharos to Timaeus and continued, "Taking on a Dark Elemental wasn't the wisest decision, my student."

Timaeus drank the elixir and responded, "I know, Master Phaedo. It's just that if I hadn't intervened, he would have claimed a dozen innocent lives."

It was the only way to prevent that from happening. "Where are they, Master Phaedo? I mean Gale and the others?" Master Phaedo quickly replied, "They're all fine, thanks to you. Zephyr confirmed their identities, and we verified their story when we saw his Dark Magic from the city, along with thunder being summoned down from the heavens."

Suddenly, Timaeus felt his strength returning, thanks to the magic elixir he had just drunk. "Where can I find them, Master Phaedo?" he asked as he got up.

Master Phaedo began escorting Timaeus out of the infirmary and replied, "You will see them in due time, Timaeus. Zephyr, Gale, and all your young friends will be waiting for us at the Royal Court."

Timaeus wore a confused expression, but then he noticed Master Phaedo take a small stone from his pocket and place it on the floor.

The stone was marked with symbols representing Central Atlantis and the Royal Court. As Master Phaedo stood over the stone, he spoke the word "Tilemetaforá," activating its magical properties. In an instant, both he and Timaeus found themselves at the entrance of the Royal Court. Master Phaedo noticed that Timaeus appeared a bit dizzy.

"Don't worry, Timaeus," he reassured him. "I felt the same way the first time I used a Teleport Rune. Now come, Byrne, Gorgias, and King Okeanos are expecting us."

The two of them entered the Royal Court, where they stood in a vast circular chamber surrounded by four towering pillars. A curved seating area encircled the centre of the court, and on the walls, directly opposite the pillars, were four large fountains shaped like dragon heads. Each fountain represented one of the four Dragon Crests.

Water cascaded from each fountain, filling the area of the chamber that separated the centre from the seating area. The seating area was occupied by Elementals and members of the Royal Guard. As Master Phaedo and Timaeus crossed the centre of the chamber, Timaeus noticed Gale and his friends sitting in the front row, being watched over by Zephyr, Hermos, Gorgas, Roc, and Ston. Once they reached the seating area, Master Phaedo approached Master Byrne, Master Gorgias, and King Okeanos, who were waiting for him while Timaeus remained behind. King Okeanos was dressed in cobalt blue robes adorned with the Dragon's Fang Crest. Four specially designed seats were crafted in the seating area for King Okeanos and the three Masters. Three of these seats were in the front row, while the king's seat was located in the second row behind the middle seat.

"Good to see you again, young Timaeus," said Master Byrne.

"Always a pleasure, Timaeus," added Master Gorgias.

"I believe we have yet to be introduced, young one," said King Okeanos.

Timaeus clenched his right hand and placed it across his shoulder. He knelt on his right knee and bowed his head. "Masters... Your Majesty," he said.

Master Phaedo rose from his seat. "Please allow me," he said. "Okeanos, this is Timaeus, my successor-to-be."

Timaeus remained on his knee with his head bowed.

"Please rise, Timaeus," said King Okeanos. "From what I've heard about your abilities, you could be all of our successors."

Chuckles echoed around the Royal Court. Timaeus stood but kept his head down, not in the mood for jokes.

"Not much of a joker, Timaeus?" King Okeanos inquired.

Timaeus looked up and replied, "Forgive me, Your Highness... It's just that with recent events, I'm not really focused on jokes."

King Okeanos understood Timaeus' perspective, and so did the other three Masters.

"It's understandable, Timaeus," said King Okeanos. "But seriously, what were you thinking when you took on a Dark Elemental by yourself?" Master Byrne questioned.

"Byrne is right, Timaeus. You're lucky to be alive right now," Master Gorgias added.

"We understand that you wanted to protect your friends, Timaeus. However, given your capabilities, a simple distraction would have sufficed," Master Phaedo stated.

"Forgive Me!" Timaeus shouted. "Masters, Your Highness, a simple distraction wouldn't have been enough. The Dark Elemental would have followed us, putting lives at risk. He already endangered someone's life once by unleashing a Chimera's Tail on our home."

Everyone in the Royal Court was shocked at what they were hearing.

"As I mentioned, Timaeus, it's understandable," said King Okeanos. "Fighting a Dark Elemental does leave a mark on us." Timaeus knelt down on his right knee once more. "Masters... Your Highness," he said, "I must ask... Who are the Dark Elementals? I was told that the Acolytes they once were have been gone for centuries but not completely wiped out. I was informed that those Acolytes are now the Dark Elementals."

King Okeanos and the three masters exchanged concerned glances before turning their attention back to Timaeus. "It seems, Timaeus," said King Okeanos, "you haven't been told the full story." He and the other three Masters then proceeded to share the origin story of the Dark Elementals with everyone in the Royal Court. What Timaeus had been told wasn't a lie, but it wasn't the complete truth either.

Centuries ago, the Acolytes were doing everything in their power to make the Archmage's prophecy of Leviathan's return a reality. However, they stood no chance against the forces of Atlantis without their master. This changed one fateful day when an Atlantean prince, known for his disregard for rules, got careless and inadvertently provided the Acolytes with what they needed to fight back.

The prince had been chosen to be his father's successor and hold the Dragon's Fang Crest. At the time, he and the successors of the Earth, Fire, and Wind Masters were young and curious. In a moment of rebellion, the young prince decided to go behind his father's back and took his three allies on a tour of the Royal Vault. There, they stumbled upon many of Atlantis' ancient treasures.

They came across a trident believed to have once belonged to Poseidon, the God of the Seas. They also found an ancient cornucopia said to have been owned by Demeter, the Goddess of the Earth, a set of armour that was said to belong to Ares, the God of War, and an ancient aegis that was rumoured to have been wielded by Zeus, the King of the Gods. The prince and his three allies were amazed at what they discovered, but their exploration eventually led them to the location of the Magic Urn that had been used to seal Leviathan.

Access to the Urn was restricted, and only a member of the Royal Family could unlock the Magic Seal. Encouraged by his three allies, the prince decided to unlock the seal. Letting his curiosity get the better of him, he touched the seal, and it opened. Inside, they found the Magic Urn containing Leviathan.

In awe of standing before the Urn that contained the ancient evil nearly responsible for the destruction of Atlantis, the prince and his three allies approached it cautiously. As the prince extended his hand toward the Urn to sense any energy emanating from it, he suddenly heard a loud shout telling him to stop. Startled, he turned around quickly, accidentally knocking the Magic Urn slightly out of its place. It turned out that the prince's younger brother had followed him and his allies into the Royal Vault.

His three allies quickly reacted to prevent the Urn from toppling over, but in the process, the lid was jarred loose, releasing a puff of black smoke. Realising the danger, the prince swiftly closed the lid of the Urn and urged his brother to run. The small puff of smoke began to expand, engulfing the prince and his allies. In a desperate move, the prince sealed off the area to prevent any of the black smoke from escaping the Royal Vault.

A few hours later, the Magic Seal unlocked once again, revealing the prince and his three allies unconscious on the ground. They were quickly rushed to an infirmary. When the four of them awoke, they were no longer who they once were; they had been corrupted by the black smoke, a manifestation of Leviathan's Dark Magic. Thus, the Dark Elementals were born.

Immediately, they turned against Atlantis, wreaking havoc wherever they went. As they battled through Central Atlantis, they sought to return to the Royal Vault to claim the Magic Urn containing Leviathan, but they found themselves outmatched by Atlantis' forces. Consequently, they fled and sought out the Acolytes, who provided them with the means to combat Atlantis' military.

Since then, they have been living in the shadows, kidnapping and corrupting Element Students with Leviathan's Dark Magic to build their own army. Their ultimate goal is to bring down Atlantis.

Eventually, the forces of the Dark Elementals grew so large that they outnumbered the Acolytes and slaughtered them all. The Dark Elementals then donned the outfits of the Acolytes as a symbol of their commitment to complete what the Archmage had started.

"Are the four Dark Elementals still alive today?" Timaeus asked

"Yes, they are," replied King Okeanos. "Leviathan's Dark Magic grants them immortality, so they cannot die of old age. Moreover, as you have undoubtedly discovered, they are also resistant to our Element Magic, making it much more difficult to defeat them in combat."

A worried expression appeared on Timaeus' face. "The Dark Fire Elemental," he said. "He mentioned Dark Elementals more powerful than him, along with his masters. How is it that they turn Element Students into Dark Elementals, Your Majesty?"

A look of devastation crossed King Okeanos' face, mirrored by the three masters.

"Students who are kidnapped are taken to the four Dark Elementals who were originally corrupted by Leviathan's Dark Magic," replied Master Phaedo. "One of them passes on a fragment of Leviathan's Dark Magic, corrupting the Element Student into a Dark Elemental. Only the original four Dark Elementals can perform this transformation, which is why you weren't corrupted by the one you fought."

A serious expression crossed Timaeus' face. "Well then," he said, prompting everyone to look at him in surprise. "It's time for me to get back to training so that the next time a Dark Elemental comes looking for me, I'll be ready."

King Okeanos and the three Masters rose from their seats. "Your determination is admirable, Timaeus," said King Okeanos. "While you were recovering, Phaedo, Byrne, Gorgias, and I discussed how you will learn to use all four forms of Element Magic. After completing your training with Phaedo, you will spend three years with each of us, starting with Byrne, then Gorgias, and finally myself."

A serious expression came over Timaeus' face as he turned to Gale and the other orphans. "Forgive me, Your Highness, but I must ask," he said. "What will happen to Gale and the others while I am training? As you may have discovered during my recovery, we are all orphans."

King Okeanos raised his hand. "You need not worry, Timaeus," he replied. "Living quarters have been arranged for all of you in Eastern Atlantis. We have also discovered that your young friends are quite formidable fighters, undoubtedly having learned to defend themselves from you. Therefore, each of them will be inducted into the Royal Guard."

This news brought a smile to Timaeus' face. "Thank you, Your Highness," he said gratefully.

"You're welcome, young one," replied King Okeanos. "I believe that concludes everything we came here to discuss today. Everyone is dismissed."

Everyone was preparing to leave the Royal Court when a voice shouted, "Ánodos Neroú!" Suddenly, the waters inside the Royal Court began to rise, blocking anyone from exiting. A young man wearing a cerulean blue robe walked confidently through the wall of water. He held a trident staff in his right hand and his left hand in the air. As he approached Timaeus, the young man lowered his left hand, causing the wall of water to recede.

"Critias, what is the meaning of this?!" King Okeanos shouted, his voice filled with authority. Critias slammed the polearm of his trident staff onto the ground and replied, "Forgive me, Father. It's just that, from what I've been told, this one is capable of defeating Hermos, Gorgas, Roc, and Ston in combat, not to mention taking on a Dark Elemental by himself. I want to see his capabilities in combat for myself."

The entire Royal Court was in an uproar, as many were eager to witness this display of power.

Master Phaedo, Master Byrne, and Master Gorgias were engaged in a discussion when Master Phaedo turned to King Okeanos. "Sorry, Okeanos," he said, "but our money is on Timaeus." This brought a serious expression to King Okeanos' face. "Challenge accepted," he replied.

After accepting the challenge from the three Masters, King Okeanos rose from his seat, raised his arms, and conjured a wall of water, much like Critias had done moments earlier. He then lowered his arms, causing the wall of water to dissipate and effectively silencing the Royal Court.

"It seems, Timaeus," said King Okeanos, "that having already defeated two successors with your abilities, everyone is curious if you can defeat the third. Do you accept my son's challenge?" Timaeus stood with a stern look on his face, reflecting on his recent battle with the Dark Elemental.

Despite this, he drew his weapons. "I accept," said Timaeus. Before the fight began, Timaeus reached into his pocket and pulled out something. "Master Phaedo!" he shouted, throwing the Green Element Stone he had found on the abandoned farmland to Master Phaedo. "I didn't earn that stone, Master," Timaeus explained. "I found it by luck, so I have no right to use it in combat."

With that, Timaeus and Critias prepared to face each other, each getting into a fighting stance. King Okeanos returned to his seat and shouted, "BEGIN!"

Critias made the opening move, attempting to strike with his trident staff. However, Timaeus easily defended himself against the prince's attack with his left sword and prepared to counterattack with his right sword. Yet, the prince was able to avoid the counter with ease.

Master Phaedo noticed a flaw in Timaeus' fighting technique. "*He left himself wide open. The boy should have easily landed that counterattack,*" thought Master Phaedo. As the battle raged on, Timaeus spotted a torch on each of the pillars surrounding the centre of the Royal Court. He raised his hands toward one of the torches and shouted, "*Éla Fotiá!*" As the flames approached, Timaeus swung both his blades upwards diagonally and shouted, "Oi Lepídes Anaflégontai!" Igniting both swords simultaneously, he quickly swung them downward diagonally, exclaiming, "Lepídes Flógas!" This created two blades of fire in the shape of an X.

Critias was astonished by Timaeus' abilities but quickly sprang into action. He extended both arms outward and shouted, "Éla Neró!" He summoned from the water that surrounded the Royal Court to his hands. At the last moment, Critias lowered his arms and then swiftly lifted them upward while shouting, "Ánodos Neroú!" This manoeuvre caused the summoned water to rise, effectively intercepting and extinguishing Timaeus' fiery attack.

Master Byrne was puzzled by Timaeus' choice to launch such a powerful attack from the very start. He thought, *"That was a strong move. Typically, Timaeus would use the first blade to distract his opponent and the second to land his main attack. Why did he go all out right away?"*

After withdrawing his blades, Timaeus faced Critias, who, having just defended against a powerful strike, decided to go on the offensive. Critias attacked Timaeus again with his trident staff, but to everyone's surprise, Timaeus did not retaliate. Instead, Critias managed to land a hit, but it caused no damage.

In a swift motion, Timaeus grabbed Critias' trident staff with his left hand and pulled Critias closer. He then delivered a solid body shot with his right hand, causing Critias to lose his grip and drop the trident staff. With his opponent disarmed, Timaeus effortlessly threw Critias over his shoulder.

Master Gorgias couldn't understand Timaeus' violent behaviour. *"His strategy allowed him to bypass his opponent's defences, but I've never seen him resort to such brutality before. The methods I've seen him use involve surprising his opponents,"* Master Gorgias thought.

King Okeanos and the three Masters then noticed Timaeus drawing his swords. "EPÍGEIA!!!" Master Gorgias shouted. Thanks to his intervention, Timaeus was unable to move. "Withdraw your weapons, young Timaeus," Master Byrne urged. Timaeus complied and sheathed his swords at Master Byrne's request.

"Why are you fighting so violently, young one?" Master Phaedo asked. King Okeanos rose from his seat and said, "I think I understand... It's because the boy is damaged from what he has been through recently.

After Master Gorgias released Timaeus, he clenched his right hand and placed it across his shoulder.

He knelt down on his right knee. "I don't understand, Your Majesty," he replied. "My injuries were healed before I came here today." King Okeanos raised his hand and shook his head in denial. "No, Timaeus," he said. "You may have healed physically, but you have not healed mentally. Up until the events of that night, everything you experienced was either training, sparring, or competitive combat. However, your encounter with that Dark Elemental involved real combat that put you in life-or-death circumstances, and the trauma from this experience has had a severe mental impact on you. You are now perceiving every opponent as threatening as that Dark Elemental."

King Okeanos' words struck Timaeus deeply, and he began to realise the effects the battle had on him. "Forgive me, Your Majesty. This is not who I am," Timaeus said as he stood up. "I not only owe you an apology, Critias, but I also owe you a challenge."

Critias turned around and walked toward the waters inside the Royal Court. He knelt down, placed his hands in the water, and spoke, "Therapéfste To Neró," healing any damage inflicted by Timaeus. With Critias healed and Timaeus mentally recovered, the two prepared to fight again, both adopting their fighting stances. King Okeanos returned to his seat and shouted, "BEGIN!!!"

Critias made the opening move, shouting, "Ánodos Neroú!!!" This created a wall of water that immediately fell and soaked both him and Timaeus in the centre of the Royal Court. As Critias attempted to attack Timaeus with his trident staff, he realised that the water had weakened his Earth Magic. In retaliation, Timaeus grabbed Critias' trident staff with his left hand, used his speed to pull Critias toward him, seized Critias' robe in the process, and threw him over his shoulder.

"*Much better. He got past his opponent's defences without using violent methods and was able to surprise him,*" thought Master Gorgias. As the battle continued, Timaeus raised his hands towards one of the torches on the pillars surrounding the centre of the Royal Court and shouted, "Éla Fotiá!" As the flames approached him, he swung both his blades upward diagonally and exclaimed, "Oi Lepídes Anaflégontai!" Igniting both swords simultaneously, he then swung his right sword downward diagonally and shouted, "Lepída Flógas!" creating a blade of fire.

Critias noticed the change in Timaeus' strategy, but he did not create the same defence as before, as he was soaked with water, which made him resistant to Fire Magic. The blade of fire struck Critias directly, but he remained unfazed by the attack.

"That was pointless," he said in disgust.

"I know," Timaeus replied confidently. "That's because the attack wasn't intended for you."

This left Critias confused but not worried. He prepared to launch his next attack when Timaeus swung his left sword horizontally, shouting, "Lepída Flógas!" This created another blade of fire.

Due to his calmness after the last attack, Critias decided to face this one head-on. However, to everyone's surprise, he was knocked back by the force of the attack.

"Nrgh!..." Critias groaned as he got back on his feet.

"How did you get past my defense?" he asked.

Timaeus stood with his blades held beside him and replied, "It's because you had no defence. As I mentioned a few moments ago, my first attack wasn't aimed at you. It was meant to evaporate the water you'd soaked yourself with, which left you vulnerable to my second attack."

The entire Royal Court applauded Timaeus' strategy. *"That was a much better attack. He not only used the first blade as a distraction but also disabled his opponent's defences in the process, making it easy to land the second attack,"* thought Master Byrne. Critias was becoming increasingly annoyed that Timaeus was outsmarting him with his tactics. In a fit of frustration, the prince tore off his robe, ran to the waters surrounding the Royal Court, and jumped in. He swam quickly in circles to confuse Timaeus. When he emerged from the water, his wounds had healed, and Critias prepared to strike with his trident staff. However, with his speed, Timaeus easily reacted to the prince's surprise attack. He defended himself with his left sword and counterattacked with his right sword, slicing Critias across the abdomen and bringing him to his knees.

Master Phaedo did not see any issues with Timaeus' fighting technique this time. He thought, *"Not only is Timaeus keeping up with Critias, but he also created a clear opening in his opponent's defence. The boy managed to land his counterattack with ease this time."* The entire Royal Court was amazed by what they were witnessing. Although Critias had been knocked down, he certainly wasn't out of the fight. Once he regained his footing, he sprinted toward the water and jumped in. He swam around and launched another surprise attack, which Timaeus easily avoided. While the prince had healed his wounds, he chose not to engage Timaeus in a direct confrontation. Instead, he kept returning to the water in hopes of catching Timaeus off-guard. However, Critias' surprise attacks proved ineffective against Timaeus' speed, although King Okeanos noticed that the prince was wearing him down.

Continuously defending himself against the surprise attacks was getting Timaeus nowhere, so he decided to withdraw his swords. Staying calm and focused, he prepared himself for Critias' next emergence from the waters. As he waited, Timaeus turned his attention to the four wall fountains. A moment later, Critias launched his next surprise attack, which Timaeus easily dodged with his speed, prompting the prince to retreat into the water again.

Wasting no time, Timaeus put his plan into action. He raised his hand toward one of the wall fountains and shouted, "Metakiníste Ti Gi!" This caused the statue of the dragon's head to close its mouth, cutting off the water from the fountain.

"Amazing," said Master Gorgias. "He used Earth Magic to manipulate the stone, making it look as though he had brought the statue to life."

Once again, Critias attempted to strike Timaeus, but he easily avoided the attack.

Each time the prince launched a surprise attack, Timaeus skilfully avoided it while closing off another fountain. "What is Timaeus up to?" Master Phaedo inquired. "Closing the fountains hasn't improved his odds in any way." With all four fountains now closed, Timaeus waited for Critias to make his next move.

"He already knows that, Phaedo," Master Byrne replied confidently. "Timaeus understands that to diminish Critias' advantage, he needs to eliminate its source. However, for this strategy to succeed, he must ensure that Critias doesn't regain access to it."

This statement intrigued King Okeanos. "That's true, Byrne," he said. "But it will take hours for the water to drain, and it appears that Timaeus won't be able to hold out much longer."

With a confident smile, Master Byrne responded, "Just wait, Okeanos... I think I know how he's planning to do it." Critias made his next attack, which Timaeus dodged with ease.

After the prince retreated back into the waters, Timaeus raised his hands and shouted, "Éla Óli Fotiá!" Flames erupted from all four pillars of the Royal Court and danced in his palms. Wasting no time, he sprinted towards the water and cried, "Fotiá Tis Kólasis!" This unleashed a fiery blaze that scorched the waters of the Royal Court.

Critias emerged from the depths, attempting to confront Timaeus, but the intense heat from Timaeus' flames kept him at bay. Within seconds, the water in the Royal Court had evaporated, leaving the area enveloped in steam.

"Therapéfste To Neró," Timaeus said, healing himself as he did so.

"I fucking knew it," Master Byrne observed. "Timaeus used Fire Magic to evaporate the water, but he had to close the fountains to prevent them from refilling. Plus, he was able to heal himself with the steam generated in the process."

Everyone was amazed. "Anemostróvilos!" Timaeus exclaimed as he created a small twister to disperse the steam. Angered at being outsmarted by Timaeus once again, Critias charged forward, attacking with his trident staff. However, Timaeus easily defended himself using his left arm, as Critias, lacking water to empower his Water Magic, couldn't penetrate Timaeus' Earth Magic defenses.

"Aerofotografía!" Timaeus shouted, summoning a powerful blast of wind that knocked Critias backwards into one of the pillars of the Royal Court. The prince quickly regained his footing and prepared to engage Timaeus once more. Both warriors dashed toward each other, intent on finishing the fight.

Critias raised his trident staff, ready to deliver a decisive blow. As he struck, Timaeus seized the trident with his right hand, pivoted on his right foot, and swung around to elbow Critias in the abdomen with his left elbow. This sudden move forced Critias to release his grip on the trident staff.

Seizing the opportunity, Timaeus took the trident staff and slid it down his arm while stepping his right foot around Critias. With another pivot of his right foot, he swung the trident staff, striking Critias' legs and bringing the prince to the ground. Timaeus then placed his left foot over Critias' chest and held the trident staff over his throat.

"Enough!" shouted King Okeanos. At this command, Timaeus removed his foot from Critias' chest and dropped the trident staff to the ground. He turned to face King Okeanos and the three Masters, clenched his right fist, and placed it across his shoulder. Kneeling on his right knee, he bowed his head.

"Rise, Timaeus," said King Okeanos. Timaeus stood up and looked at him and the three Masters with a look of strong determination on his face. The king rose from his seat, and the three Masters applauded alongside the Royal Court, which erupted in applause and cheers for Timaeus and his impressive demonstration.

Timaeus turned to Critias and offered to help him up, which Critias accepted. "I don't fear defeat," said Critias, "but I'm prepared to accept it." The two shook hands. "Don't worry," replied Timaeus. "I promised Hermos and Gorgas a rematch, and I'm promising you one as well."

He then focused on the four wall fountains and said, "Metakiníste Ti Gi," causing the statues to open and allowing the waters to flow back to the Royal Court.

"What we witnessed here today was remarkable," said King Okeanos. "In time, it will no doubt become incredible... and eventually, indescribable. But for now, we cannot look back. It's time for all of us to prepare for what lies ahead. With that said, now that everything has been concluded here today, everyone is dismissed."

Chapter Seven
The Valley

After everyone was dismissed from the Royal Court, Master Phaedo and Timaeus decided to focus on completing Timaeus' training. Master Phaedo offered his successor the Green Element Stone, but Timaeus declined, insisting that he needed to earn it properly since he had found it. With that, they returned to their training.

Meanwhile, in an unknown location, the Dark Fire Elemental that Timaeus had faced reported back to his masters. He stood before the four Dark Elementals who had originally been corrupted by Leviathan's Dark Magic. All four of them wore black hooded robes, their faces obscured by the shadows of their dark powers.

"What is this madness you speak of?" asked the Dark Elemental of Fire.

Trembling before his masters, the Dark Fire Elemental replied, "Forgive me, my lady, but it is true. This little shit possesses the ability to use all four forms of Element Magic. Despite being merely a Wind Student, his power is fucking formidable. And what's worse, he has been chosen to bear the Dragon's Eye Crest."

The Dark Elemental of Earth sat quietly, chuckling to himself. "Haha... As we know, the four Elementals who originally defeated Leviathan had to combine their abilities to do so. What's the point of reviving it if one person could accomplish this alone?"

The Dark Elemental of Water stood up in anger. "No... This is not possible. If what took four Elementals to achieve can be done by just one, then all our efforts will have been for nothing," he said.

The Dark Fire Elemental approached his masters. "Forgive me, masters," he said. "But based on my experience with the little shit, he can't combine the four forms of Element Magic into one."

The Dark Elemental of Water glared at him and replied, "That you know of! For all we know, this could be something he learns during his training."

The Dark Fire Elemental stood, fear evident in his eyes. "You seem to be overlooking something," said a voice. Everyone turned to see the Dark Elemental of Wind standing by a ledge, facing away from them.

"While what you're saying is true, this Element Student is meant to bear the Dragon's Eye Crest. It is indeed possible that he could learn a power that might jeopardise everything we aim to achieve. However, in order for us to obtain the Dragon's Eye Crest, he has to die first. By the time we resurrect Leviathan, he will have been killed by one of us."

This brought smiles to the others' faces. "For delivering us this information," said the Dark Elemental of Wind. "Your life shall be spared."

The Dark Fire Elemental let out a sigh of relief. "Thank you, master," he said. "But may I ask that when the time comes, you allow me to kill that fucking little shit? He got the better of me through sheer luck, and he was barely alive when I left. The only reason he survived is because of Phaedo and his fucking lackeys."

The Dark Elemental of Wind stood with his back to the others and said, "By all means... if he hasn't been killed before you two meet again." With a vengeful expression, the Dark Fire Elemental walked away to prepare for the day he would confront Timaeus again. As he departed, another Dark Elemental approached, accompanying a kidnapped male Water Student. The Dark Elemental of Water moved toward the young boy and infused him with a piece of Leviathan's Dark Magic, corrupting him into a Dark Elemental.

"Another one for our endless army," he remarked.

"It would seem so," replied the Dark Elemental of Wind.

The young boy was taken away while the other three Dark Elementals joined the Dark Elemental of Wind at the ledge, overlooking an entire legion of Dark Elementals.

In Eastern Atlantis, Timaeus continued his training under Master Phaedo. In a short amount of time, he was able to refine his Wind Magic while also practising the other forms of Element Magic when he wasn't training with Master Phaedo. He frequently visited Gale and the other orphans who were being trained to become members of the Royal Guard, helping them with their training and putting his skills into practice.

As part of his training, Timaeus worked with the weaponsmiths of Eastern Atlantis and soon became a skilled blacksmith. With this training, he was able to forge a new weapon in preparation for when he would start his training with Master Byrne. He crafted a broadsword that could split into two, allowing him to switch between the weapons of the Fire Elementals and the Wind Elementals whenever he desired. This versatility would also make it easier for Timaeus to add a bow to his arsenal in the future.

As Timaeus' training progressed, he learned to combine his Wind Magic with his new weapon. By the time his training was complete, he wielded a blade that enabled him to cut through the wind itself. After three years, the moment had finally come to put his skills to the test.

"You've come a long way since your abilities were discovered, Timaeus," said Master Phaedo. "But, like all Wind Students before you, it is time for you to face the final trial. It is time for you to earn your Element Stone."

Timaeus placed his clenched right hand on his left shoulder and bowed his head. "Yes, Master Phaedo," he replied. "What must I do? I've seen many Wind Students earn their Element Stone, but I've never been told anything about the final trial."

Master Phaedo placed his hand on Timaeus' shoulder and replied, "We don't reveal any information about the final trial because, in the past, students were lost after receiving such details. Their arrogance led them to attempt the trial before they were ready. The information I'm about to share with you must remain a secret. Understood?"

Timaeus placed his clenched right hand on his left shoulder and bowed his head once again. "Understood, Master Phaedo," he replied. "You have my word." With that, Master Phaedo revealed the final trial to Timaeus.

"You must venture to the valley on the northeastern side of Eastern Atlantis," said Master Phaedo. "Once there, you will find the Element Stone atop its highest cliff. Your abilities will undoubtedly make this task easier than it sounds, which is why Byrne, Gorgias, Okeanos, and I have agreed that during this final trial, you are limited to using only the Element Magic you are currently being trained in. Once you have retrieved the Element Stone or if you wish to withdraw from the trial at any time, take this Teleport Rune, and you can return here immediately."

With that, Timaeus set out to find his Element Stone.

Timaeus' journey led him back to the abandoned farmland where he had lived three years prior. As night fell, he decided to stay there until morning. Reflecting on his time there, Timaeus walked down to the river to catch his dinner and cooked it over a campfire. This brought back some painful memories of the night he was attacked by the Dark Fire Elemental. Although those memories were difficult to face, Timaeus resolved not to let them affect him as they had three years ago.

After a restful night, morning arrived, and Timaeus continued on his journey. Eventually, he reached the valley where he could see, in the distance, the highest cliff rising above the forest. Atop that cliff awaited his Element Stone. Despite the calmness of the valley, Timaeus sensed that something was lurking nearby; otherwise, the journey would have been too easy, especially considering all the training he had undertaken to prepare for this moment.

Timaeus ventured into the forest within the valley. After walking for several hours, he finally arrived at the cliff where he would find his Element Stone. Without wasting any time, he began to climb the cliff face. At first, he had no trouble, but as he continued to ascend, he struggled and nearly slipped to his death on several occasions. Exhausted from the climb, Timaeus hung on the cliffside as he neared the top. Despite his fatigue, he summoned the last of his strength, and as evening approached, he finally reached the summit.

To Timaeus' surprise, after hours of climbing, he found nothing there. Although this was strange, he knew his journey wasn't over yet. After catching his breath for a moment, Timaeus began to explore the area. He discovered huge white feathers and two sets of large footprints. Suddenly, a large creature emerged, letting out a terrifying cry, and struck Timaeus across the face with its tail.

Timaeus instantly jumped to his feet and drew his blade, splitting it into twin swords. Everything about this final trial began to make sense, especially why no information had been disclosed beforehand to anyone until they were truly prepared. He recalled a story he had heard many years ago about a valley in Atlantis that very few people ventured into and even fewer returned from. The final trial was not the valley itself but rather what lay within it. Timaeus had been sent to Griffin Valley.

He swung his swords at the beast but failed to land a single hit. The Griffin retaliated, knocking one of Timaeus' swords from his hand.

A fierce clash ensued between man and beast, but the Griffin struck Timaeus back with its wing. Undeterred, he charged at the creature again, but it skilfully evaded his attack and slashed his right arm with its left talon.

Timaeus quickly recovered and launched another assault at the Griffin, yet it continued to defend itself and avoid all of his strikes.

The Griffin attacked Timaeus with its right talon, pushing him closer to the edge of the cliff. As the battle intensified, Timaeus' blade began to glow. He brought his sword from his right side to his left shoulder and swung it horizontally, shouting, "LEPÍDA ANÉMOU!" This manoeuvre cut through the wind, creating a small whirlwind that distracted the Griffin.

Taking advantage of this moment, Timaeus quickly retrieved his other sword, aiming to land a fatal blow. However, the Griffin countered with its right wing, striking him across the torso with its left talon. Heavily injured and losing stamina, Timaeus felt hopeless against the creature.

Just as the Griffin prepared to finish him off, Timaeus noticed a familiar green glow behind it—the whirlwind had uncovered the Element Stone he had been searching for. Merging his swords back into one, he skilfully avoided the Griffin's imminent attack, rolling beneath the creature to get behind it. There, he seized the Element Stone, which revitalised him with its stamina-increasing effects.

The Griffin, undeterred, slashed at Timaeus once more. With the Element Stone's power, he shouted, "MEGÁLOS ANEMOSTRÓVILOS!" This conjured a powerful tornado around him, hurling the Griffin aside. With the creature momentarily incapacitated, Timaeus stabbed it through the shoulder with his sword, finally defeating it.

Chapter Eight
The Mountain

With the trial complete, Timaeus set the Teleport Rune given to him by Master Phaedo on the ground, preparing to report his success. Just as he was about to recite the incantation to activate the rune, he heard a faint groan. It was the Griffin; it had survived Timaeus' final attack. Despite the danger that the creature had put him in, Timaeus didn't want to feel as if he were taking the life of an innocent being.

He approached the Griffin, took out a small amphora, and poured the water inside onto the creature's wound. As he did so, he spoke the words, "Therapéfste To Neró," causing a blue glow to appear as it healed the Griffin's injury. However, this healing caused Timaeus to take on the creature's pain in his right shoulder.

A short while later, the Griffin awoke, fully healed from Timaeus' attack. It stood up and looked toward Timaeus. He raised his left hand in front of him and said, "Easy... easy," as the creature approached.

To Timaeus' surprise, the Griffin lowered its head toward his left hand, allowing him to stroke its forehead. The Griffin was expressing gratitude for Timaeus saving its life. Happy to have made a new friend in the Griffin, Timaeus decided it was time to return. He approached the Teleport Rune he had placed on the ground earlier.

As he was about to speak the incantation to activate it, the Griffin let out a loud cry and lay on the ground, which Timaeus mistook for an unwillingness to let him leave. He picked up the Teleport Rune and approached the Griffin to say goodbye to his new friend, but the creature cried out again, flapped its wings, and then placed its head on the ground.

Confused by this behaviour, Timaeus sensed that the Griffin wanted him to do something. He walked around to its left side, and the Griffin lifted its head, looking towards Timaeus while flapping its wings and chirping at him.

It soon became clear that the Griffin wanted Timaeus to mount it. He placed his hand on its left side and climbed onto the creature's back. With that, the Griffin ran toward the edge of the cliff and took to the skies. As the creature soared out of Griffin Valley, the Dark Elemental of Wind appeared atop the cliff and approached the spot where the wounded Griffin had been moments before.

He knelt down and picked up some of the creature's blood from the wound Timaeus had inflicted upon it. As he did so, he watched Timaeus and the Griffin soaring off into the sunset. Timaeus was enjoying the beautiful spectacle of the sunset while riding on the Griffin, but he had no idea where the creature was taking him. To prevent being carried away to an unfamiliar location, Timaeus decided to improvise by using his Wind Magic to guide the Griffin. Eventually, he succeeded in steering the creature back to the training grounds in Eastern Atlantis.

Master Phaedo, Zephyr, and Gale were anxiously awaiting Timaeus' return. "Do you think something has happened to him, Master Phaedo?" Gale asked. Shaking his head, Master Phaedo replied, "I don't know, Gale... I have seen many Wind Students succeed and fail this trial. So, I'm afraid only time will tell."

Gale and Zephyr exchanged worried glances about their friend, but Master Phaedo was even more concerned because he had expected Timaeus to be back by now. Suddenly, all three of them heard a loud cry. They looked up to the sky and saw a Griffin heading towards them. Not realising that Timaeus was riding the creature, Master Phaedo, Zephyr, and Gale prepared to defend themselves.

As the Griffin landed in front of them, they raised their weapons, causing the creature to rear in defence. "How the fuck do we handle this thing?" Zephyr exclaimed as the Griffin let out another loud cry.

"Hold on," said a familiar voice. As Master Phaedo, Zephyr, and Gale reacted to the sound, the Griffin reared again, knocking Timaeus off its back. Despite their attempts to reach Timaeus, the creature stood its ground, preventing them from getting past it.

"Stop!" Timaeus shouted as he got back up. With the Griffin still holding its position, Timaeus walked around it and stroked its forehead, saying, "Easy... easy." The creature calmed down and lay down on the ground.

Amazed by what they were witnessing, Master Phaedo, Zephyr, and Gale put away their weapons.

"What the fuck is going on here, Timaeus?" Zephyr asked. Timaeus turned around and explained what had transpired in Griffin Valley, emphasising that he wasn't going to let an innocent creature die. After hearing Timaeus' story, Zephyr inquired, "Does your new friend have a name?"

As Timaeus was about to answer, Master Phaedo stepped forward and said, "You were only allowed to use Wind Magic during this trial, Timaeus."

Timaeus placed his right hand across his left shoulder and replied, "I understand that, Master Phaedo. However, as I just explained, I had already completed the trial. The Water Magic wasn't for my benefit; it was for the benefit of another."

Hearing this impressed Master Phaedo, and he responded, "Very well, Timaeus. You didn't use any other Element Magic to complete the trial, so you did not gain any advantage. It seems you have formed quite a bond with this Griffin; he shows great affection and loyalty toward you."

Gale was confused by Master Phaedo's words. "He shows?" Gale asked. Master Phaedo turned towards him and replied, "Yes, Gale. This is a male Griffin. Males have white feathers, while females have brown feathers. I must ask, though, Timaeus, how did you tame the beast so quickly to get it to bring you back here?"

Timaeus then explained, "I didn't. I had to use Wind Magic to guide him back here." Master Phaedo was impressed by Timaeus' intuition.

"What's his name?" Zephyr asked for the second time. After a few moments of thought and while stroking his new friend on the forehead, Timaeus replied, "His name is Stratos." The Griffin chirped happily.

"I think he likes it," said Master Phaedo. "The name suits him. These creatures are strong enough to take on an army! Hehe. Now that your new friend has been given a name, we have other important matters to discuss. After retrieving your Element Stone, you are now officially an Elemental, and soon, it will be time for you to start your training with Master Byrne in North Atlantis."

Timaeus placed his right hand across his left shoulder and replied, "Yes, Master Phaedo." Master Phaedo felt proud of the warrior Timaeus was becoming. "With that, let us retire for the night," he said. As everyone began to leave, Stratos started to follow Timaeus. "I have a feeling that Stratos won't be returning to Griffin Valley any time soon," he mused. "During the time before I leave for North Atlantis, I think it would be wise to train him so that next time, he will know where to go instead of me having to use magic to guide him. Plus, he needs to learn to distinguish friend from foe."

Stratos chirped happily at this idea, and with that, the five of them retired for the night. Timaeus brought Stratos back to where he, Gale, and the other orphans resided. Upon their arrival, dinner was being prepared over a campfire. Everyone was glad to see Timaeus and Gale, but they were wary of Stratos, particularly because of the way he was looking at them. "Calm down, Stratos," Timaeus said.

The Griffin let out a loud cry and charged toward one of the orphans standing near the campfire. Fearing for the boy's safety, Gale drew his weapon. However, Timaeus noticed that Stratos had begun to slow down, and to everyone's surprise, he stopped when he reached the boy. Stratos started sniffing at what the boy was holding in his hand, drawn in by the smell of fish cooking over the campfire. Without harming the boy, Stratos quickly snatched the fish on the stick from his hands and ran off with it.

"It seems like your new friend likes fast food," Gale remarked, prompting laughter from everyone. Afterwards, they all sat around the campfire while Stratos munched on the fish he had taken.

Meanwhile, in the unknown location where the Dark Elementals resided, the Dark Elemental of Wind returned with a sample of Stratos' blood that he had taken from the site where the Griffin fought Timaeus. He walked past his comrades to the edge of a cliff overlooking his ever-growing army of Dark Elementals.

"It appears we will need to be at our zenith if we are to defeat the one who can wield all four forms of Element Magic," he said. A worried look crossed the face of the Dark Elemental of Fire. "What the fuck do you mean?" she asked.

Looking back over his shoulder, the Dark Elemental of Wind replied, "The one who can use all four forms of Element Magic has now been promoted to an Elemental." The other three Dark Elementals were at a loss for words. The Dark Elemental of Earth merely laughed it off.

"Haha... So what?" he teased. "Why not just kill him and be done with it? Why all this worry?"

The Dark Elemental of Wind revealed a sample of Griffin's blood that he had obtained and showed it to the other three Dark Elementals. "Because the little shit has his uses," he explained. "Most Element Students simply obtain their Element Stone and escape the beast guarding it, but this one drew blood from a Griffin. This could work to our advantage if he were able to collect blood from the other beasts that guard the Element Stones."

The Dark Elemental of Water erupted in fury. "If he were to obtain blood!" he shouted. "If he doesn't gather any blood from the other beasts, then by the time we confront this little shit, he will have mastered all four forms of Element Magic and acquired four Element Stones! Who knows what the fuck else he might gain!"

The Dark Elemental of Wind turned to face his comrade and replied, "As I said, we will need to be at our zenith."

Turning back to look over his army of Dark Elementals, the Dark Elemental of Wind returned the sample of Stratos' blood to his robes.

In the coming weeks, Timaeus successfully tamed Stratos. He began by teaching him to distinguish between friend and foe by having him learn everyone's scent. Next, Timaeus introduced certain commands to help Stratos understand right from wrong. Finally, he trained Stratos to respond while airborne, allowing him to guide the creature to various destinations without using Wind Magic.

The weeks flew by, and soon, it was time for Timaeus to depart for North Atlantis to begin his training with Master Byrne. He entrusted Gale with their living quarters while Stratos stood guard as a watchful protector. After saying goodbye to everyone, Timaeus gently stroked his loyal companion's forehead, reassuring him that he wouldn't be gone forever.

Afterwards, Timaeus set a Teleport Rune on the floor, marked with symbols representing North Atlantis. He then spoke the words, "Tilemetaforá," activating the rune's magic. In an instant, he found himself in North Atlantis, where Master Byrne awaited him.

"Greetings, young Timaeus," Master Byrne said. Timaeus placed his right hand across his left shoulder, bowed his head, and replied, "Not so young anymore, Master Byrne." Master Byrne placed his right hand over Timaeus' left shoulder and chuckled, "Hehe. I must say, young Timaeus, surviving Griffin Valley is no easy task, but being able to tame a Griffin is extraordinary."

As Master Byrne and Timaeus walked toward the training arena in North Atlantis, a familiar voice interrupted them. "Well, well," it said. "Long time, no see, you little shit." Timaeus turned to see

Hermos in hooded scarlet robes. The two approached each other and embraced.

Timaeus noticed that she had earned her Element Stone. Master Byrne approached the two of them and said, "Now that you two have reacquainted, come with me, young Timaeus. You're welcome to join us, Hermos. A small living quarter has been prepared for you while you're training here in North Atlantis. Once you're settled in, your training will begin tomorrow."

Timaeus crossed his right hand over his left shoulder, bowed his head, and replied, "Yes, Master Byrne."

After settling in, Timaeus retired for the night. The next day, he started his training with Master Byrne. Just as he had with Master Phaedo, he refined his Fire Magic while practising the other forms of Element Magic. He frequently sparred with Hermos, putting his training into practice.

Using his weaponsmith training from Eastern Atlantis, Timaeus forged his own bow and quiver. He chose a recurve bow because it provided great energy and speed for the arrows. In no time, he became a skilled archer.

Timaeus also studied magic with the Mages in Northern Atlantis as part of his training. As he progressed, he crafted a wand for himself and learned how to create various items for battle. During his magical studies, Timaeus developed a Teleport Rune, allowing him to return to Eastern Atlantis, and created another rune to return to Northern Atlantis, bringing Stratos along with him, and introduced the Griffin to Hermos and Master Byrne.

Although Dark Magic was frowned upon, Timaeus explored many spellbooks. By the end of his training, he managed to learn the spell that he had first seen used by the Dark Fire Elemental, which allows its user to conceal their weapon in plain sight.

After three years, the time had finally come for Timaeus to put his training to the test. "You've come a long way during your time here, young Timaeus," said Master Byrne. "Now it is time for you to face the final trial of Northern Atlantis and earn your next Element Stone." Timaeus placed his clenched right hand on his left shoulder and bowed his head. "Yes, Master Byrne," he replied. "What can I expect during this trial? After my experience in Griffin Valley, I assume a beast will be guarding the Element Stone I am to claim?"

Master Byrne chuckled and replied, "You are correct, young Timaeus. However, I'm not going to give you the usual speech about not revealing information regarding the final trial. The only detail that must remain secret is the identity of the beast you will face because if you already know what you're up against, it's not truly a trial. And what Phaedo told you about arrogant students trying to face the trial before they are ready is indeed true."

Timaeus placed his clenched right hand on his left shoulder and bowed his head again. "Understood, Master Byrne," he replied. "And as I mentioned to Master Phaedo, you have my word." With that said, Master Byrne revealed the final trial to Timaeus.

"You must venture to the mountain on the far northern side of Northern Atlantis," said Master Byrne. "Once there, you will find the Element Stone atop the highest point of the mountain. As with the trial in Griffin Valley, you are restricted to using only the Element Magic you are currently being trained with. After retrieving the Element Stone, or if you wish to withdraw from the final trial, you can use a Teleport Rune to return here immediately. However, I will allow you to take Stratos with you as far as the mountain. The poor boy could use the exercise."

Stratos happily chirped in response to Master Byrne's words. "You can ride Stratos to the base of the mountain," Master Byrne said. "Once he lands there, he will go no further." With that, Timaeus set out with Stratos to search for his next Element Stone. Their journey to the mountain took just over an hour. After Stratos landed at the mountain's base, Timaeus dismounted and began his ascent.

The path started off straight but soon turned into a circular route. For three hours, Timaeus followed the winding trail up the mountain, where he would either find his next Element Stone or face death in his quest. The heat intensified as he climbed higher, but despite the discomfort, Timaeus refused to pull out his Green Element Stone.

At last, he reached the top, where he discovered the Red Element Stone waiting for him, resting on a stone altar.

This seemed very strange to Timaeus, as the Element Stone he went to find in Griffin Valley wasn't waiting for him, but this one was. As he approached the stone altar, he heard a strange growl and said, "Emfanízetai I Lepída," causing his weapon to appear. When he turned around, he saw what looked like a giant goat-like creature. As it walked toward him, Timaeus stepped back and then heard a hissing sound that resembled a serpent.

Reaching the stone altar, he backed away as far as he could. The creature tilted its head back, revealing a lion's head, and lifted its tail, which turned out to be a serpent, explaining the hissing sound. Everything suddenly made sense; Timaeus was on Chimera Mountain.

The Chimera's lion head let out a loud roar, and fire erupted from its mouth, engulfing Timaeus in flames. However, when the flames subsided, Timaeus found himself unharmed. He had picked up the Red Element Stone, which now granted him immunity to fire.

The Chimera lunged to attack with its left arm. Timaeus quickly jumped onto the stone altar to avoid the assault and plunged his sword into the altar for leverage. The Chimera's lion head was preparing for another strike at Timaeus. Aware of the limited magic available from the Red Element Stone, Timaeus drew his bow, selected an arrow from his quiver, and, using his impressive archery skills, shot the Chimera's lion head between the eyes, killing it.

Timaeus withdrew his bow, picked up his sword from the altar, and split it into two twin swords. As the Chimera prepared to attack again, Timaeus countered with his left sword and leapt over the beast, using his right sword to behead its serpent tail. He was determined not to take any chances after his previous encounter with a Chimera's Tail years ago. With two heads out of the way, only one remained.

Seeing a flicker of fire on the ground, Timaeus ran toward it as the Chimera stood on its hind legs, ready to attack again. When his blades touched the flames, Timaeus shouted, "Anáflexi Lepídas!" igniting them. As the Chimera lunged forward, Timaeus countered by using his right blade to stab through its left shoulder and his left blade to stab through the base of the Chimera's goat head. With a swift pivot to the left on his back leg, Timaeus threw the Chimera to the ground, defeating it in the process.

Merging his swords into one again and surveying the beast's lifeless body, Timaeus heard a strange noise behind him, followed by the sound of slow clapping. "Impressive," said a voice. Timaeus slowly turned around to find the Dark Elemental of Wind standing before him. "Impressive indeed," the Dark Elemental remarked as he approached Timaeus.

Raising his blade defensively, Timaeus responded, "You're one of the Elementals originally corrupted by Leviathan's Dark Magic, aren't you?" The Dark Elemental of Wind, impressed by Timaeus' insight, replied, "Smart as well as strong."

Not wanting to take any risks, Timaeus split his blade into twin swords. "I did not come here to fight," the Dark Elemental of Wind said. Timaeus stood his ground and replied, "The last time I encountered a Dark Elemental, we fought because he didn't get what he wanted, so I'm not taking any chances."

The Dark Elemental of Wind removed his cloak and replied, "He is a fool and has a serious score to settle with you. However, if you're willing to die here and now, boy, then so be it... Fight me."

The Dark Elemental of Wind charged at Timaeus, landing a punch to his abdomen before he could raise his defences, causing him to drop one of his swords in the process. With a powerful kick to the face, Timaeus found himself on his back while the Dark Elemental picked up his fallen sword. As the Dark Elemental swung the sword down at Timaeus, he managed to block it with his left arm, sustaining no injury due to his use of Earth Magic. With his left hand free, Timaeus delivered a left hook to the Dark Elemental, who was taken aback by his opponent's resilience.

A fierce duel ensued, with Timaeus forced to remain on the defensive. "You should feel proud," remarked the Dark Elemental of Wind. "This is the longest anyone has lasted against me in centuries."

Timaeus knocked the sword in his opponent's hand to the right and delivered a kick to the abdomen with his left leg, sending his opponent crashing to the ground. Realising that his opponent couldn't defend himself as effectively, Timaeus prepared to deliver the finishing blow. However, the Dark Elemental of Wind threw the sword at him, and it stabbed through his right shoulder.

"As impressive as your skills are, boy," the Dark Elemental of Wind said, "and despite how long you managed to last, you had no hope of defeating me."

Timaeus knelt down and placed his sword on the ground. He then reached into his supply satchel and pulled out a Magic Gem. With the help of his Green Element Stone, he gathered the strength to throw the gem into the air. "Ektyflotikó Fos!" he shouted, causing the gem to emit a powerful red light.

The Dark Elemental of Wind kicked Timaeus to the ground and said, "It doesn't matter what colour of light the gem emits; nobody would be able to see it from here. Even if they did, they wouldn't be able to save you in time." Timaeus lay there in pain. "Who said anything about the light being a signal for a person?" This puzzled the Dark Elemental of Wind, but he dismissed it, believing Timaeus was just stalling for time. He pulled the sword out of Timaeus' shoulder, ready to finish him off, when suddenly a loud cry echoed from the skies. Stratos landed in front of the Dark Elemental of Wind and slashed him with his right talon, causing him to stumble and drop the sword. Seizing this opportunity, Timaeus grabbed the sword, merged them both back into one, mounted Stratos, and the two quickly made their escape.

Chapter Nine
Flame Wind

Barely escaping with their lives, Stratos and Timaeus flew away from Chimera Mountain. The Dark Elemental of Wind let them go because, for the time being, he was not concerned with them. He had come to Chimera Mountain to collect blood samples from the Chimera's corpse. After gathering what he needed, Timaeus and Stratos were far out of sight and headed back to the training grounds in Northern Atlantis.

Master Byrne and Hermos were waiting for their return.

"The amount of time he's been gone suggests he should have already reached the top of Chimera Mountain by now," Hermos said, worry evident in her voice.

Master Byrne placed a reassuring hand on her shoulder. "I know, Hermos," he replied. "However, facing a Chimera is no easy trial. For all we know, he could have been killed, burned, or poisoned by it. I doubt that very much, though, considering how skilful Timaeus is. So, all we can do for now is wait."

A few seconds later, Master Byrne and Hermos heard Stratos cry out from the skies. The two of them signalled him with Fire Magic, and he flew down to them, landing right beside them.

"Where is he, boy?" Master Byrne asked. Stratos lay on the ground, carrying a severely injured Timaeus on his back. Clutching an Element Stone in both hands, he had gathered the strength to survive the journey. Master Byrne and Hermos could hardly believe what they were witnessing.

"No Chimera could have done this," Hermos said, her voice filled with disbelief. Master Byrne focused on the wound on Timaeus' shoulder.

"No, it couldn't," he replied. "The wound is too clean. A Chimera would have torn someone to pieces. This wound was made by a blade. Come, Hermos, let's get him down and take him to an infirmary."

Stratos angrily chirped at Master Byrne and Hermos, indicating his concern.

"Easy there, boy," said Master Byrne. "We'll make sure he's alright." After hearing Master Byrne's words, Stratos allowed him and Hermos to take Timaeus off his shoulders so they could bring him to the infirmary.

"W... Water," Timaeus said in a weak voice. Master Byrne and Hermos exchanged glances, knowing that Timaeus could heal himself immediately with Water Magic.

"There's no water around for him to use," Hermos said. Stratos let out a loud cry upon hearing this and ran across the training grounds before taking to the sky.

"Stratos!" Master Byrne shouted. "Where the fuck is that idiot bird going?"

Stratos flew out of the city to a small river on the outskirts. He landed next to the river and walked in, soaking himself before emerging and taking to the skies again. Upon returning to the training grounds, he landed in front of Master Byrne and Hermos, letting out a loud cry to warn them not to take Timaeus any further.

"Stratos, that's enough, boy!" Master Byrne yelled. "We'll make sure Timaeus is safe." Stratos refused to back down. Angry, he glared at them before turning to the side and shaking off the water, splattering it onto Timaeus, Hermos, and Master Byrne.

"What the...? What are you doing, Stratos?!" Master Byrne shouted. Stratos simply chirped in response.

"Master Byrne, look," said Hermos as a faint blue glow began to appear. Timaeus, in a weak voice, recited, "Therapéfste... To... Neró." The spell was working, but due to Timaeus' weakened state, he wasn't healing as quickly as he normally would. Once the wound closed, he took a deep breath and repeated, "Therapéfste To Neró."

At that, the rest of his injuries healed, and he was able to stand without the support of Master Byrne and Hermos. He stepped forward and hugged Stratos, grateful for his friend's help and relieved to be alive.

Master Byrne stepped forward and asked, "What the fuck happened to you up there, Timaeus? Those injuries weren't caused by a Chimera." Hermos then interjected, "No, those injuries came from a weapon." Turning around, Timaeus replied, "You're right... My weapon." Hermos looked confused, but Master Byrne was beginning to understand. "Someone else was up there. Who attacked you, Timaeus?" he inquired.

Stratos lay on the ground as Timaeus leaned against him and responded, "A Dark Elemental." Master Byrne and Hermos were stunned by his revelation. "Was it the same Dark Elemental who attacked you many years ago?" Master Byrne asked. Timaeus looked down at the floor and shook his head. After a moment, he looked up and replied, "No. The one who attacked me on Mount Chimera is one of the four who were originally corrupted by Leviathan's Dark Magic."

Hermos was at a loss for words. Master Byrne, on the other hand, inquired, "Which one was it?" Timaeus looked up at Master Byrne and replied, "I don't know, Master Byrne. This Dark Elemental didn't use any magic; he relied on fighting tactics and even used one of my own swords against me."

Master Byrne pressed for more details. "Was this Dark Elemental a man or a woman?" he asked. Timaeus thought for a moment and then responded, "It was a man, Master Byrne."

Pleased with Timaeus' answer, Master Byrne continued, "So, it wasn't the Dark Elemental of Fire. What was his behaviour like? Was he calm, quick to anger, or always laughing?"

Timaeus stood up straighter and replied, "He was calm. He said he hadn't come there to fight, but I wasn't willing to take any chances."

With this information, Master Byrne was able to piece everything together. "You've encountered the leader of the Dark Elementals, young Timaeus," he said, turning away as he walked. "The man you've just described is the Dark Elemental of Wind." This revelation brought looks of confusion to both Timaeus and Hermos.

"I thought the Water Elemental was their leader?" Hermos asked, recalling that those who bore the Dragon's Fang Crest were all from royal blood.

Master Byrne turned to face his students and replied, "Originally, that was the case. The Dark Elemental of Water led the group until Leviathan's Dark Magic had corrupted him so much that it drove him mad. The Dark Elemental of Wind then took over. Despite the madness caused by the Dark Magic, he remains a formidable opponent."

This brought a frightened look to Timaeus and Hermos. "Believe me, my students," said Master Byrne. "The Dark Elementals are not to be trifled with, but for now, let's drop the matter." Both Timaeus and Hermos placed their right hands across their left shoulders and replied, "Yes, Master Byrne."

Master Byrne then turned his attention to Timaeus. "On that note, now that you've retrieved your Red Element Stone, young Timaeus, it will soon be time for you to leave North Atlantis and start your training with Master Gorgias in Southern Atlantis." He shook Timaeus' hand, impressed with the warrior he had trained.

Stratos then got up and walked over to Master Byrne, rubbing his head against him. "Yes, Stratos. I'm going to miss you too, boy... I think it's time we all retired for the night."

Hermos then turned her attention to Timaeus. "I think that's a good idea because you've got to be up early in the morning. Don't forget, you little shit, before you leave for Southern Atlantis, you owe me a rematch."

Everyone started laughing, and with that, they all retired for the night.

Meanwhile, in the unknown location where the Dark Elementals resided, the Dark Elemental of Wind returned with samples of Chimera's blood that he had obtained from Chimera Mountain. As he walked past his comrades, they all noticed the wound he had received from Stratos' talon.

"No way is he that fucking powerful?" the Dark Elemental of Fire asked. The Dark Elemental of Wind shot her an angry look and replied, "No... The one who can use all four forms of Element Magic is impressive in combat, and he survived against me longer than anyone has in centuries. But it wasn't him who did this to me."

This left the other three Dark Elementals confused. The Dark Elemental of Fire then asked, "Well, if it wasn't the little fucking shit, then who was it?"

Looking down at his wound with an angry expression, the Dark Elemental of Wind replied, "The one who can wield all four forms of Element Magic summoned his Griffin companion using a Magic Gem he had created to signal the beast."

The Dark Elemental of Water stood up in a fit of rage. "I FUCKING WARNED YOU!" he cried. "No doubt he learned from his magic studies in Northern Atlantis, and now he possesses two fucking Element Stones. Soon, he will also gain fucking knowledge from Southern Atlantis."

The Dark Elemental of Wind approached his comrade in anger, while the Dark Elemental of Earth simply laughed it off. "Haha... Despite his craziness, he has a point," he said. "You should kill the fucking little shit now before he utilises his training into something much more powerful."

Fuelled by anger, the Dark Elemental of Wind approached his comrade and said, "Before he called his Griffin companion, I had him at death's door. I hesitated for a moment when he claimed that the Magic Gem he used wasn't meant for signalling people. I thought he was getting desperate, so I decided to deliver the finishing blow. It was then that the creature attacked me. As impressive as his skills are, he stood no chance of defeating me. I need him to obtain blood from the last two beasts."

This made the Dark Elemental of Water even angrier. "You're taking too much of a fucking risk!" he shouted. "Although the fucking little shit has drawn blood from the first two beasts, you're overlooking something that could jeopardise your entire fucking plan. He will undoubtedly draw blood from the third beast because he has to fight it hand-to-hand, but there's no guarantee you'll get blood from the fourth because that creature is fought in water. You wouldn't be able to retrieve any blood from it."

As irritated as he was by his comrade's words, the Dark Elemental of Wind stood by his cliff, examining the wound Stratos had inflicted on him. He took out the samples of blood he had collected. The Dark Elemental of Water then retrieved a small amphora and poured water over his comrade's wound, saying, "Therapéfste To Neró," which healed his injuries.

The Dark Elemental of Wind glanced at his comrade with a sinister grin before returning the blood samples to his robes. He surveyed the army of Dark Elementals gathered below from his cliff.

The following morning in Northern Atlantis, Timaeus awoke and headed straight to the training arena, where Master Byrne, Hermos, and the other Fire Elementals and students awaited him. Upon reaching Master Byrne, Timaeus placed his right hand across his left shoulder. A few moments later, Master Phaedo arrived to witness the results of Timaeus' training. After greeting his master, Timaeus and Hermos took their positions in the centre of the arena.

"Before you begin," said Master Byrne, "I have something to share with everyone." He raised his arms and spoke loudly to the assembled crowd. "Several years ago, I found a small boy who was slacking off and punished him by making him face Hermos in combat. It was on that day that we witnessed something we thought impossible: a boy able to use all four forms of Element Magic. Now, several years later, we will see if that boy has transformed from a slacker into Master Phaedo's true successor by having him face Hermos in a rematch."

Everyone in the arena cheered as Timaeus and Hermos shook hands. "Draw your weapons," said Master Byrne. "Remember what I told you years ago, young Timaeus. This isn't about making friends; this is punishment."

A smile spread across Timaeus' face as he replied, "Yes, Master Byrne." He then extended his hand in front of him and declared, "Emfanízetai I Lepída," causing his weapon to materialise. He split it into twin blades. Hermos drew her broadsword in preparation. Master Byrne raised his hand and shouted, "Now! Let's see if young Timaeus can hold his own against Hermos this time!" The crowd erupted in cheers, eager for the match to begin. Master Byrne then brought his hand down and shouted, "BEGIN!"

Hermos made the first move, just as she had during their last sparring session, by raising her sword and swinging it downwards towards Timaeus. He quickly raised both of his swords to defend himself. Capitalising on his speed, Timaeus launched a counterattack with the sword in his right hand. Hermos barely had time to defend herself, and unlike their previous match, she could not push Timaeus back. This allowed him to land a strike on her right shoulder with the sword in his left hand.

A fierce sword duel ensued, with Timaeus using his two swords and agility to block Hermos' incoming attacks. His training and their previous sparring sessions enabled him to identify several openings in her defence. The spectators were amazed at how effectively Timaeus was keeping Hermos on the defensive.

"Timaeus is doing quite well," remarked Master Phaedo. "You trained him well, Byrne."

Master Byrne turned his head towards Master Phaedo. "He's doing as I anticipated," he replied, turning his gaze back to the action. Master Phaedo then interjected, "But Hermos hasn't been trying? Hehe... Byrne, neither of them has been putting in their full effort; this is merely a warm-up. This time, it's us who don't know what we're in for." This remark brought an excited look to Master Byrne's face.

Timaeus was still keeping Hermos on the defensive when suddenly she ceased her attack. "I think that's enough for a warm-up," said Hermos. "It's about time we started taking this battle seriously." Timaeus looked back at her, an intense expression on his face. "Why not?" he replied, preparing himself to continue.

Hermos then glanced at a fire torch at the edge of the training arena, raised her hand, and spoke, "Éla Fotiá," summoning the fire from the torch into her palm.

Hermos placed the flame to her sword and spoke the incantation, "Anáflexi Lepídas," causing the blade to ignite. Timaeus was surprised to see Hermos using the same strategy she had employed when they first met.

"Now... let's start taking things seriously," Hermos declared as she continued her assault. However, this time, her attacks did not pose the same difficulty for Timaeus, allowing him to maintain his defence while launching his own counterattacks.

"Éla Fotiá!" Hermos shouted, summoning fire from another torch into her free hand. She then raised her hand toward Timaeus and yelled, "Ékrixi Flógas," shooting the flame directly at him.

Unlike their previous encounter, Timaeus did not use Wind Magic to defend himself. Instead, he stood his ground, allowing Hermos' magic to hit him.

"Anemostróvilos," Timaeus said, conjuring a small twister to clear the smoke. He stood confidently, a smile on his face and his Red Element Stone in his hand.

Master Byrne and Master Phaedo were left confused. "What was Hermos doing?" Master Byrne wondered. "She knows perfectly well that with that Red Element Stone, Timaeus is immune to fire."

Despite the truth in Master Byrne's words, Master Phaedo replied, "Unless what we just saw wasn't Hermos' intention... As you said, Byrne, she knows full well that Timaeus is immune to fire because of his Red Element Stone. However, what we just witnessed was most likely a distraction, and we have yet to see Hermos' real intentions."

His words intrigued Master Byrne. Timaeus chuckled, "Hehe, not gonna work out the same way it did last time, Hermos."

Despite his words, Hermos remained undeterred. Standing firm with her sword, she said, "Éla Fotiá," drawing fire from the blade. She then shouted, "Ékrixi Flógas!" and sent the flame towards Timaeus.

Standing his ground, Timaeus let Hermos' magic hit him again, knowing it would have no effect on him. *"What is Hermos doing?"* he thought. *"She knows we're both immune to fire, so I don't know what else she could—Hold on!"* Suddenly, everything became clear. "AAARGH!" Timaeus screamed as an arrow struck him in the right shoulder. "Now we're even for the attack you landed on me during the warm-up," said Hermos.

Master Phaedo and Master Byrne were amazed by what they had just witnessed. "Of course," said Master Byrne. "You were right, Phaedo; it was a distraction." Master Phaedo was stunned. "I can't believe I didn't see it," he said. "She knew he was immune to fire, so she used the smokescreen as cover to hide her true intentions."

Hermos continued her assault on Timaeus, showcasing her archery skills. Although Timaeus used his swords to defend himself from the arrows being fired at him, he struggled to mount a full defence with his right arm due to the arrow still lodged in his shoulder. Hermos fired three arrows at once, holding her bow diagonally. Timaeus managed to block two of the arrows, but because he couldn't fully defend himself with his right arm, the third arrow struck the centre of his right leg, lacerating the skin and bringing him down onto his right knee. He dropped the sword from his right hand in the process.

"Éla Fotiá," said Timaeus, drawing the fire from Hermos' sword. "You're not singeing me this time, Hermos," said Timaeus. Hermos withdrew her bow and replied, "Did you actually think you stood a chance against me?"

Still kneeling, Timaeus looked up at Hermos with a smile and said, "It's a good thing I didn't stay the same pathetic piece of shit I was all those years ago." He then raised the sword in his left hand, pulled the arrow out of his shoulder, and prepared to stand up.

"Finish him, Hermos!" Master Byrne shouted. Hermos picked up her sword and ran toward Timaeus to end the match before he could get back up. As he stood up, Timaeus' emotions were as furious as fire, yet he remained as calm as the wind. He raised his right hand towards Hermos, which still held the fire he summoned from her sword.

As Hermos was about to reach Timaeus, he shouted, "Flóga Ánemos!" This created a whirlwind of flames that sent Hermos flying backwards across the training arena. The entire arena was left in awe at what they had just witnessed. Not only did Timaeus use two forms of Element Magic at once, but he also managed to unite them into one powerful attack.

Though visibly shaken, Hermos stood up and reached for her sword. After grabbing it, she showed signs of injury. Master Byrne couldn't understand how Hermos had been injured so easily. "What is going on?" he wondered. "Despite Timaeus sending her across the arena, that shouldn't have caused such severe injuries."

After observing the scene, Master Phaedo shared his thoughts. "I don't think it was Timaeus' force that injured her, Byrne. I believe it was the magic Timaeus used against her that caused this damage."

Master Byrne wore a confused expression as Master Phaedo continued, "Although Hermos is immune to fire due to her Red Element Stone, the magic that Timaeus just used against her united both Wind and Fire Magic. This likely allowed it to bypass the protection offered by her Element Stone to some extent. The way Hermos appears now—looking as though she's spent hours on Chimera Mountain searching for her Red Element Stone—suggests that Timaeus' magic has left her exhausted. Fortunately, there are no signs of burn damage."

Master Phaedo's words brought a worried look to Master Byrne's face. "As much as I enjoy seeing what the little shit is capable of," he said, "we shouldn't let this continue. Years ago, we understood what we were dealing with because it involved each of the four forms of Element Magic. However, this is new and could be dangerous territory for all of us."

A sigh of relief escaped Master Phaedo. "A wise choice, Byrne," he replied. Just as the two were about to call off the fight, Hermos picked up her sword, ready to continue. "Don't think you've beaten me, Timaeus," she challenged. Timaeus raised his swords and stood in a defensive position. "Bring it," he responded.

Hermos charged toward Timaeus while he stood his ground. Once they were within range, Hermos swung her sword to attack, but Timaeus raised his swords to defend himself. After successfully blocking Hermos' attack, Timaeus shouted, "Ánodos Anémou!" A gust of wind surged upward, lifting him into the air, away from Hermos.

While airborne, Timaeus held his swords outward and swung them downward, exclaiming, "Anemostróvilos!" This created a small tornado that surged toward Hermos, lifting her into the air and causing her to drop her sword.

When Timaeus landed back on the ground, he let Hermos fall, withdrew his swords, and quickly ran to where she would land. He caught her in his arms just before she hit the ground. Holding Hermos, Timaeus looked down at her and said, "How do you like this pathetic piece of shit now?"

Hermos gazed back up at him. "You're not pathetic, I'll give you that," she replied, "but a piece of shit all the same." With the last bit of strength she had, Hermos managed to get out of Timaeus' arms, picked up her sword, and made one final attempt to strike him. However, using Earth Magic, he caught her sword and stopped her attack.

"That's enough!" Master Byrne shouted. Timaeus released Hermos' sword. "Yes, Master Byrne," he replied, accepting that she could no longer continue. Hermos, in a weakened tone, acknowledged, "Yes, Master," but due to her exhaustion, she collapsed back into Timaeus' arms.

"Oh no," Master Byrne said with a worried tone as he stood up. "Timaeus, take my amphora!" Master Phaedo shouted, tossing his amphora to Timaeus. After catching it and opening it, Timaeus set Hermos down on the floor and turned his attention toward a torch in the arena.

Timaeus raised his hand and shouted, "Éla Fotiá!" summoning fire from the torch. "Flóga," he said, increasing the flame's temperature. He then poured the water from the amphora over the flame, causing it to turn into steam. With both himself and Hermos enveloped in steam, Timaeus spoke, "Therápefsé Mas To Neró," healing both of them while surrounded by the steam.

Hermos awoke just moments later, with Timaeus standing over her, offering his hand to help her up. As she took his hand and got to her feet, Hermos said, "You got me again, you little shit."

Bringing a smile to Timaeus' face, he replied, "It seems history is repeating itself. You've awakened another ability within me that I had no idea I was capable of." This also brought a smile to Hermos' face.

"An ability we now need to discuss," said Master Byrne as he and Master Phaedo approached the two of them. Timaeus and Hermos placed their right hands over their left shoulders as their masters approached.

"Don't worry, Masters," said Timaeus. "I think I might be able to explain this one." Master Phaedo was eager to hear what his student and successor had to say. "Please, tell us, Timaeus," he said with excitement.

Timaeus then began to explain, "The way I see it is like this: Unlike many years ago when I first used Fire Magic and could only feel anger, this time my emotions were very different. Not only did I have the rage of fire, but I was also able to remain as calm as the wind. This, for the time being, is the only explanation for how I was able to unite Wind and Fire Magic."

Timaeus' theory intrigued both Master Phaedo and Master Byrne. "Could you demonstrate it again, young Timaeus?" Master Byrne asked. Not wanting to disappoint, Timaeus replied, "I'll try, Master Byrne, but I can't promise anything."

Turning towards a torch in the training arena, Timaeus spoke, "Éla Fotiá!" and summoned fire to his hand. He extended his hand in front of him and tried to focus his emotions. "Flóga Ánemos," he said, but nothing happened. "Flóga Ánemos!" Timaeus shouted, but still nothing occurred.

"My apologies, masters. I did say that I couldn't promise anything," he said. Master Phaedo placed his hand on Timaeus' shoulder and replied, "It's alright, Timaeus... There's plenty of time to figure this out."

Master Byrne stepped forward and said, "Phaedo's right, young Timaeus. You still have two more forms of Element Magic to learn. Who knows how many more secrets about your abilities you'll discover along the way?"

Timaeus placed his right hand across his left shoulder. "However, let's focus on the here and now," Master Byrne continued. "You'll soon begin your training with Master Gorgias in Southern Atlantis."

He then turned to everyone in the training arena and shouted, "What we witnessed here today was not only powerful combat but also amazing skill. Let's hear it for Hermos and Timaeus!" Everyone in the training arena stood up and cheered for both warriors.

Chapter Ten
The Labyrinth

A few days later, Timaeus and Stratos flew back home to Eastern Atlantis to check on everyone. Zephyr was growing into a strong Wind Elemental but was struggling with the trial in Griffin Valley. Meanwhile, Gale and the other orphans were progressing well in their training, showing enough promise to become future members of the Royal Guard.

Timaeus decided to stay for a few days to train with Zephyr, challenging him to get past Stratos so that he would be prepared for his next trial in Griffin Valley. After several days of training, Timaeus and Stratos set off for Southern Atlantis. Master Gorgias was waiting for Timaeus, and as soon as he spotted Stratos above the city, he lit a beacon to signal where they should land.

"It's nice to see you again after all this time, Timaeus," said Master Gorgias.

Timaeus dismounted Stratos, walked towards him, placed his right hand across his left shoulder, bowed his head, and replied, "It's great to see you too, Master Gorgias."

Master Gorgias walked past Timaeus and approached Stratos. "And this must be the mighty Stratos I've been hearing so much about," he said. Stratos chirped as he lay down.

"Yes, Master Gorgias," replied Timaeus. "Don't worry; you'll get better acquainted so he can learn friend from foe."

Master Gorgias then turned to face Timaeus. "I hear you found and befriended this mighty creature in Griffin Valley, and that he saved your life on Chimera Mountain," he said. "And you had a recent confrontation with the Dark Elemental of Wind?"

Timaeus stood firm and replied, "Yes, Master Gorgias. I wouldn't be standing here today if it weren't for Stratos... Unfortunately, I don't know much else. I don't know why he was on Chimera Mountain or what he was looking for."

Master Gorgias turned back toward Timaeus. "His intentions will eventually reveal themselves," he said. "But for now, we will have to let things unfold."

Master Gorgias and Timaeus walked toward the South Atlantis training arena, with Stratos following closely behind them. Suddenly, a familiar face approached them. Timaeus turned to see Gorgas approaching, dressed in hooded yellow robes adorned with a medallion. As Gorgas drew nearer, Timaeus noticed that he had earned his Element Stone.

"It's been a long time, and we still have a score to settle," Gorgas said, pointing his finger at Timaeus. Stratos reared up and let out a loud cry, mistaking Gorgas' approach for a threat. Timaeus quickly stepped in front of Stratos, raising his arms in a calming gesture.

"Whoa, whoa! Easy, boy," he said. "Apologies, Master Gorgias. Once he gets acquainted with everyone, he'll know who is friend and who is foe."

Just then, two more familiar figures appeared: Roc and Ston.

"Unless you two want to end up as this Griffin's dinner," Gorgas warned, "I suggest you wait to settle any scores until after you've gotten to know him."

Roc and Ston were at a loss for words. "Now that the rest of us have reacquainted ourselves, come, Timaeus. While you were training in North Atlantis, we have prepared living quarters for you during your training here in South Atlantis. Once you're settled, your training will begin tomorrow." Timaeus crossed his right hand over his left shoulder, bowed his head, and replied, "Yes, Master Gorgias."

After getting settled, Timaeus retired for the night. The next day, he began his training with Master Gorgias. Just like during his training in the East and the North, he refined his Earth Magic while practising other forms of Element Magic and trying to discover the secret to uniting them. He frequently sparred with Gorgas, Roc, and Ston, putting his training into practice. Timaeus also worked with the armoursmiths of Southern Atlantis as part of his training, which greatly improved his blacksmith skills.

With his training in armoursmithing, Timaeus was able to forge a new piece of equipment that would allow him to harness each form of Element Magic to its fullest potential. He created two wrist gauntlets, each capable of holding two Element Stones. This innovation meant that Timaeus could use all of his Element Stones simultaneously, rather than being restricted to one at a time.

Additionally, drawing on his magical training from Northern Atlantis, he crafted an Enchanted Medallion that protected its wearer from harm; the purer their heart, the more invincible they became. As Timaeus' training progressed, he learned to combine his Green and Red Element Stones effectively. By the time his training was complete, his power and stamina had reached new heights.

After three years of rigorous training, the moment had finally come to put his skills to the test.

"Like during your training with Phaedo and Byrne, you've come a long way, Timaeus," said Master Gorgias. "Now it is time for you to face Southern Atlantis' final trial and earn your next Element Stone."

Timaeus placed his clenched right hand on his left shoulder and bowed his head. "Yes, Master Gorgias," he replied. "I know something will be guarding the Element Stone, but you can't tell me what it is."

Master Gorgias smiled and responded, "You are correct, Timaeus... So you don't need to hear everything that Phaedo and Byrne told you."

Timaeus bowed his head again, placing his right hand on his left shoulder once more. "No, Master Gorgias," he said. "And as I told Master Phaedo and Master Byrne, you have my word that I will not reveal what is guarding the Element Stone."

With that said, Master Gorgias revealed to Timaeus the final trial. "You must venture to the caves on the southern side of Southern Atlantis," instructed Master Byrne. "Once there, you will find the Element Stone hidden within a labyrinth inside the caves. As you already know, you are limited to using the Element Magic you have been training with. Like the previous trials, once you have retrieved the Element Stone, or if you wish to withdraw from the final trial, you can use a Teleport Rune to return here immediately. Feel free to take Stratos with you to the caves; let him stretch his wings." Stratos chirped happily at Master Gorgias' words. "Stratos can go with you to the caves," said Master Gorgias, "but he will not enter with you." With that, Timaeus set out with Stratos to find his next Element Stone.

Their journey to the caves took less than an hour. After Stratos landed outside, Timaeus dismounted and ventured inside. Oddly, he found himself walking through a narrow passage that seemed to lead in only one direction, which was confusing since he wasn't navigating a labyrinth but simply walking straight. However, after a short while, everything became clear. Timaeus arrived at a large underground chamber where the labyrinth was located. He could see the Element Stone shining at its centre, but strangely, there were no beasts in sight.

Timaeus made his way along the edge of the cave to the entrance of the labyrinth. He started navigating the maze based on what he had memorised from his earlier descent, which made it feel almost too easy. As he continued through the maze, the ground suddenly began to rumble.

Timaeus initially believed that the beast guarding the Element Stone was hunting him through the labyrinth. However, he soon realised that it wasn't a creature causing the ground to rumble; rather, it was the walls of the labyrinth themselves. The walls were shifting, cutting off certain pathways and opening up new ones, making the labyrinth increasingly difficult to navigate.

As Timaeus continued through the maze, he found that the more he explored, the more it transformed. What troubled him most was the absence of any beast attempting to stop him from reaching the Element Stone. The labyrinth itself could not be the beast.

After navigating the ever-changing maze for several hours, Timaeus finally reached the centre, where he discovered the Element Stone.

It sat on an altar like the Red Element Stone on Chimera Mountain, except this altar had a statue behind it. Timaeus noticed something strange; he thought he could hear breathing, but throughout his time navigating the labyrinth, he hadn't encountered a single living creature. As he approached the altar to claim the Element Stone, he heard something hit the ground behind it, and the breathing sound became louder.

Suddenly, the statue came to life. What Timaeus had perceived as a statue was actually the legendary guardian of the labyrinth: the Minotaur. The mighty beast lunged to attack Timaeus with a powerful punch, but Timaeus used his speed to dodge it. The Minotaur's fist slammed against the labyrinth's wall, taking a chunk out of it in the process.

Timaeus decided to attack the Minotaur while its back was turned, but his efforts were in vain. The beast quickly retaliated by swinging its massive arm, knocking Timaeus backwards against the wall. The Minotaur then charged at him, but Timaeus narrowly avoided the attack just in time.

As the walls of the labyrinth began to shift again, Timaeus found himself cut off from the Element Stone. The Minotaur, using its immense strength, tore down the labyrinth's walls in search of Timaeus.

Avoiding the creature had been useful, but Timaeus realised he would eventually have to fight back.

Amidst the remnants of the destroyed walls, an idea sparked in Timaeus' mind. "Pétrini Ánodos," he called out, causing a segment of stone to levitate. "Vlastós Pétras!" he shouted, launching the levitated stone at the Minotaur.

The stone did no harm to the beast, and it continued to hunt Timaeus while demolishing the labyrinth around them. Repeating the same strategy over and over wasn't getting Timaeus anywhere. However, after some time, he decided to stand his ground. His plan was to distract the Minotaur with the smaller remnants of the labyrinth walls while using the larger pieces to block the beast's path.

Focusing his Earth Magic, Timaeus shouted, "PÉTRINI ÁNODOS!" He levitated all of the larger stone remnants directly above the Minotaur and let them fall onto the beast. With the Minotaur down, Timaeus went to claim his third Element Stone.

As he picked it up, he suddenly heard the pile of rocks behind him beginning to stir. The Minotaur wasn't finished yet; it erupted from under the debris in a fit of rage.

With the Gold Element Stone in his hand and a small remnant of the labyrinth wall in the other, Timaeus knew it was time to fight back. The Minotaur charged toward him, and this was his chance to end the battle. Timaeus stood his ground, getting into a fighting position as the beast closed in.

As the Minotaur raised its arms to slam them down on him, Timaeus countered with incredible speed, throwing his fist at the creature and shouting, "GÍNETE ÉNA ME TI GI!" His fist struck the Minotaur's face with tremendous force, knocking the beast onto its back.

Timaeus stood there, amazed that his plan had worked. Using the power of the Gold Element Stone and holding the remnant of the labyrinth wall, he turned his entire forearm to stone, giving him the extra strength needed to bring the beast down.

The Minotaur did not get back up; the force of Timaeus' attack had broken the beast's neck, defeating it; its corpse lay there on the ground with blood pouring from its mouth. A moment later, Timaeus heard a familiar sound that he hadn't heard since his trial on Chimera Mountain.

"We meet again," he said as he turned around to find the Dark Elemental of Wind standing behind him.

"Indeed we do," the Dark Elemental responded. "You've become even more impressive since our last encounter; that's the third beast you've defeated... You're becoming quite the little Windslash these days."

Keeping a close watch on his opponent, Timaeus replied, "So what does that make you? Darkslash?"

An evil grin spread across the Dark Elemental's face. "I like monikers," he said. "I've had Leviathan's Dark Magic coursing through me for so many centuries that I've forgotten my own name... But I must admit, Darkslash has a nice ring to it."

He then began to walk towards Timaeus, who stood his ground and asked, "What do you want?" Darkslash simply grinned as he walked past Timaeus and replied, "Nothing you need to concern yourself with."

Timaeus secretly slipped on his gauntlets and turned around to see what Darkslash was up to. He noticed Darkslash collecting some of the Minotaur's blood from the floor. "That day on Chimera Mountain," Timaeus said, "were you there for the Chimera's blood?"

Darkslash stood up, turned to face Timaeus, and replied, "As I said, it's nothing you need to concern yourself with. Just take your new Element Stone, and let's leave it at that until we meet again."

Timaeus continued to stand firm. "You remember what happened last time," Darkslash warned. "Things didn't end well for you, and your Griffin friend won't be able to save you like he did before."

Not intimidated by Darkslash's words, Timaeus replied, "Things aren't quite the same as they were last time." He then revealed his gauntlets, showcasing the Red and Green Element Stones on his right gauntlet, and added a Gold Element Stone to his left gauntlet.

"Oh fuck," Darkslash said, unable to believe what he was seeing. Timaeus wasted no time; he rushed at Darkslash, picking up a small remnant of the labyrinth walls in both hands. He shouted, "GÍNETE ÉNA ME TI GI!" as he transformed his forearms into stone.

He punched Darkslash in the face with his right hand and struck him in the abdomen with his left. Then, he kicked him aside and prepared for another attack. However, Darkslash seized both of Timaeus' arms, stopping him. "Nobody attacks me like that and lives," he said. Darkslash threw Timaeus aside, but Timaeus quickly sprang back to his feet, and their battle continued.

Timaeus decided to stick to hand-to-hand combat to avoid the risk of Darkslash taking his weapon from him again. Darkslash raised his right hand in front of him and shouted, "Aerofotografía!" This unleashed a powerful blast of wind. Timaeus quickly countered by shouting, "Gínete Éna Me Ti Gi!" which turned his entire body to stone, making him immune to the Wind Magic.

Once Darkslash's wind subsided, Timaeus launched his attack, delivering a left hook to Darkslash's face, followed by a right-hand body shot to his abdomen. He then seized Darkslash's right arm with his left hand and threw him over his shoulder. Darkslash sprang back to his feet and said, "Well, well... I must say I'm very impressed. But don't think for a second that you've won; I'm just going to have to up my game."

With that, Darkslash extended his hands in front of him and declared, "Emfanízontai Lepídes," causing his swords to materialise.

He took the swords and immediately charged at Timaeus. Before Timaeus had time to react, Darkslash slashed at his right arm with his left sword. "AARGH!" Timaeus cried out in pain. Darkslash continued to rush back and forth, slashing Timaeus with each pass, causing him immense pain. In desperation, Timaeus tore a piece from his robes and knelt on the floor.

Due to the labyrinth's walls being made of limestone, Timaeus found two pieces of flint and used them to create sparks, igniting a piece of torn clothing. "Éla Fotiá," he said, summoning the flames to his right hand.

"A little flame isn't going to help you," Darkslash said, approaching Timaeus. "Nor will it summon your Griffin friend." He continued, "I've enjoyed our fight today, Windslash. Things weren't quite the same as last time, but you were never going to defeat me."

Timaeus was filled with rage, but he remained calm at the same time. "I think we're done here for today, don't you?" said Darkslash. "Let this painful encounter be a lesson to you about challenging an opponent you have no hope of defeating." He then raised his sword in his left hand to strike Timaeus one last time.

As Darkslash was about to deliver the blow, Timaeus raised his right hand and shouted, "Flóga Ánemos!" This created a whirlwind of flames that knocked Darkslash back and spread through the remnants of the labyrinth. With his opponent down, Timaeus escaped from the labyrinth and left the cave. Despite his injuries, he was able to continue on, aided by his Green Element Stone.

Outside, he found Stratos waiting for him. Timaeus mounted him, and together, they headed back.

Chapter Eleven
Sandstorm

Darkslash awoke to find that Timaeus had left the cave. Infuriated at having been outsmarted again, he couldn't help but feel frustrated, especially since Timaeus had knocked him down without assistance this time. However, he decided not to dwell on it too much, as he had already accomplished what he came for. Still, he couldn't shake his worries after witnessing Timaeus' ability to unite Element Magic.

Timaeus rode Stratos back to the training grounds in Southern Atlantis, where Master Gorgias, Gorgas, Roc, and Ston were waiting for their return.

"Hehe," chuckled Gorgas. "I wonder if that little idiot has managed to navigate the labyrinth yet."

Roc and Ston laughed at Gorgas' words. A smile crossed Master Gorgias' face as he replied, "Now, come on, Gorgas. If I recall correctly, it took you roughly six hours to navigate the labyrinth. Roc and Ston took even longer, but you all retreated with a Teleport Rune as soon as you saw the Minotaur. With all the training Timaeus has received, I wouldn't be surprised if he chose to stay behind and fight the Minotaur, just as he did with Stratos—and don't forget the Chimera."

A frown appeared on the faces of Gorgas, Roc, and Ston, but they did not disagree with Master Gorgias' words. Moments later, they heard a cry from Stratos in the sky. Without Fire Magic, Roc and Ston lit a signal beacon for Stratos to follow. He flew down and landed next to the beacon.

"Stratos, where is Timaeus?" Master Gorgas asked. Stratos lay on the ground, and Timaeus dismounted him. Although he had made the journey without any trouble, he was suffering from excruciating pain. Master Gorgias, Gorgas, Roc, and Ston were shocked by the extent of his injuries.

"I take back what I said, Master Gorgias," Gorgas admitted. "Though it seems the Minotaur gave him a rough time." Timaeus sat on the ground and leaned against Stratos, while Master Gorgias examined his injuries.

"Yes, it did, Gorgas," he replied. "However, the Minotaur does not wield a sword," he added, pointing out the blade wounds to Gorgas.

"Couldn't the Minotaur's horn cause an injury like this?" asked Roc. Master Gorgias shook his head from side to side. "No," he replied. "Look closer, Roc. While you are correct that the Minotaur's horn can damage the skin, these cuts are too clean to have been made by the beast's horn. Come, let's get Timaeus some medical attention."

Stratos chirped multiple times at Master Gorgias as he went to help Timaeus up. "It's alright, Stratos," Master Gorgias said. "He'll be fine, trust me." Timaeus lay against Stratos, breathing heavily. "I'm alright, Master Gorgias," he said. "I just need some water, and I'll be able to heal myself."

Master Gorgias chuckled and replied, "That's what I meant, Timaeus. Ston, would you please fetch an amphora of water?" Ston placed his arm across Timaeus' shoulder and replied, "Yes, Master Gorgias."

While Ston went to fetch an amphora of water, Master Gorgias asked, "How did you end up like this, Timaeus?" Laying against Stratos and breathing heavily, Timaeus replied in a weak voice, "Darkslash." This response brought a confused look to the faces of Master Gorgias, Gorgas, and Ston. "What is Darkslash?" Master Gorgias asked. Before Timaeus could answer, Ston returned with the amphora of water. He poured the water over Timaeus, who then said, "Therapéfste To Neró," causing a blue glow to appear. Within less than a minute, Timaeus' injuries were healed.

"Thanks, Ston," said Timaeus as he got up, shaking his hand in the process. "Last time, Stratos flew out of the city and soaked himself to get the water I needed to heal myself." Stratos happily chirped, seeing that his friend was alright. "Hehe," chuckled Master Gorgias. "I do recall Byrne telling me about that... You have made a fine companion in this Griffin."

Master Gorgias approached Stratos and gently stroked his forehead before turning his attention to Timaeus. "Now," said Master Gorgias, "I must ask you again, Timaeus... How did you come to be injured like that? And what is this 'Darkslash'?"

Roc stepped forward and explained, "Master Gorgias told us that those cuts were too clean to have come from the Minotaur's horn." Timaeus stood there and replied, "I had another encounter with the Dark Elemental of Wind. It was his weapons that inflicted those cuts."

Worried looks crossed the faces of Master Gorgias, Gorgas, Roc, and Ston as Timaeus continued, "He mentioned how much he enjoys his monikers, so I decided to give him one of his own... Darkslash." The expression of concern on everyone's faces remained.

"Yes," replied Master Gorgias, "the Dark Elemental of Wind does indeed enjoy his monikers. He only bestows them upon those who impress him, so you must have made quite an impression to earn a moniker of your own, which allowed you to give one to him."

Timaeus stood there, looking at the floor, and replied, "Yes, Master Gorgias. He's impressed that I've defeated the beasts guarding the Element Stone during the final trial and that I've been able to face him in combat." Out of curiosity, Master Gorgias asked, "What does he call you?"

Timaeus, appearing a bit embarrassed, answered, "Windslash." This elicited a slight chuckle from Master Gorgias, Gorgas, Roc, and Ston. "It actually suits you," said Master Gorgias. Gorgas stepped forward and added, "I agree; it has a nice ring to it." A faint smile appeared on Timaeus' face.

"Does anyone else have a moniker?" he asked. Master Gorgias paused before replying, "He has names for the four who hold the Dragon Crests since we've had several encounters with the Dark Elementals. He calls Phaedo 'Fade Away,' Byrne 'Burnout,' Okeanos 'No Keanos,' and he calls me 'Gorges'."

Everyone laughed. "But enough about names for now," said Master Gorgias. "What was the Dark Elemental of Wind doing there?" With a concerned look on his face, Timaeus replied, "The same thing he wanted when I was on Chimera Mountain, and no doubt when I was in Griffin Valley... He wants the blood of the beasts that guard an Element Stone." Everyone was shocked by Timaeus' words.

"But how could he have the blood of all the ones you've faced so far?" Gorgias asked. "Unlike the Minotaur and the Chimera, you didn't kill Stratos. Plus, the two of you left Griffin Valley."

Timaeus walked up to Stratos and pointed to where he had stabbed him through the shoulder many years ago. "I stabbed Stratos through the shoulder, which drew blood from him," he said. "Although I healed the wound, some of his blood ended up on the floor. Darkslash no doubt collected it when Stratos and I left Griffin Valley because he didn't confront me after I obtained my first Element Stone."

Intrigued by Timaeus' words, Master Gorgias asked, "Do you know why he wants the blood of the beasts?" Timaeus stepped away from Stratos and replied, "Unfortunately, no, Master Gorgias. Each time I confront him, I ask what he wants, but he keeps that to himself. I have no idea what his intentions are." This left everyone puzzled.

"Could it be some kind of spell?" Roc asked. Ston then chimed in with an idea, "Could he use magic to create copies of the beasts with the blood?" Ston's idea intrigued everyone, but Master Gorgias responded, "I highly doubt that, Ston. If that were the case, he would have already done it with the Griffin and Chimera blood. However, a spell wouldn't surprise me, as there is a lot of powerful magic involving blood."

Hearing Master Gorgias' words, Roc presented another idea: "Imagine a creature created using the blood of all four beasts."

This idea caught Gorgas' attention. "He likely needs the blood of all four beasts," he said. "That's why he appears when Timaeus gains his Element Stones; he's the only one who has defeated and extracted blood from the beasts." Gorgas' words made sense and pieced together several clues.

"However, there's still something puzzling me, Timaeus," said Gorgas. "How were you able to survive and walk away from the fight against that Dark Elemental?" Timaeus looked down at his gauntlets and replied, "After obtaining my Gold Element Stone and thanks to my training, I was able to put up a fight against him. This forced him to use his magic and weapons. Despite the immense pain he inflicted with each attack from his swords, I managed to create fire using a piece of torn cloth and some flint I found. By doing so, I was able to knock him down and escape by using an ability I hadn't been able to access for three years."

This caught everyone's attention. "What is this ability?" Gorgas asked. Timaeus looked at Gorgas and replied, "It's the ability to use two forms of Element Magic and unite them into one—specifically, Wind and Fire Magic." Master Gorgias, Gorgas, Roc, and Ston could hardly believe what they were hearing.

"Could you demonstrate this ability now?" Master Gorgias asked. Unsure if he could, Timaeus responded, "I don't know... I've been trying to figure it out during my time here, but I've had no success. Darkslash was able to recreate the circumstances that allowed me to use it the first time. The pain he caused me fuelled my emotions, but I managed to stay calm at the same time."

Upon hearing Timaeus' words, Master Gorgias came up with an idea. "Instead of relying on your emotions as you would in training or combat, try to put yourself back in those original circumstances. Focus on the pain to fuel your emotions, while also remaining calm."

Timaeus focused his attention on a torch in the training arena. He raised his hand toward it and said, "Éla Fotiá," summoning the flame to his palm. Following Master Gorgias' advice, Timaeus concentrated on the pain he had experienced to fuel his emotions while remaining calm. After a moment of focus, he shouted, "Flóga Ánemos!" Unfortunately, nothing happened.

"I'm sorry, Master Gorgias," he muttered. In response, Master Gorgias encouraged him, "Try again... but this time, don't worry about disappointing anyone; that will help you stay calm."

Taking this to heart, Timaeus focused solely on the pain to fuel his emotions while keeping his composure. Moments later, he shouted, "Flóga Ánemos!" This time, he managed to create a gust of flames, though it wasn't as powerful as the ones he had conjured before.

"Amazing," said Master Gorgias. "It's a shame we couldn't have worked on this more. Speaking of which, now that you have your Gold Element Stone, your time in Southern Atlantis will soon come to an end. You will be starting your training with King Okeanos in Western Atlantis."

He placed his hands on Timaeus' shoulders, feeling amazed at what Timaeus had accomplished during his training. Stratos chirped happily at Master Gorgias. "I will be sad to see you go too, Stratos," he said. "Let us retire for the night."

Timaeus and Gorgas then turned to each other. "Hermos got her rematch," said Timaeus, "so you will have yours as well, Gorgas." This brought a smile to Gorgas' face. "We best be up early tomorrow then," he replied, "as I want to see what Windslash is capable of."

The two shook hands, their competitive spirits apparent, and with that, they all retired for the night.

Meanwhile, in the unknown location where the Dark Elementals resided, Darkslash returned with a sample of the Minotaur's blood that he had obtained from the labyrinth. His comrades were astonished when they saw his battle injuries from his fight with Timaeus.

"Haha," laughed the Dark Elemental of Earth. "Did you have a run-in with the Minotaur?"

Darkslash glared at him in frustration. "The Minotaur was dead when I arrived," he replied. "The little Windslash is becoming increasingly impressive in combat. He fought back using hand-to-hand techniques that forced me to use my weapons against him."

The Dark Elemental of Fire could hardly believe what she was hearing. "This is fucking ridiculous," she said. "How the fuck could he have damaged you so badly using only hand-to-hand combat?"

Darkslash turned to her with an angry expression.

"You've always had quite the flare, despite how annoying it is," he said. "That's it... Dark Flare... It suits you." Darkslash's choice of moniker brought an evil smile to her face.

"What are the monikers for these two fuckers?" she asked, pointing towards the Dark Elementals of Earth and Water. Darkslash glanced at the Dark Elemental of Earth.

"Dark Gaia," he said. Dark Gaia chuckled at the name. "Gaia is known as Mother Earth," he noted. "So, I take it I'm Father Earth?"

Dark Flare looked at Dark Gaia and replied, "You fucking idiot."

Dark Gaia turned his attention to Dark Flare and laughed, "Haha. Speaking of fucking idiots... What's the waterfall's moniker?"

The Dark Elemental of Water glared at Dark Gaia and said, "Dark Tide." This response infuriated Darkslash.

"Monikers are my speciality," he declared. "Although, I must admit, that one does suit you."

Dark Tide's face was still marked with rage. "Now that we have your foolish monikers sorted out," he said, "you still need to explain how you became so injured. Surely it wasn't the little Windslash, especially if he was fighting you hand-to-hand."

Angered by Dark Tide's words, Darkslash turned away from his comrades and replied, "The little Windslash has forged two special gauntlets, each containing two Element Stones, allowing him to use all of them at once."

This revelation caught the attention of all his comrades. "As intriguing as that sounds, Darkslash—or whatever the fuck your name is," said Dark

Flare, "that shouldn't have made the little fucker strong enough to injure you that badly."

Darkslash turned around furiously and replied, "You're right. With three Element Stones, he was able to fight me in a way that forced me to use my weapons against him. With my swords, I initially caused him excruciating pain, but what he did next left me in disbelief. Using a piece of torn clothing and some flint, he created fire to unleash Fire Magic against me. I wasn't concerned at first because, under normal circumstances, it wouldn't have helped him. So, I raised my sword, intending to teach him a lesson about challenging me. But then the little Windslash combined his Wind and Fire Magic into one attack, knocking me down and causing the injuries you see before you."

His comrades could hardly believe what they were hearing. "YOU FUCKING IDIOT!" cried Dark Tide.

Darkslash furiously rushed towards his comrade and shouted, "Enough!" The two of them looked each other in the eye. "I only need the little Windslash to obtain blood from the last beast," said Darkslash. "Then I will kill him, especially after what he did to me in the labyrinth."

His words only intensified Dark Tide's anger. "Don't you see the fucking risk you're taking? The last beast he has to fight will be in water, so any blood he draws from it could be lost to the depths! He hasn't even started training with Water Magic yet, but he has already found a way to use all of his Element Stones at once. He's become so capable that you were forced to use your weapons against him! And this new ability you mentioned, which allows him to unite two forms of Element Magic... Hasn't it crossed your mind that he could eventually unite other forms or, even fucking worse, unite all four forms? That's how Leviathan was originally defeated!"

Dark Tide's words were impacting Darkslash in a significant way. "SILENCE!" he cried. Dark Tide then handed Darkslash a small amphora of water, which he poured over himself. "Therapéfste To Neró," said Dark Tide, healing Darkslash. The two exchanged menacing glares, and then Darkslash turned and walked toward his cliff.

"Haha," laughed Dark Gaia. "He does have a point, you know. There's no guarantee you'll get the last beast's blood because it could be lost in the water."

Dark Flare then stepped forward and said, "Plus, if this fucking Windslash— or whatever you call him— learns to unite all four forms of Element Magic, and considering how fucking strong you're saying he is... as crazy as it sounds, he could probably become fucking powerful enough to take down Leviathan by himself."

Darkslash stood silently by his cliff, taking out the blood samples he had collected. Holding them in his hand and looking over the edge at the army of Dark Elementals, he said, "No matter whether I get the last beast's blood or not, the next time Windslash and I meet, he dies." This remark brought evil smiles to all of his comrades' faces.

The next morning in Southern Atlantis, Timaeus awoke and headed straight for the training arena, where Master Gorgias, Gorgas, Roc, Ston, and the other Earth Elementals and students awaited him. Upon reaching Master Gorgias, Timaeus placed his right hand across his left shoulder. A moment later, Master Phaedo and Master Byrne arrived to observe Timaeus' training progress.

Suddenly, everyone heard a loud cry, and Stratos came running across the training arena toward Master Byrne. "Haha," laughed Master Byrne as he stroked Stratos. "It's good to see you too, old friend." Stratos happily chirped in response.

"Has he been getting along with you as well, Gorgias?" Master Phaedo asked. Master Gorgias looked at Master Phaedo and Master Byrne and replied, "We got off to a bad start, but we eventually saw eye to eye."

Stratos gave Master Gorgias an intimidating look. "Of course you did," Master Byrne said sarcastically, stroking Stratos. After everyone had greeted one another, Timaeus and Gorgas took their places in the centre of the arena. Stratos lay at the side of the arena in front of Master Byrne.

"Before you begin," Master Gorgias said, standing up. He cleared his throat and addressed everyone in a loud voice. "Almost a decade ago, I witnessed three of my students bullying two Wind Students in Eastern Atlantis. On that day, I saw something remarkable—a Wind Student using all four forms of Element Magic. Now, nearly ten years later, we gather to see if one of them has remained the bully and the other the victim, or if they have truly earned the right to hold the Dragon Crests by facing each other once more in a rematch."

Everyone in the arena cheered as Timaeus and Gorgas shook hands. "Take your places," said Master Gorgias. "As I mentioned many years ago, Timaeus... you'll need to be ready if you want to impress the King." Timaeus smiled at Master Gorgias and replied, "Yes, Master Gorgias." The two competitors then assumed their fighting positions.

Master Gorgias raised his hands and shouted, "Now! Let us see what the future holders of the Dragon Crests are made of!" The crowd erupted with cheers as they prepared for the battle to begin. Master Gorgias lowered his hands and declared, "BEGIN!"

Neither Timaeus nor Gorgas made an immediate move; instead, they began to circle each other, searching for an opening in each other's defences. After a moment, Gorgas made the first move, rushing toward his opponent and swinging his right arm at him. Timaeus blocked the attack with his left arm, opting not to evade.

Timaeus grabbed Gorgas' right forearm with his left hand and placed his right arm underneath Gorgas' to throw him over his shoulder. With Gorgas landing on the floor, Timaeus prepared to punch him with his right arm. However, Gorgas activated his Gold Element Stone. As he noticed the sand on the training ground, Gorgas shouted, "Gínete Éna Me Ti Gi!" This allowed him to transform his entire body into sand, evading Timaeus' attack and escaping his grip.

A few seconds later, Gorgas reformed right in front of Timaeus and launched an attack, swinging his right arm followed by several hook punches. Timaeus, relying on his speed, easily dodged every strike. Taking advantage of an opening, Timaeus delivered a body shot with his left hand, but Gorgas defended it with his right arm. As Timaeus aimed for a shot to Gorgas' head, Gorgas shouted, "Gínete Éna Me Ti Gi!" again, turning his body into sand to avoid the attack and reformed seconds later.

Gorgas launched another attack on Timaeus, using only hook punches that were once again easily dodged. However, Gorgas' fighting style forced Timaeus to defend himself against one of the strikes with his right arm. Timaeus managed to counterattack with a left uppercut, making Gorgas stumble backwards.

"Lucky shot?" Timaeus asked.

"Hehe," chuckled Gorgas. "No, no, you got me... But this time, I didn't take the full force because last time, I wasn't aware of your capabilities."

Both fighters began to circle each other again, searching for openings in each other's guard. Gorgas made his next move, throwing his right arm straight at Timaeus. This attack was dodged, allowing Timaeus to counter with an uppercut that caused Gorgas to drop to his knees.

Seizing the opportunity, Timaeus threw his right arm straight at Gorgas, but Gorgas caught the attack with his right hand and shouted, "Gínete Éna Me Ti Gi!" He then transformed his body into sand to evade Timaeus.

Reforming a few seconds later, Gorgas launched another volley of hook punches at Timaeus, who dodged them with ease. Sensing an opening in his opponent's defence, Timaeus threw a right hook, but Gorgas caught his punch with his left hand and countered with a right hook that connected with Timaeus' left cheek. The entire training arena erupted in amazement that Gorgas managed to land a hit on Timaeus.

"It seems Gorgas is gaining the upper hand on Timaeus," said Master Gorgias. Master Byrne shook his head from side to side with a smile on his face. "Hehe," he chuckled. "Not even close, Gorgias. The real battle hasn't even started yet; Phaedo will tell you." Master Phaedo, sitting nearby with a smile, added, "This is only the warm-up."

This comment brought a shocked expression to Master Gorgias' face while Masters Phaedo and Byrne laughed, knowing that the real battle was still to come.

Timaeus stood there with a smile on his face. "I can hardly believe it myself, Gorgas," he said. "You actually managed to hit me." A smile broke out on Gorgas' face. "Hehe," he chuckled. "Now that we've finished the warm-up, Timaeus... show me what Windslash is capable of."

Accepting Gorgas' challenge, Timaeus got into a fighting position and raised his right hand towards a torch in the training arena, shouting, "Éla fotiá!" He summoned fire from the torch. Gorgas prepared himself by taking a fighting stance and said, "Timaeus, you know Earth Elementals are resistant to Fire Magic; your strategy is pointless."

However, Timaeus didn't listen to Gorgas' warning. Remaining confident, he aimed his right hand at his opponent, focusing on his pain but staying calm. He shouted, "Flóga Ánemos!" A whirlwind of flames erupted, astonishing everyone in the training arena.

Gorgas quickly responded to his opponent's attack by shouting, "Gínete Éna Me Ti Gi!" He transformed his entire body into stone. Once

Timaeus' flames subsided, Gorgas reverted to his normal form, completely unscathed, leaving everyone confused. "EPÍGEIA!!!" he shouted, immobilising Timaeus.

In a bid to escape, Timaeus attempted to turn his body into sand to reform himself. He began to chant, "Gínete Éna Me!... ARGH!" However, before Timaeus could finish the spell, Gorgas seized the opportunity and rushed towards him, delivering a powerful uppercut that knocked Timaeus backwards onto the ground.

Master Byrne asked in astonishment, "How was Gorgas able to do that? I thought he was only capable of holding his opponent in place." Master Gorgias, sitting nearby with a smile, responded, "You are correct, Byrne. As you mentioned, Gorgas is only at the level where he can hold his opponent in place, which is exactly what he did. While rushing towards Timaeus, he maintained his grip on him, allowing him to deliver that counterattack."

Although this resolved one question, another continued to trouble Master Byrne. "Gorgas' strategy to prevent Timaeus from escaping his counterattack is one thing," he said. "What I still can't understand is how Gorgas managed to withstand Timaeus' ability to unite two forms of Element Magic and remain unscathed. Phaedo, do you have any ideas?"

Before Master Phaedo could share his thoughts, Master Gorgias interjected, "Last night, we explored this ability and discovered how to unite the two forms of Element Magic without requiring Timaeus to be in the same circumstances as before. Unfortunately, it wasn't as powerful as it had been in the past."

However, Master Phaedo had a different perspective. "No, I don't think it's about the power," he said, drawing curious looks from Master Byrne and Master Gorgias.

"Unlike what happened three years ago during Timaeus' battle with Hermos, this situation is not about uniting two forms of Element Magic that allow Timaeus to bypass the protective effects of an Element Stone. Instead, he has combined two forms of Element Magic that Earth Elementals are resistant to. This explains how Gorgas was able to withstand the attack by using his Element Stone to turn his body into stone." Master Phaedo's words surprised both Master Byrne and Master Gorgias.

"So Timaeus wouldn't have gained the upper hand, no matter how strong he was?" Master Gorgias asked. Despite the circumstances, Master Byrne responded, "It would seem that way, Gorgias. Timaeus still has much to learn about this ability of his, and we don't yet know its full extent. However, I wouldn't count him out just yet; he's getting back up."

Timaeus got back to his feet and walked toward Gorgas. "Nice ability, Timaeus," Gorgas remarked. "But you, of all people, should know that Wind Magic and Fire Magic don't work against Earth Elementals. I was expecting a challenge from Windslash." Timaeus got into a fighting position, ready for another round. "I had to see for myself what happens when Element Magic is united against you," he replied. "Though it seems that uniting those two particular forms doesn't allow me to bypass your defences, so I'll have to find another way."

Not intimidated by Timaeus' words, Gorgas rushed at him, throwing a straight punch with his right arm. Timaeus dodged the attack by slipping to his left and countered with a body shot to Gorgas' abdomen, knocking him backwards to the ground. Gorgas quickly got back up, shooting Timaeus a challenging look. "Now we're even," he said as he prepared for his next move.

Rushing toward Gorgas with remarkable speed, Timaeus aimed another punch at his opponent's abdomen. However, this time, Gorgas managed to stay on his feet, stepping back on his right leg to resist the blow. This left everyone puzzled; they couldn't understand why Gorgas hadn't been knocked back as he had been during their previous encounter.

Timaeus soon realised that Gorgas had caught his punch. Gorgas then lifted Timaeus and delivered a powerful blow, sending him sprawling across the training grounds. "Now we're even," Gorgas remarked, referencing their previous battle in the courtyard all those years ago.

Timaeus got back up with a smile on his face. His fight with Gorgas ignited a mix of emotions within him—determination combined with a sense of calm. As he stood, circles of wind began to swirl around him, lifting sand from the ground in the process.

Not feeling threatened by Timaeus' actions, Gorgas charged in for his next attack. However, as Gorgas approached, Timaeus shouted, "Ammothýella!" In an instant, his body transformed, causing Gorgas to halt in his tracks. Everyone in the training area was in disbelief as it appeared that Timaeus had become a living sandstorm.

"What's going on?" Master Gorgias asked, bewildered. A smile spread across Master Byrne's face as he glanced at Master Phaedo. "He's done it again, hasn't he, Phaedo?" Master Phaedo, equally amazed, replied, "Yes, Byrne, I do believe he has. This time, he's combined the determination of the Earth Elementals with the calmness of the Wind Elementals. The only question that remains is: what is this combination capable of?"

Timaeus began walking toward Gorgas, maintaining his guard. "Let's see what Windslash's latest ability can do," he said.

In an instant, Timaeus' body dispersed into a violent sandstorm and reformed behind Gorgas. He swung his arm to strike his opponent, but it passed straight through Timaeus' form. Seizing the opportunity, Timaeus landed a right hook to Gorgas' face, causing him to stumble backwards.

"What the...? How the fuck were you able to hit me?" Gorgas exclaimed. Timaeus looked back at him with a smile on his face. "Lucky shot," he replied sarcastically. Despite the sarcasm, Gorgas couldn't help but smile, though it also irritated him.

Gorgas then attempted a straight punch aimed at Timaeus' head, but again, his fist went right through him. Timaeus countered with a strike to Gorgas' abdomen. Enraged, Gorgas unleashed a flurry of attacks using every technique he knew. However, each blow only met with Timaeus' counterattacks, ultimately bringing Gorgas down to one knee.

Chapter Twelve
Earth and Thunder

With his opponent down on his knee and nearly defenceless, Timaeus prepared to attack by throwing a straight punch. Not one to give up easily, Gorgas instinctively reached out to catch the punch, just as he would against any opponent. To everyone's surprise, he successfully caught Timaeus' hand. As Gorgas looked up, he was shocked to see Timaeus in his usual form. However, a few seconds later, Timaeus' appearance changed, and his body became intangible again.

"So that's how he did it," muttered Master Byrne. "The little shit." His words piqued the interest of Master Phaedo and Master Gorgias.

"Care to enlighten us, Byrne?" asked Master Gorgias.

"Hehe," chuckled Master Byrne as he began to explain. "I'm surprised you didn't notice this, Gorgias. This new ability allows Timaeus' body to become intangible, but it solidifies the moment he attacks."

Amazed by Master Byrne's revelation, Master Phaedo responded, "That's an intriguing discovery, Byrne. However, I doubt we've seen the full extent of this new ability yet."

Gorgas got back up and threw a punch straight through Timaeus' intangible body. Timaeus countered with an attack, which Gorgas anticipated, knowing that Timaeus' body would become solid when he struck. Just before Timaeus' form became intangible again, Gorgas executed a quick punch and managed to hit Timaeus in the face.

The two resumed their battle, with Gorgas not only dodging his opponent's attacks but also successfully countering several of them. Now that Gorgas had figured out how to fight back against his new ability, Timaeus needed to rethink his strategy.

Glancing at one of the torches in the training arena, he raised his left hand towards it and shouted, "Éla fotiá!" He summoned fire from the torch, and as soon as the flames reached Timaeus' hand, it transformed into glass. Timaeus dispersed his body and reformed with his hand intact, which sparked an idea in his mind.

"Éla Fotiá!" he shouted, summoning fire from the torch again, but stopped the flames before they reached him. Gorgas stayed back, keeping his guard up. "Not going to transform your whole body this time, are you?" he asked.

Timaeus stood confidently and replied, "No, but I'd be prepared if I were you." He then extended his hands outwards, causing the fire he had summoned to expand horizontally. With this newfound ability, he created a small but powerful sandstorm and sent it through the flames, generating hundreds, if not thousands, of shards of glass that flew straight at Gorgas.

With little time to react, Gorgas shouted, "Gínete Éna Me Ti Gi!" and turned his body to stone, allowing him to withstand the glass shards without taking any damage. Once the shards had hit the ground, Gorgas reverted back to his original form and prepared to strike back.

"Éla Fotiá!" Timaeus shouted again, summoning fire from the torch and spreading his hands to the side, ready to execute the same technique that would keep Gorgas on the defensive.

"Gínete Éna Me Ti Gi!" Gorgas shouted, turning his entire body into sand to hide from Timaeus and force him to revert to a solid state. As Gorgas reformed behind his opponent, Timaeus returned to normal and quickly swung his left arm, shouting, "Flóga Ánemos!" To everyone's surprise, a wind of flames erupted, knocking Gorgas onto his back. When Gorgas fully reformed, his body was covered in burn marks.

"Stone is immune to fire," Timaeus remarked, "but sand isn't." Determined to finish Timaeus off, Gorgas rose to his feet and shouted, "Gínete Éna Me Ti Gi!" He then transformed his body to stone and approached Timaeus like a living statue, intending to deliver a blow strong enough to knock Timaeus out, knowing he couldn't get past his defences if Timaeus fought back.

In response, Timaeus shouted, "Gínete Éna Me Ti Gi!" and turned his body to stone to match Gorgas' strength.

The two stone golems exchanged blows equally, neither able to gain the upper hand. They paused and began to circle each other, searching for a way to breach each other's defences. Timaeus remained calm when he suddenly felt a shock on his arm, similar to a spark of electricity. This distraction allowed Gorgas to land a punch on Timaeus.

Feeling the jolt, Timaeus decided to implement an all-or-nothing strategy using his Green and Gold Element Stones. He transformed back to his normal state and extended his arms downward. The green and gold stones began to glow, and thunder crackled around him as he manipulated the electrical currents in the air. With no time to waste, Gorgas charged forward, throwing his fist directly at Timaeus.

Drawing on the determination of Earth Elementals and the calmness of Wind Elementals, Timaeus shouted, "Gíne Éna Me Ti Gi Kai Ti Vrontí!"

Timaeus' body began to transform into stone as he caught Gorgas' punch. A few seconds later, the stone started to crack, and Timaeus' body returned to flesh, emitting sparks of electricity. His clothes glowed a vivid lime-green. Once again, he had united two forms of Element Magic, this time merging with earth and thunder. He swiftly threw Gorgas' arm to the side, causing Gorgas to stumble backwards.

Undeterred, Gorgas launched another attack, but Timaeus skilfully dodged it. He countered with a quick and powerful punch to Gorgas' abdomen, followed by a right hook to the face. Despite using his Gold Element Stone to transform his body into stone, Gorgas felt the impact, and it seemed as though Timaeus' attacks had cracked Gorgas' own form, causing him to fall to the ground.

He lay on the ground as his body returned to its normal state, but he was unable to continue because he had been knocked out. "Timaeus is the winner!" Master Gorgias shouted. The crowd in the arena erupted in cheers for Timaeus' victory. As he regained his composure, he turned toward Master Gorgias, Master Byrne, and Master Phaedo, placing his right arm across his left shoulder.

Suddenly, Timaeus heard Gorgas begin to groan. "Master Byrne," Timaeus called out. "Could you please throw some water over Stratos and send him over here?" Master Byrne recalled how Stratos had helped him a few years ago by providing a water source for Timaeus to heal himself. "I'll send him right over, Timaeus," he replied. "Stratos, come here, boy."

Master Byrne, along with Masters Phaedo and Gorgias, used their amphoras to soak Stratos with the water inside them.

"Go on, boy," said Master Byrne, sending Stratos over to Timaeus. Standing between Timaeus and Gorgas, Stratos shook the water off of himself, splashing it onto them. Timaeus then spoke the words, "Therápefsé Mas To Neró," which healed both himself and Gorgas. However, this caused Timaeus to feel the pain of Gorgas' burn marks. He awoke a moment later and got to his knees, with Timaeus standing before him, offering to help him up. Taking Timaeus' hand to rise, Gorgas exclaimed, "Fuck... So that is what Windslash is capable of." A smile spread across Timaeus' face as he replied, "Well... It's what Windslash can do at the moment. There's still more to discover. Unlike the last time, when I was able to take on you, Roc, and Ston by myself, this time, I had to unite Element Magic just to face you." This made Gorgas smile as well.

Master Gorgas stood up and addressed everyone in the training arena. "After what we've witnessed here today—both a powerful display of strength and amazing strategy—I think it's safe to say that the Dragon Crests chose wisely. These two truly are the ones worthy of holding them. Let's hear it for Gorgas and Timaeus!" The crowd erupted in cheers for both warriors.

A short while later, the training arena was cleared. Master Phaedo, Master Byrne, and Master Gorgas approached Timaeus and Gorgas, who both placed their right hands over their left shoulders. "I can explain most of what happened this time, Masters," Timaeus said, "but unfortunately, not everything." Master Phaedo was intrigued by Timaeus' words. "Please, tell us what you can, Timaeus," he urged, eager to listen.

Timaeus continued to explain, "Last time, when I combined Wind Magic and Fire Magic against Hermos, my emotions were different. This time, my determination and ability to remain calm allowed me to unite Wind Magic and Earth Magic. What I can't quite explain is how I was able to damage Gorgas so easily."

Masters Phaedo, Byrne, and Gorgias sought to understand how Timaeus was capable of inflicting such damage on Gorgas so they could better assess the situation. "Would you be able to demonstrate those abilities again, Timaeus?" Master Gorgias asked.

With a confident expression, Timaeus replied, "Now that we've learned more about how I can unite Element Magic, I'll see what I can do."

He took a few steps back, focused his emotions, and shouted, "Ammothýella!" In that moment, he combined his Wind Magic and Earth Magic, transforming his body into a living sandstorm.

Amazed by what he was witnessing, Master Phaedo said, "This ability is extraordinary. Ordinarily, Wind Elementals can't become intangible due to instability. However, by uniting Wind Magic and Earth Magic, Timaeus gains the stability he needs to maintain this intangible form." This statement brought a smile to Master Byrne's face. "Indeed, it does, Phaedo," he chuckled. "Though, from what we've seen, this intangible form is vulnerable to fire, Timaeus was able to use that vulnerability to his advantage against his opponent."

Master Gorgias stepped forward and added, "There's no doubt he came up with a clever way to use his other combination against Gorgas. The shards of glass were a distraction; he was counting on Gorgas using his Element Stone to turn into sand, which would then make him vulnerable to the combination of Wind Magic and Fire Magic. Am I right, Timaeus?"

Reverting to his normal state, Timaeus smiled and replied, "You figured me out, Master Gorgias... But what I still don't understand is how I was able to damage Gorgas so easily with the other ability." He looked at his student and successor with confidence.

"Well then," said Master Phaedo, "let's try and find out." Eager to explore the capabilities of his new ability, Timaeus extended his arms downward. As before, his Green and Gold Element Stones began to glow, and thunder crackled around him as he manipulated the electrical currents in the air.

Focusing on his emotions, Timaeus shouted, "Gíne Éna Me Ti Gi Kai Ti Vrontí!" Just like last time, his body started to transform into stone. A few seconds later, the stone began to crack, allowing Timaeus' flesh to emerge once again, emitting sparks of electricity. As before, his clothes glowed with a vibrant lime-green.

"Remarkable," said Master Gorgias. "Now, let's see if we can find an explanation for what this ability is capable of. Gorgas, we need you to turn your body into stone." Gorgas placed his right arm over his left shoulder and replied, "Yes, Master Gorgias." He then stepped in front of Timaeus and said, "Gínete Éna Me Ti Gi," causing his body to transform into stone.

"Now, let's start with something simple," Master Gorgias continued. "Both of you, place your fists against one another." Timaeus and Gorgas nodded and replied, "Yes, Master Gorgias." They then placed their right fists together, but nothing happened.

"Hmmm," exclaimed Master Byrne. "This time, try punching your fists against one another." Timaeus and Gorgas stood firm and responded, "Yes, Master Byrne." They then punched their fists together, and this time, the impact seemed to crack Gorgas' hand.

"It seems we're making progress," said Master Byrne. "This time, I want Timaeus to attack while Gorgas defends." Timaeus and Gorgas assumed their fighting positions and responded, "Yes, Master Byrne."

Timaeus launched several attacks, and Gorgas successfully defended against each one, creating the illusion that Gorgas' body was cracking under the pressure.

"Good, we're making more progress," Master Byrne said. "Gorgas, is there anything you can share with us?"

Reverting to his normal self, Gorgas replied, "It's hard to describe, Master Byrne. When we placed our fists together, I could feel the sparks of electricity around Timaeus' body. And just now, when we punched our fists together, and Timaeus threw those attacks for me to defend against, everything felt as it would under normal circumstances."

Gorgas' words intrigued Master Byrne.

"So, it felt like you were taking attacks as you normally would?" he asked. Looking back on the battle from a short while ago and the exercises they had just done to figure out Timaeus' new ability, Gorgas replied, "Yes, Master Byrne. That's exactly how I would describe it."

Master Phaedo's face suddenly lit up. "That's it," he said. "Timaeus' new ability isn't causing Gorgas' body to crack while it's transformed into stone. What this new ability does is allow Timaeus to bypass any enhancements created by magic. That's why all of Timaeus' attacks feel normal to Gorgas instead of being resisted by the enhancements of Gorgas' Earth Magic."

Everyone was amazed by Master Phaedo's explanation. "Hehe," chuckled Master Byrne. "You never cease to amaze me, Phaedo... and neither do you, young Timaeus."

Master Gorgias stepped forward. "Indeed he doesn't Byrne," he said. "With the amount of secrets to his abilities he's uncovered so far, and no doubt he'll uncover in the future... He certainly won't cease to amaze us when he discovers them... However, let's focus on the matters at hand... With your progress and what we witnessed here today, you will definitely impress the King... You are ready to begin your training with King Okeanos in Western Atlantis."

Chapter Thirteen
The Lake

Timaeus and Stratos flew back home to Eastern Atlantis a few days later to check on everyone. Thanks to his training with Timaeus and Stratos a few years earlier, Zephyr had finally passed his final trial in Griffin Valley and obtained his Element Stone. Gale and several of the other orphans had trained so well that they were inducted into the Royal Guard, and the training of the remaining orphans was progressing smoothly; they, too, would soon be ready for induction.

Timaeus spent a few days with those he had always considered family, sharing stories of his training, the abilities he had discovered, and his encounters with Darkslash. After their time together, Timaeus and Stratos set off for Western Atlantis. King Okeanos was waiting for Timaeus, and as soon as Stratos was spotted, a beacon was lit to signal him where to land.

"You're certainly not the young boy I met all those years ago, Timaeus," said King Okeanos. Timaeus dismounted Stratos and walked towards him. He placed his right hand across his left shoulder, bowed his head, knelt on his right knee, and replied, "Your Majesty... It certainly has been a long time."

King Okeanos then approached him. "Please stand, Timaeus," he said. "And please introduce me to your friend." Timaeus rose to his feet, his right hand still on his left shoulder. "Certainly, Your Majesty," he said. "I want him to get acquainted with everyone so he can learn friend from foe."

They both stopped as they reached Stratos. "Gorgias tells me he almost devoured Gorgas a few years back," said King Okeanos. A smile spread across Timaeus' face. "Haha," he laughed. "That's a bit of an exaggeration, if I may say so, Your Highness... Stratos mistook Gorgas' challenging behaviour for a threat. If I hadn't reacted quickly enough, he might have actually devoured him. But once he learned who was friend and who was foe, everything was fine."

Stratos chirped and bowed his head toward King Okeanos, surprising Timaeus because Stratos usually takes longer to get used to strangers.

"Good boy, Stratos," Timaeus remarked as Stratos continued to chirp. "It normally takes him longer to become acquainted with someone. If I may ask, what is your secret, Your Majesty?"

King Okeanos gently stroked Stratos' forehead and replied, "I don't know... He was likely able to tell that I was a friend and not a foe from our greeting." Timaeus was intrigued by King Okeanos' words. "I think you may be right, Your Majesty," he said. "If so, you'll be giving Master Byrne some competition."

King Okeanos liked the sound of Timaeus' words, which made Stratos chirp happily. "Byrne has told me about this amazing creature," King Okeanos said. "He's also shared how you met and what you have faced together. Phaedo has been telling me about the incredible abilities you've been discovering, and Gorgias mentioned your recent encounter with the Dark Elemental of Wind. I've heard that you were able to hold your own against him and that he's been collecting the blood of the beasts that guard an Element Stone."

Timaeus faced King Okeanos, placed his right hand on his left shoulder, bowed his head, and replied, "Everything you've been told is correct, Your Majesty. However, as I mentioned to Master Gorgias, I don't know what he is collecting the blood for. We have put our heads together, and the best explanation we can come up with is that he needs the blood of all four beasts and plans to use them for some kind of spell."

King Okeanos raised his hand to calm Timaeus. "Calm down, Timaeus," he said. "Gorgias has already informed me of what you told him and the possibilities you considered. However, we still do not know what this spell could entail, so we must ensure he does not obtain the blood of the last beast. Gorgias also mentioned the title he gave you: Windslash, is that correct?"

Timaeus placed his right hand on his left shoulder, bowed his head again, and replied, "You have been informed correctly, Your Majesty."

King Okeanos smiled at Timaeus' response. "Hehe," he chuckled. "It suits you. As for the Dark Elemental of Wind, we know what he wants; we just need to understand the reason behind his desires." With that, King Okeanos and Timaeus walked toward the West Atlantis training arena, with Stratos following behind them.

"Well, if it isn't Windslash," said a familiar voice. Timaeus turned to see Critias, clad in hooded, cerulean blue robes. As he approached,

Timaeus noticed that Critias had earned his Element Stone. "You've certainly come a long way since we last met," Critias said, extending his hand for a handshake.

Stratos let out an angry chirp. Timaeus quickly turned around and raised his left arm towards the creature. "No, no, Stratos. Easy, boy," he said. "Apologies, Your Majesties. He learns to distinguish friend from foe pretty quickly after he gets acquainted with you."

Stratos chirped again before lying down on the ground. "It's possible he was suspicious of the handshake," King Okeanos stated. "He didn't react while Critias was walking toward you." Timaeus and Critias pondered King Okeanos' words.

"Now that we're all reacquainted," the king continued, "Come, Timaeus. A living quarters has been prepared for you while you're training here in West Atlantis, just like during your training in North and South Atlantis. Once you're settled in, your training will begin tomorrow." Timaeus crossed his right hand over his left shoulder, bowed his head, and replied, "Yes, Your Majesty."

After settling in, Timaeus retired for the night. The next day, he began his training with King Okeanos. Similar to his training in the East, North, and South, he was able to refine his Water Magic, allowing him to practice all four forms of Element Magic fully. He also focused on uniting them.

Using his blacksmith skills, he devised a method to combine the hilts of his twin swords, creating a double-edged sword. This innovation enabled him to wield his combined weapons like a Water Elemental's trident staff.

Timaeus frequently sparred with Critias to put his training into practice. He also studied the art of foresight with the Seers of Western Atlantis as part of his training. As he progressed, the Seers gifted him an Enchanted Chalice, which he used to practice foresight both during his time with them and on his own. His magical training from Northern Atlantis further refined his foresight skills.

Additionally, the gauntlets he forged in Southern Atlantis allowed him to learn how to use the three Element Stones he had acquired in combination. As Timaeus continued his training, the power of his Red Element Stone increased due to its proximity to the other two stones. By the time Timaeus completed his training, he had become so skilled in foresight that he could predict both what could happen and what would happen.

Unfortunately, he could not use foresight without his Enchanted Chalice, and none of his visions could help him find Darkslash or understand his intentions. After three years, the time had finally come for him to put his training to the test.

"After training with all four masters and learning the four forms of Element Magic, you've certainly come a long way over the past twelve years, Timaeus," said King Okeanos. "Now it is time for you to face the final trial of Western Atlantis and earn your final Element Stone."

Timaeus placed his clenched right hand on his left shoulder, bowed his head, and knelt on his right knee. "Yes, Your Majesty," replied Timaeus. "I am already familiar with how the final trials work, so there's no need to go over everything. However, I assure you that I will not reveal the identity of the beast that guards the Element Stone."

King Okeanos chuckled and replied, "That's all right, Timaeus. I didn't think it would be necessary to go over everything." He remained kneeling on his right knee as Timaeus placed his clenched right hand on his left shoulder and bowed his head again. "No, Your Majesty," he replied.

With that, King Okeanos revealed the final trial to Timaeus. "You must venture to the lake on the southwestern side of Western Atlantis," said Master Byrne, "Once there, you will find the Element Stone hidden at the bottom of the lake. Please rise, Timaeus; there's no need for me to reiterate the rest. You already know that you are limited to using the Element Magic you have been training with. Although you haven't used one to withdraw or return from the previous trial, I advise that you take a Teleport Rune with you. I don't mind if Stratos accompanies you; it would do him some good."

Stratos happily chirped at King Okeanos' words. "Though I'd advise against taking him all the way," said King Okeanos. "If he were to go all the way with you to the lake, he'd be in danger from the beast that awaits you there." With that warning in mind, Timaeus set out with Stratos to find his final Element Stone. Their journey to the lake took roughly an hour. Timaeus heeded King Okeanos' advice and had Stratos land outside the woodlands surrounding the lake to keep him safe from the beast he was about to encounter, as well as from Darkslash. Timaeus dismounted from Stratos and ventured into the woodlands. After walking for a short while, he arrived at the lake. The shorelines were surrounded solely by the woodlands he had just traversed. It felt as though the entire area was filled with evil.

Unlike the final trials across the rest of Atlantis, Timaeus did not find the beast waiting for him. As he approached the lake and gazed upon its waters, it felt as if he were looking into a reflection of darkness itself. A few minutes later, while walking along the shoreline, Timaeus noticed a blue glow emanating from the depths of the lake, revealing the location of the Element Stone at the bottom. Now that he knew where to find the stone, Timaeus wasted no time and jumped into the water. He swam down, following the blue glow, and moments later, he discovered the object of his quest—he had finally obtained his last Element Stone.

Despite achieving his goal, Timaeus felt uneasy; everything had seemed too easy, unlike the challenges he had faced in the other trials. His concerns were confirmed when he suddenly sensed movement in the water.

He looked around, trying to locate what was lurking in the water. Thanks to his Water Magic, Timaeus had no fear of drowning, so he decided to lie in wait. He could still feel the movements beneath the surface and sensed that it was a large creature. However, no matter how hard he searched, he could not see it. To make things easier, he reached into his supply satchel and released a Magic Gem into the water, anchoring it in place with his Water Magic.

As he remained still, he felt the creature approaching closer and closer. When it was almost upon him, Timaeus put his plan into action. Without wasting any time, he recited the incantation despite being underwater: "Ektyflotikó Fos!" His muffled chant caused the Magic Gem to produce a powerful blinding light, which not only revealed the creature but also temporarily stunned it.

Timaeus could hardly believe his eyes as he rushed to the surface. After jumping out of the water, he found that with the Blue Element Stone in his possession, he could walk on water. However, he was still in danger; the lake's waters began to ripple violently as the beast approached the surface. Realising the imminent threat, Timaeus quickly executes a fast evasive manoeuvre just as the beast emerges, determined to capture its prey.

With his hand outstretched, Timaeus commanded, "Emfanízetai I Lepída," causing his weapon to materialise. He swiftly split it into twin blades, then merged the hilts to form a double-edged sword. Just as he prepared for battle, the beast lunged at him. Timaeus easily evaded the attack and countered, striking the creature across the face and causing a minor bleed. This reminded him that he must not let Darkslash get his hands on the creature's blood. To ensure this, he knew he had to kill the beast and let its body sink to the bottom of the lake.

Timaeus and the beast faced each other, each preparing for their next move. Just as it seemed the creature was about to launch the same attack again, it surprised Timaeus with a sneak attack, using its tail to knock him across the water. Fortunately, he quickly recovered and managed to avoid being devoured. When he returned to the surface, he stood on the water, thanks to his Blue Element Stone. The creature resurfaced just moments later. Despite everything he had encountered so far, Timaeus struggled to identify what this beast was. At first glance, he thought it might be a sea serpent, but a lake wasn't its natural habitat. He understood why King Okeanos had recommended bringing a Teleport Rune, given how intelligently the creature hunted and fought its prey. Unable to discern what he was up against, Timaeus decided to end the encounter quickly, just in case the beast had any more surprise attacks in store.

Standing in a fighting position and staring down the creature with his double-edged sword in his right hand, Timaeus threw his left hand upward and shouted, "Ánodos Neroú!!!" This incantation caused the water between him and the creature to rise, momentarily distracting it. The beast then leapt through the water in an attempt to attack Timaeus, only to find that he had vanished.

Seconds later, he emerged from the water behind the creature and hurled his double-edged sword at it, spinning it like a disc. The weapon made a direct hit, decapitating the beast. "Éla Neró!" Timaeus shouted, summoning his sword back to him, using a tactic taught to him by Critias that took advantage of the wet environment.

With that, Timaeus walked across the water back to the shoreline. However, just a few minutes later, as he continued on his way, the waters began to ripple, and a three-headed creature emerged. Everything was starting to make sense: the oppressive evil filling the area and the waters reflection of darkness were both linked to the beast before him. Timaeus realised he had been sent to Hydra Lake.

Despite having pieced together a plan, Timaeus now faced a new challenge. It was difficult enough dealing with the Hydra when it had only one head, but now he had to contend with three. The middle head attacked first, but Timaeus easily dodged it. However, the left and right heads launched a double attack, which he narrowly escaped by retreating underwater, causing the heads to collide with each other.

Timaeus decided it was best to lure the Hydra back out onto the lake before striking back, as they were too close to the shoreline to ensure that none of its blood would spill onto land. After resurfacing, Timaeus stood on the water's surface, ready to fight back. He knew he couldn't decapitate the Hydra again, as it would only grow more heads. This time, the left and right heads continued to attack as a distraction while the middle head waited for the perfect moment to strike.

Timaeus evaded and countered every attack from the Hydra's left and right heads with his speed and his double-edged sword. However, both he and the middle head of the Hydra knew he couldn't keep this up forever. The Hydra's middle head was patiently waiting for an opening in Timaeus' defence, and because he was preoccupied with the left and right heads, he had no opportunities to heal himself with his Water Magic.

As Timaeus gradually began to wear down, the middle head of the Hydra bided its time. Finally, during one of Timaeus' counterattacks, he made a misstep, and the Hydra's middle head seized the moment to strike. With little time to react, Timaeus retreated underwater and shouted, "Pagoméno Neró!" This spell caused the water above him to freeze into a thick layer of ice, preventing the middle head from devouring him.

When Timaeus resurfaced, he called out, "Therapéfste To Neró," effectively healing himself.

The ice inspired Timaeus with a brilliant idea. Focusing his Water Magic, he prepared for the Hydra's next attack. As the beast drew closer, Timaeus braced himself for an all-or-nothing attempt to stop it. When the Hydra was within range, all three of its heads were poised to strike. In that moment, Timaeus threw his arms upward and shouted, "To Neró Anevaínei Kai Pagónei!" This incantation caused the waters to rise around the beast and freeze, effectively immobilising it.

Timaeus' plan had succeeded; he had defeated the Hydra without killing it. He walked across the frozen surface of the lake and returned to the shoreline. Looking back at the Hydra trapped in ice, Timaeus heard a familiar sound for the first time in three years. "I was wondering when you would arrive... Darkslash," he said, planting his weapon firmly in the ground and continuing to gaze across the lake.

"What the fuck have you done, Windslash?" Darkslash replied in a furious tone.

"By freezing the Hydra out on the lake and denying me access to it, you've ruined everything." Timaeus grinned and secretly slipped on his gauntlets. "You mean you can't collect its blood," he said as he turned to face Darkslash. "We've figured out that you're collecting the blood of the beasts that guard the Element Stones. The only thing that still eludes us is what you're collecting it for."

Darkslash looked at Timaeus with an infuriating glare and replied, "As I told you three years ago, Windslash, that's nothing you need to concern yourself with." Timaeus got into a fighting stance and stood his ground. "The fuck it doesn't," he responded angrily. "If it threatens Atlantis, it has everything to do with me."

Darkslash began to walk toward Timaeus and spoke, "Emfanízontai Lepídes," summoning his weapons.

"You barely escaped last time, Windslash, and unless you free the Hydra and allow me to obtain its blood, you won't be escaping at all." Timaeus placed his Blue Element Stone into his left gauntlet and pulled his weapon from the ground.

"It didn't help you last time," Darkslash retorted, "and you won't be able to outsmart me like you did in the labyrinth."

Not intimidated by his opponent's words, Timaeus replied, "A lot has changed over the past three years, Darkslash. So much, in fact, that this time, I won't need to resort to outsmarting you."

Timaeus' words brought a confused look to Darkslash's face, but he remained unperturbed. Without hesitation, Timaeus rushed at Darkslash and swung his double-edged sword, but Darkslash easily defended against the attack. A furious sword duel ensued, with both combatants matching each other's blows. Eventually, Timaeus managed to knock Darkslash's swords upward, seized hold of his cloak, and threw him along the shoreline.

He quickly got back to his feet and looked towards Timaeus. The two of them ran toward each other, dragging their swords along the ground. Once they were within range, they swung their blades at one another, locking them together. Darkslash blocked Timaeus' double-edged sword with just one of his own. Before Timaeus could counterattack, Darkslash continued his assault, effortlessly blocking each of Timaeus' attacks with his left-handed sword.

"What's this, Windslash?" Darkslash asked mockingly. "Are you starting to wonder how you ever got the better of me before?"

With that, Darkslash made three precise strikes against Timaeus with his right-handed sword and then kicked him to the ground. Seizing the opportunity, Darkslash jumped and performed a somersault, preparing to impale Timaeus with his swords.

"GÍNATE ÉNA ME TI GI!!!" Timaeus cried as he turned his body into soil, allowing him to hide from Darkslash and narrowly escape his attack. However, this tactic left Timaeus' weapon behind. He reformed a few seconds later.

"Very impressive," Darkslash said, observing him. "I didn't think you'd have enough time to escape... That was quite a clever tactic."

Timaeus stood behind Darkslash and replied, "You like that one? It's great for an instant, tactical escape."

Darkslash turned around and said, "I know... But I think it's time we stopped playing games, Windslash." With that, Darkslash lunged at Timaeus again with his swords.

"Éla Gi!" Timaeus shouted, summoning his double-edged sword from the soil, just in time to block Darkslash's attack.

Knowing he wouldn't be able to hold his defence for long, Timaeus shouted, "Gíne Éna Me Ti Gi Kai Ti Vrontí!" His body then transformed into soil and emitted sparks of electricity. A few seconds later, Timaeus' form returned to flesh, still sparking with electricity, and his clothes glowed a vibrant lime-green.

Darkslash could not believe what he was seeing. Using this opportunity, Timaeus used his double-edged sword to bring Darkslash's right arm downwards, jamming his right-handed sword into the ground and also bringing his left arm upwards, creating an opening; Timaeus then delivered a powerful punch to his opponent's abdomen.

"ARGH!" Darkslash cried as the impact caused him to drop both his swords. Timaeus' double-edged sword emitted sparks of electricity and swung around, delivering a clean strike across his opponent's chest.

"AAARGH!!!" he screamed, feeling pain that he hadn't in a long time. Darkslash shot Timaeus an infuriated look. "How is this possible, Windslash?!" he demanded. Timaeus stood his ground and replied, "It's an ability I learned three years ago. It allows me to bypass any enhancements created by magic, which seems to include the enhancements you gain from Leviathan's Dark Magic. I don't know if this is limited to Element Magic, but Leviathan's Dark Magic is what created your Dark Element Magic."

Timaeus quickly approached Darkslash to deliver another strike, but the sparks of electricity faded, and his clothes stopped glowing. Darkslash then grabbed Timaeus' double-edged sword to stop his attack. He raised his right hand in front of Timaeus and shouted, "Aerofotografía!" A powerful blast of wind erupted, knocking Timaeus backwards along the shoreline.

"It seems that your ability is limited to the magic from your Element Stones, Windslash," Darkslash remarked, picking up his swords as he walked toward Timaeus. Timaeus lay on the ground with his right arm extended towards the lake and whispered secretly, "Liósimo Tou Neroú." Afterwards, he rose, ready to face his opponent once more.

"It seems you're right, Darkslash," Timaeus admitted. "I haven't mastered the Gold Element Stone yet, so its magic runs out faster. However, I have mastered my first two Element Stones. Mastering the Red Element Stone gives me access to something without needing to ignite it." As he spoke, Timaeus' Red Element Stone began to glow, igniting his body in flames. This caused a look of concern to spread across Darkslash's face, prompting him to quickly grab his weapons from the ground.

Timaeus charged toward him, shouting, "Flóga Ánemos!" A gust of fiery wind blast swept Darkslash off his feet, sending him toward the edge of the shoreline and causing flames to spread across the lake area.

As Darkslash lay at the edge of the shoreline, struggling to recover from the recent attack, Timaeus noticed something lying on the ground that had fallen from Darkslash's robes. He picked it up and discovered it was a Teleport Rune, but the markings on it were unusual. Just then, a sword swiped across Timaeus' hand, causing him to drop the Teleport Rune, which Darkslash caught in midair.

"I take it that's something else I don't need to concern myself with?" Timaeus asked.

Darkslash returned the Teleport Rune to his robes and replied, "That is correct, Windslash."

Despite Darkslash's answer, Timaeus remained curious about the strange markings on the Teleport Rune. "That's quite an unusual Teleport Rune," he remarked. "From what I can tell by the markings, it's meant to cover all of Atlantis. No Teleport Rune is that powerful."

Timaeus' curiosity began to annoy Darkslash. "As I keep telling you, Windslash," he replied, "it's nothing you need to concern yourself with." Despite Darkslash not answering any of his questions, Timaeus started to piece things together, and it began to make sense. "That's it!" he exclaimed. "That's why you need the blood of the beasts. That Teleport Rune currently only allows you to travel anywhere in Atlantis, but with the blood of the beasts, you can enhance its magic to bring as many as you want to Atlantis."

This revelation only served to anger Darkslash. "Phaedo has taught you well, Windslash," he retorted. "However, you've only uncovered part of my intentions." His words didn't bother Timaeus at all. "I'm not going to bother asking what they are," he said, "because I know what the answer will be. Nevertheless, with what I know so far, figuring out the rest shouldn't be too difficult."

Darkslash was infuriated by Timaeus' words. "Well then," he replied, "if that's the case, Windslash... you won't be leaving here alive." The two charged at each other, resuming their battle and matching each other blow for blow.

A moment later, the waters of the lake began to ripple violently, capturing both of their attention. "What have you done, Windslash?" Darkslash asked, concern evident in his voice. Timaeus looked Darkslash in the face and replied, "A little while ago, when you knocked me along the shoreline, I cast a spell to cause the ice restraining the Hydra to melt. I couldn't concentrate on it long enough to speed up the process, so I used a combination of my Wind and Fire Magic to accelerate it."

Just then, the Hydra emerged from the water and wasted no time attacking Timaeus and Darkslash with its three heads.

The two of them managed to avoid the beast's attack, but the middle head then lunged at Timaeus. "GÍNETE ÉNA ME TI GI!!!" he cried, turning his body into soil to hide from the creature. The beast redirected its attention to Darkslash. The three heads toyed with their new prey, attacking one at a time randomly. However, Darkslash was able to hold his own against the Hydra. Realising this, the beast decided to change its strategy, mimicking what it had done to Timaeus. The left and right heads would distract Darkslash while the middle head waited for the perfect moment to strike. Darkslash skilfully evaded and countered the attacks of both heads with his speed and swords, all the while keeping a watchful eye on the middle head, knowing it was looking for an opening to attack. Timaeus reformed from the ground and watched as Darkslash fought back against the Hydra, but he noticed that, despite all the counterattacks, no blood had spilt from the creature's body.

Timaeus recalled his previous battles with Darkslash. In their first encounter, he bled heavily when his own weapons were used against him. However, during their second fight, despite being struck multiple times by Darkslash's swords, he didn't bleed at all. Now, he understood the importance of obtaining the blood of the beasts.

With a renewed purpose, Timaeus ran toward the Hydra and shouted, "Ánodos Anémou!" This invocation summoned a gust of wind that lifted him into the air, allowing him to land on the Hydra's middle head. He raised his double-edged sword horizontally, and the Green Element Stone embedded in his right gauntlet began to glow.

At that moment, Timaeus cried, "KALÓ TI VRONTÍ KÁTO APÓ TOUS OURANOÚS!!!" A powerful bolt of lightning surged down from the heavens, striking the Hydra and electrocuting it, ultimately killing the beast and securing his victory.

The evil surrounding Hydra Lake began to dissipate following the death of the beast. Timaeus leapt off the corpse of the Hydra and landed in front of Darkslash, who was staring at the body in shock. "WHAT HAVE YOU DONE?!!!" he cried.

Timaeus reached into his supply satchel and replied, "I've disrupted your plans in one important way. Despite the damage you can inflict with those blades of yours, no blood can be extracted from the wounds you inflict on your victims. That's why you needed me to extract the blood from the beasts for you."

Darkslash turned and glared fiercely at Timaeus. "NRGH!!!" he grunted. "It isn't the blades that stop the wounds from bleeding; it's the Dark Magic of Leviathan. Otherwise, I could have obtained the blood of the beasts a long fucking time ago. You'll pay for this Windslash!" At that moment, Timaeus threw a Magic Gem into the air and shouted, "Ektyflotikó Fos!" This created a powerful red light to signal Stratos.

"You'll be dead before that feathered piece of shit gets here," said Darkslash. Timaeus took a fighting stance, stood his ground, and replied, "I doubt it... Battling that Hydra has left you exhausted; me, on the other hand." He then raised his hand toward the lake. "Éla Neró!" he shouted, summoning water from the lake. He pulled his arm toward him, causing the summoned water to splash onto his body, soaking him in the process. With that, Timaeus declared, "Therapéfste To Neró!" healing himself.

Despite this, Darkslash didn't back down and continued his offensive. Timaeus was easily able to defend against Darkslash's attacks, but despite his opponent's weakened state, he struggled to break through Darkslash's defence. Just then, a loud cry echoed from the woodlands, and Stratos came running toward them, positioning himself between the two.

Darkslash was not about to back down and prepared to fight back. However, Stratos reared up and slashed Darkslash's right arm with his left talon, causing him to fall to the ground. Darkslash was too weak to get back up.

"Easy, Stratos," said Timaeus as he walked past the creature. He then held his double-edged sword in front of Darkslash and said in a threatening tone, "This is your final warning." Too weak to resist, Darkslash had no choice but to concede.

Timaeus then separated the hilts of his weapon, transforming it back into two swords, and merged them once more into a broadsword. The two of them then spoke in unison, "Apókrypsi Lepídas," concealing their weapons. Timaeus turned around and mounted Stratos. As Darkslash got back to his feet, he said, "This is far from over, Windslash... So don't think for a second that this is the end of anything." Timaeus, sitting atop Stratos, replied, "I didn't expect it to be." With that, Timaeus and Stratos headed back.

Chapter Fourteen
Wind Mist

Darkslash watched as Timaeus and Stratos made their way back. He was enraged, not only because he had been outsmarted and outmatched in battle but also because Timaeus had forced him into submission. The recent events deeply affected him; his opponent had discovered an ability that allowed him to bypass enhancements from magic, including Leviathan's Dark Magic. To make matters worse, Timaeus had denied him what he had come for.

"ARGH!!!" he cried in frustration as he approached the dead body of the Hydra. Still furious, Darkslash's attention was suddenly caught by something near the Hydra, which brought an evil smile to his face.

Meanwhile, Timaeus rode Stratos back to the training grounds in Eastern Atlantis, where King Okeanos and Critias were waiting for their return.

"He should've been back by now," Critias said. "Even I wasn't foolish enough to face that Hydra."

King Okeanos looked at his son and replied, "He's fought and killed every beast that guards an Element Stone so far, my son. It wouldn't surprise me if he found a way to kill the Hydra as well. Plus, each time he defeats one of the beasts, the Dark Elemental of Wind shows up to claim its blood, so that must also be taken into account." Critias listened carefully to his father's words; as crazy as they sounded, he knew his father made a valid point.

A few moments later, they heard Stratos' cry, and the signal beacon was ignited with Fire Magic before anyone could reach it. Stratos flew down and landed next to the beacon. Timaeus quickly dismounted from Stratos and rushed over to King Okeanos and Critias to inform them about the events at Hydra Lake.

"Your Majesties," he said hurriedly, "I know what Darkslash is after and what he's planning."

King Okeanos held up his hand to signal Timaeus to slow down. "Please, Timaeus," he said calmly. Timaeus placed his right hand on his left shoulder, bowed his head, and knelt on his right knee. "Forgive me,

Your Majesty," he replied. King Okeanos stood before him and continued, "Please rise, Timaeus. You've done nothing wrong; you were just speaking too quickly for us to understand."

Before Timaeus could begin explaining what he had discovered, Critias stepped forward and said, "Before you share anything, Timaeus, there's something I'd like to know." Timaeus stood silently, waiting for Critias to ask his question.

"What I'd like to know is how you returned from Hydra Lake unscathed," Critias asked. "From what you've told us already, it's clear that you had another encounter with the Dark Elemental of Wind."

Timaeus approached Critias, placing his hand on his shoulder, and replied, "If you had waited a moment, my friend, you would have found out, but since you're so eager to know, I'll tell you... The reason I'm unscathed is that I didn't encounter him in Griffin Valley, and there's no water on Chimera Mountain or in the Labyrinth." This brought a smile to King Okeanos' face. He chuckled, "Hehe, now that you've answered Critias' question, what was it you wanted to tell us? Talk slowly this time."

Timaeus crossed his right arm over his left shoulder and bowed his head. "As I mentioned, Your Majesty," he said as he raised his head, "I know what Darkslash is after and what he's planning. He needs the blood of the beasts for a Teleport Rune he has created. Currently, it allows him to travel anywhere in Atlantis, but with the blood of the beasts, he can strengthen its magic, enabling him to bring as many as he wants to Atlantis. He is undoubtedly planning an invasion. Fortunately, he did not obtain the Hydra's blood."

King Okeanos and Critias were at a loss for words, seized by fear. "Are you sure he hasn't obtained the Hydra's blood?" Critias asked. Timaeus stood firmly and replied, "I'm quite sure. The Hydra is dead, and Leviathan's Dark Magic prevents any wounds he inflicts on his victims from bleeding. That's why he waited for me to face the beasts; I'm the only one who has drawn blood from them."

Despite Timaeus' answer, King Okeanos and Critias still had more questions. "How did you kill the Hydra?" King Okeanos inquired. Timaeus placed his right arm on his left shoulder and responded, "At first, I froze it in the lake. However, when Darkslash showed up, even though my ability to bypass enhancements from magic also works against

Leviathan's Dark Magic, it wasn't enough. So I set the Hydra free, and it went after Darkslash. After realising that he couldn't make the beast bleed, I used Wind Magic to electrocute it by summoning thunder. As for Darkslash, he was left exhausted after battling the Hydra, which allowed me and Stratos to force him into submission."

Though they could hardly believe what they were hearing, King Okeanos and Critias remained concerned. "It's incredible that you were able to defeat the Hydra and the Dark Elemental of Wind by yourself," said Critias. "However, considering what you've just shared about his intentions, I don't want to take any chances. We need to ensure he hasn't obtained any blood from the Hydra's body."

With an intense expression, Timaeus responded, "I only forced him to surrender; I still can't defeat him on my own. However, I agree that we should confirm he hasn't acquired any blood."

King Okeanos approached Timaeus and Critias. "Take this Teleport Rune," he instructed. "It will allow you to travel to Hydra Lake. Timaeus, you still have the rune you took with you that allows you to return here. We need to find out as quickly as possible if he obtained the Hydra's blood, so Stratos will need to remain here."

Stratos chirped in an upset manner. King Okeanos approached him, stroked his forehead, and said, "Nothing against you, my friend, but we need to find out as quickly as we can." King Okeanos' words lifted Stratos' spirits a little, but he was still disappointed that he wasn't allowed to accompany Timaeus and Critias.

Placing the Teleport Rune on the ground, Critias spoke the activation phrase, "Tilemetaforá." In an instant, the two of them arrived at the entrance of the woodlands surrounding Hydra Lake. Wasting no time, they ventured straight through the forest, and upon reaching the lake, they saw the Hydra's lifeless body by the shoreline.

"Is this how you left it?" Critias asked. After gazing at the body for a few moments, Timaeus replied, "Yes, without a doubt... This is exactly how I left it before I returned. Darkslash hasn't touched it."

Despite Timaeus' earlier response, Critias remained concerned. "Let's check the shoreline," he suggested. "Just in case any blood fell on land." Timaeus looked at Critias and replied, "Very well... Although I kept the battle confined to the lake, I did wound the beast, so it's wise to check if the wound reopened at any point."

Both Timaeus and Critias walked along opposite sides of the shoreline, but when they met up on the other side of the lake, they found no signs of blood. They retraced their steps, scanning the area in case either of them missed something, but still found nothing.

As they returned to where the Hydra's body lay, the two were about to leave when Critias noticed something. "Timaeus," he said with a worried tone, "look... the Hydra's left head." They approached the Hydra's body, and their worst fears were realised as they took in the sight before them.

Although Timaeus had killed the Hydra by electrocuting it, he didn't realise at the time that this had caused the left head's nose to bleed. "FUCK!" he cried angrily. "And Critias, look! The blood's been wiped; now he has the blood of all four beasts."

With what they had discovered, Critias urged, "Hurry, Timaeus. We must report our findings back to my father." Without hesitation, Timaeus set his Teleport Rune on the ground and spoke the activation phrase, "Tilemetaforá." In an instant, the two of them found themselves back at the training grounds in Western Atlantis, where King Okeanos awaited them along with Stratos.

Immediately, Timaeus placed his right hand on his left shoulder and knelt on his right knee. "Your Majesty," Timaeus said hurriedly in a worried tone, "we've discovered something, and it's worse than we thought."

King Okeanos raised his hand to stop Timaeus. "Rise, Timaeus," he said. "Now, one at a time... and please, speak slowly." Timaeus stood up and allowed Critias to go first, as he didn't want to take all the credit.

"It's like this, Father," Critias began. "When we arrived at the lake, the Hydra's body hadn't been moved, and there was no blood on the shoreline. However, as we were leaving, we noticed something. I'll let Timaeus explain this part."

Timaeus stepped forward. "Thank you, Critias," he said. "As we were leaving, Your Majesty, Critias noticed something on the left head of the Hydra's body. As I mentioned before, I killed the Hydra by electrocuting it, which caused the blood vessels in its nose to rupture, leading to bleeding from the left head's nose. Additionally, the blood had been wiped clean, meaning Darkslash now possesses the blood of all four beasts."

King Okeanos trembled with fear. "So, the Dark Elemental of Wind can now bring his forces to Atlantis whenever he wants," he said, "depending on how long it takes to prepare the Teleport Rune." Despite the general apprehension, Timaeus stepped forward. "Forgive me, Your Majesty, but I must ask... Where are the Dark Elementals hiding? Wouldn't it be better to find them and end this before it begins?"

King Okeanos turned, feeling anxious and helpless. "Even if we sought them out, Timaeus," he replied, "this conflict began centuries ago." Timaeus pressed on, "Then where are they hiding, Your Majesty?"

Before he could finish, King Okeanos turned, his anger flaring. "They're hiding on the mainland, Timaeus! They gather their forces on the Atlas Mountain!"

Timaeus placed his right hand on his left shoulder and bowed his head. "Forgive me, Your Majesty," he said. King Okeanos walked towards Timaeus, placed his hand on his shoulder, and replied, "I should be the one asking for your forgiveness, Timaeus. What you're suggesting is something we've all desired for centuries, but it is a suicide mission. Now that the Dark Elemental of Wind has acquired the blood of all four beasts, it's only a matter of time before he brings down Atlantis."

Despite the grim situation, a glimmer of hope suddenly appeared on Timaeus' face. "What can you tell me about Darkslash, Your Majesty?" he asked, eliciting a confused look from both King Okeanos and Critias.

"You must have encountered him several times, Your Majesty. How would he go about enacting his plan?" Despite not knowing where Timaeus was headed with this question, King Okeanos replied, "Well, as you surely know, he reveals little to no information to his opponents in order to keep them in the dark and guessing. By doing this, his opponents let their guard down, making it easier for him to defeat them. So, he would undoubtedly set his plan in motion when you'd least expect it, as you don't know the full extent of his strategy or how long it will take him to execute it."

This remark brought a smile to Timaeus' face. "Which is exactly why we're going to turn his own tactics against him," he said, eliciting a surprised look from King Okeanos and Critias. "I left Hydra Lake thinking he couldn't obtain the beast's blood, so he likely believes we don't know he managed to acquire it. This means he can prepare without us realising his plan has succeeded, allowing him to invade Atlantis while our guard is down. However, he doesn't know that we are aware he obtained the Hydra's blood. This gives us a chance to prepare for when he enacts his plan, as he will think we are oblivious to his intentions and that our defences will be lowered when he strikes."

A smile spread across King Okeanos' and Critias' faces. "Hehe," chuckled King Okeanos. "You never cease to amaze me, Timaeus." Critias approached King Okeanos. "He never ceases to amaze me either, Father," he said.

Both turned their attention back to Timaeus. "Speaking of which," said King Okeanos, "now that you've obtained your final Element Stones, your training is complete. It is time for you to return to Phaedo in Eastern Atlantis until the moment arrives for you to become the new guardian of the Dragon's Eye Crest."

Timaeus placed his right hand on his left shoulder and knelt down on his right knee. King Okeanos stood in awe of the warrior bowing before him, unable to believe what Timaeus had achieved. He could hardly fathom that he stood before an Elemental who could not only wield all four forms of Element Magic but had also mastered their use.

"Please rise, Timaeus," said King Okeanos. "You bow to no one."

Feeling honoured by the King's words, Timaeus stood up. Stratos, the Griffin, happily chirped at King Okeanos, who affectionately stroked Stratos' forehead.

"It will be such a shame to see you leave, Stratos," the King remarked. "After everything that has transpired, I think it's time for us to retire for the night."

A serious expression crossed Critias' face. "Despite what has happened, I believe I have a way to prepare for when the Dark Elemental of Wind enacts his plan."

This sparked a curious look from Timaeus. "Go on," he replied, eager to learn more.

Critias stepped closer to Timaeus. "You still owe me a rematch," he said. "So, let us all retire for the night. Tomorrow, we will see if Windslash is ready."

A competitive glint appeared in the eyes of both Timaeus and Critias as they shook hands. King Okeanos chuckled at Critias' words, and with that, they all retired for the night.

Meanwhile, on the Atlas Mountains, where the Dark Elementals resided, Darkslash returned with a sample of the Hydra's blood that he had obtained at Hydra Lake. When his comrades saw how injured he was from his battle with Timaeus, they were at a loss for words. "That is fucking impossible," said Dark Flare. "No way could an Elemental inflict that much fucking damage on you." Darkslash didn't respond, as he was in too much pain to speak.

"Hehe," chuckled Dark Gaia. "Windslash probably cut off the Hydra's heads too many times and left him to fend for himself." Still not responding, Darkslash approached Dark Tide. He poured a small amphora of water over Darkslash and said, "Therapéfste To Neró," healing him. "How powerful has he become this time?" Dark Tide asked, giving Darkslash an evil glare.

"He froze the Hydra out on the lake, so I couldn't obtain its blood," he replied. "Windslash has become so much more powerful that I had to use my weapons right from the start. He couldn't get past my defences, and I managed to land a few clean hits on him, but the little shit used Earth Magic to evade my finishing attack." Wanting to know more, Dark Flare asked, "So, how the fuck did Windslash manage to cause that much fucking damage to you?"

Darkslash turned to her, anger etched on his face. "Windslash has learned a new ability by combining Wind and Earth Magic. This allows him to bypass magical enhancements, including Leviathan's Dark Magic. I couldn't believe the pain he was able to inflict on me with this ability." His comrades were stunned, unable to process what they had just heard.

"I FUCKING TOLD YOU THIS WOULD HAPPEN!" cried Dark Tide. Darkslash turned towards him and angrily replied, "This ability of his is limited! He can only sustain it for a short time, and once it had worn off, I had the upper hand over him again."

Dark Tide glared furiously at Darkslash. "It's limited now," he said. "However, now that he's learned how to use all four forms of Element Magic and obtained all four Element Stones, he'll undoubtedly figure out how to sustain it for longer." Not wanting to hear any more from Dark Tide, Darkslash turned and walked away towards his cliff.

"Haha," laughed Dark Gaia. "I'm with Dark Tide on this one; he has been telling you to kill that little shit for years." Ignoring Dark Gaia's comments, Darkslash continued the story.

"Despite knocking him down, Windslash then sets a plan in motion to free the Hydra. Because he couldn't concentrate, he used his Wind and Fire Magic combination to melt the ice faster. After knocking me down, he discovered my Teleport Rune, and he fucking figured out why I needed the blood of the beasts. He's no doubt pieced together the fucking rest by now, but it doesn't matter."

His comrades didn't understand what he meant. "What do you mean, 'it doesn't fucking matter?" Dark Flare asked furiously. "He's figured out what you were fucking planning, and from what I can tell, he's fucking thwarted what you've been waiting twelve years to achieve."

Darkslash then took the Hydra's blood from his robes and turned toward his comrades, showing it to them. "You haven't heard the best part yet," he said. "Despite setting the Hydra free, it attacked both of us. Windslash ended up killing the beast by electrocuting it, so no blood fell from its body. He then summoned his Griffin friend using a Magic Gem and healed himself with water from the lake. Neither of us could penetrate each other's defences, but once that Griffin arrived, it knocked me down, and I was forced to surrender."

Dark Flare was disgusted by what she was hearing.

"You fucking surrendered to him," Darkslash ignored her. "Haha," laughed Dark Gaia. "I'm with Dark Flare about him forcing you to surrender. However, if Windslash defeated the Hydra, how did you obtain its blood?"

An evil smile crept onto Darkslash's face. "After Windslash and his Griffin friend left," he said, "I thought he'd ruined everything. But when I looked at the Hydra's body, I noticed that the left head's nose was bleeding. The electrocution must have ruptured the blood vessels in its nose, causing it to bleed."

Dark Flare, intrigued by what she was hearing, asked, "So, when do we invade Atlantis?" Darkslash smiled mischievously at her question and replied, "I need to prepare the Teleport Rune with the blood of the beasts first, but I plan to wait a while to make Windslash think he has foiled my plan." His words filled Dark Tide with anger.

"That's a bad idea!" he shouted. "If you wait too long, he could learn how to use his magic in much more powerful ways! He's already figured out how to bypass enhancements from magic; he could end up learning how to nullify them! I say that after you've strengthened the Teleport Rune using the blood of the beasts, we invade Atlantis immediately!"

Dark Tide's words were beginning to annoy Darkslash. "NO!" he cried. "It seems you're overlooking something this time. Windslash is unaware that I obtained the Hydra's blood, so Atlantis' guard will be down when we invade, especially if we wait and let them think my plan has been foiled."

Dark Tide was agitated and had lost his words. "Haha," chuckled Dark Gaia. "Dark Tide still has a point about Windslash learning to use his magic in more powerful ways."

Darkslash turned to look over the cliff's edge. "Maybe so," he said, tucking the Hydra's blood back into his robes. "But with their guard down, Atlantis won't see us coming until it's too late." Satisfied that his comrades understood, Darkslash stood tall and gazed out at the chaos he planned to unleash upon Atlantis.

The next morning in Western Atlantis, Timaeus woke up and headed straight to the training arena, where King Okeanos, Critias, and the other Water Elementals and students were waiting for him. When he reached King Okeanos, Timaeus placed his right hand on his left shoulder. The King then held out his left hand and said, "Remember, Timaeus, you bow to no one." Not wanting to seem disrespectful, Timaeus lowered his head and replied, "Thank you, Your Highness." Moments later, Master Phaedo, Master Byrne, and Master Gorgias arrived to witness Timaeus' abilities now that his training was complete.

Suddenly, everyone heard a loud cry as Stratos came running across the training arena toward Master Byrne. "Haha," laughed Master Byrne as he stroked Stratos. "It's good to see you too, Stratos. I've missed you, old friend." Stratos chirped happily in response.

"How has he been getting along with you, Okeanos?" asked Master Phaedo. A curious look appeared on Master Gorgias' face as he asked, "He hasn't tried to devour Critias, has he?" This brought a smile to King Okeanos' face.

"Hehe," he chuckled. "Actually, we've been getting along just fine ever since Stratos and Timaeus arrived. He adjusted to us very quickly and hasn't tried to devour anyone." Stratos chirped happily at King Okeanos' words.

"Good thing I gave you a heads-up about him, Okeanos," said Master Byrne, chuckling while stroking Stratos. After everyone had greeted each other, Timaeus and Critias prepared to take their places in the centre of the arena.

"Hold on, both of you," said King Okeanos. Timaeus and Critias looked towards him, slightly confused by his words. "The reason I've stopped you both is that this training arena isn't filled with water. Unlike your rematches with Hermos and Gorgas, you wouldn't be able to showcase your full potential here. That's why I think we should have this rematch at the same place as your original match: the Royal Court."

King Okeanos' words brought smiles to their faces, and Stratos let out a loud and upset cry. "Haha," he chuckled. "No worries, Stratos. You can come along too."

King Okeanos then stepped forward and placed a Teleport Rune on the ground. Everyone present at the training arena gathered around him as he spoke, "Tilemetaforá," activating the rune. In an instant, everyone in his vicinity was teleported to the Royal Court.

When they arrived, Gale and the other orphans who had once lived with Timaeus were present; all of them were now part of the Royal Guard. Sitting next to them were Zephyr, Hermos, Gorgas, Roc, and Ston. As before, other members of the Royal Guard, as well as various Wind, Fire, and Earth Elementals, were also in attendance. Everyone who had just arrived took their seats in the seating area while King Okeanos and the three masters settled into their places.

Stratos sat in the third row of the seating area behind King Okeanos and the three masters. Timaeus and Critias took their positions at the centre of the Royal Court.

"Before we begin," said King Okeanos, "there is something I would like to share with everyone first." The King rose from his seat, took a deep breath, and spoke loudly to the assembly.

"Twelve years ago, my son faced a challenge and lost to a Wind Student who had not only defeated Byrne's and Gorgias' successor in combat but had also triumphed over a Dark Elemental. This Wind Student had become Phaedo's successor two days prior, not just because of his victories but also due to something we had always believed to be impossible: his exceptional ability to wield all four forms of Element Magic. Now, here we are, twelve years later. That Wind Student has not only become an Elemental but has also been trained in all four forms of Element Magic. Today, we will witness a rematch between Phaedo's successor and my own son, to see what he is capable of now that his training is complete."

Everyone in the Royal Court cheered as Timaeus and Critias shook hands. "Draw your weapons," said King Okeanos. "Remember what we talked about all those years ago, Timaeus, regarding the trauma of facing a Dark Elemental and its severe mental effects on you. Don't let what you discovered last night have the same impact."

A smile spread across Timaeus' face as he turned to King Okeanos and replied, "I won't, Your Majesty." He then extended his hand in front of him and spoke, "Emfanízetai I Lepída," causing his weapon to materialise. He split it into twin blades and then merged the hilts together to form a double-edged sword. Critias drew his trident staff.

King Okeanos extended his right arm in front of him. "NOW!" he shouted. "Let us see what being trained to use all four forms of Element Magic has enabled Timaeus to accomplish against the heir to the throne of Atlantis!" The entire Royal Court erupted in cheers as they anticipated the start of the battle. King Okeanos then returned to his seat and shouted, "BEGIN!"

Unlike last time, Critias didn't make the opening move, nor did Timaeus. Instead, the two exchanged intimidating glares without saying a word. Timaeus' double-edged sword crackled with sparks of electricity. This display caught the attention of Master Gorgias, who thought to himself, "Is he really going to attack Critias violently like he did twelve years ago?" Fortunately, Master Byrne quickly interpreted Timaeus' actions. "No, that's not his intention," he replied. "The sparks of electricity around Timaeus' weapon serve as a warning... A warning to prevent Critias from using the same strategy he employed twelve years ago, as the electricity would enable Timaeus to counter it more effectively." King Okeanos found Master Byrne's insight intriguing. "You make a valid point, Byrne," he commented. "However, the circumstances are not quite the same as they were twelve years ago."

Master Phaedo had something to say in response to King Okeanos' words. "That is true, Okeanos," he replied. "Both of them have come a long way in the last twelve years. However, just like twelve years ago, our money is still on Timaeus." The King and the three Masters erupted in laughter.

A moment later, both Timaeus and Critias made their opening moves, locking their weapons together in a fierce struggle, neither able to overpower the other. Less than ten seconds passed when swirling circles of wind began to surround them, growing faster as Timaeus and Critias continued to clash.

"Ánodos Anémou!" Timaeus shouted, unleashing a surge of wind that lifted both combatants into the air, sending them in opposite directions. Timaeus executed a somersault backwards, landing gracefully at the edge of the central platform. Critias attempted to do the same, but the powerful winds threw him off balance, and he landed on his back at the edge of the platform.

Despite this, Critias raised his arm toward one of the fountains on the wall of the chamber and said, "Éla Neró," summoning water from the fountain. He pulled his arm toward him, letting the summoned water hit his body and soak him. Then, he spoke, "Therapéfste To Neró," healing himself from the fall.

Getting back to his feet, Critias raised his arm and shouted, "Ánodos Neroú!" This caused the water circling the central platform to rise and form a wall. He then lowered his arm, allowing the water to cascade down over the centre of the platform.

With little time to react, Timaeus jumped into the air, holding his weapon horizontally above his head, with the blades facing front to back. He landed in the centre of the platform, slamming his blade into the surface, and shouted, "Apólyto Midén!!!" This caused all the water crashing down to freeze, capturing Critias in the process.

With his opponent trapped in ice, Timaeus shouted, "Diamantoskóni!" The command caused the ice to shatter, inflicting immense pain on Critias. However, despite being soaked by the ice, he managed to speak slowly, "Therapéfste... To... Neró," healing himself. Although he healed the damage, Critias still felt cold from being trapped in the ice.

As Timaeus charged towards him for his next attack, Critias' Element Stone began to glow. He then uttered, "Sóma... Neroú," and in an instant, his body transformed into water, allowing Timaeus' attack to pass straight through him, splashing water everywhere. The Element Stone lay on the floor behind Timaeus. A few seconds later, Critias reformed but remained in his watery state.

As Timaeus turned around, Critias launched a punch, and the force of the water knocked Timaeus to the ground.

"I take it what we've been seeing so far is just the warm-up?" asked King Okeanos. The three masters sat together, laughing as they replied, "Yes." Despite their answer, King Okeanos wasn't surprised; he was eagerly anticipating when the real battle would begin.

Timaeus got back to his feet, and Critias returned to his normal stance, both exchanging menacing looks. "Unlike my sandstorm ability," Timaeus said, "I can't hit you, but because of the pressure of the water, you can still hit me."

Critias planted the polearm of his trident staff on the ground. "I think that's enough for the warm-up, Timaeus," he said. "Now... it's time to find out what Windslash can do." Not backing down from Critias' challenge, Timaeus assumed a fighting position and prepared to engage again. His Green and Gold Element Stones began to glow.

Critias took up a fighting stance. "Once I turn my body into water, your two forms of Element Magic will be of little use to you," he said as his Blue Element Stone began to glow. "Sóma Neroú."

Not worried about Critias shapeshifting into water again due to the stone surface they were standing on, Timaeus shouted, "Gíne Éna Me Ti Gi Kai Ti Vrontí!" Uniting his Wind and Earth Magic, Timaeus transformed his body into stone, which crackled with electricity. A few seconds later, the stone began to crack, and Timaeus returned to flesh, still emitting sparks and donning lime-green glowing clothes. The entire Royal Court was mesmerised by the spectacle.

Both Timaeus and Critias launched their attacks. Timaeus threw a punch with his right hand, which Critias evaded. In response, Timaeus counterattacked with his double-edged sword, slashing across Critias' abdomen. Critias felt the impact, as Timaeus' ability allowed him to bypass the enhancements from magic. He followed this attack with a left hook to Critias' face.

Both attacks made it seem as though Critias' abdomen and face had reverted to normal. "Therapéfste To Neró," he said, causing his face and abdomen to shapeshift back into water after healing the damage inflicted by Timaeus. Despite his ability to bypass enhancements from magic, Timaeus decided to end things quickly and resumed his offensive. However, just as he was about to land his next attack, his clothes stopped glowing, and the sparks of electricity faded, causing Timaeus' weapon to pass straight through Critias' body, sending water splashing everywhere.

Quickly scanning for the Blue Element Stone, Timaeus maintained his distance from it as Critias' body began to reform. "What's going on?" asked Master Byrne. "When Timaeus used that ability against Gorgas, he was able to defeat him in an instant." Master Gorgias recognised the problem immediately.

"While that is true, Byrne," he replied, "the circumstances in this battle are different. When Timaeus fought Gorgas, he left Gorgas vulnerable by using his Wind and Fire Magic while Gorgas was reforming after shapeshifting into sand. This allowed Timaeus to quickly end the battle after uniting his Wind and Earth Magic with the power of his Green and Gold Element Stones."

With Master Gorgias' words, Master Phaedo was able to identify the problem. "Everything you both said is correct," he explained. "However, in this case, the issue is that Timaeus hasn't mastered his Gold Element Stone. When he first combined his Green and Gold Element Stones to unite his Wind and Earth Magic, he managed to defeat his opponent with minimal effort after weakening him. But that initial attack would have probably been all he could manage at that point because he had only just acquired his Gold Element Stone. Now, although he has learned to use the Gold Element Stone at an advanced level, he can only maintain that ability for a limited time. Plus, he is facing an opponent who is not only at full strength but also has the ability to heal himself using Water Magic."

King Okeanos sat behind the three Masters, slowly clapping his hands. "Plus, Timaeus can't even things out," he remarked. "Timaeus has only just acquired his Blue Element Stone, while Critias has mastered his. Therefore, the battle can't be balanced, and there's not much else Timaeus can do."

Master Phaedo looked on in disagreement. "I wouldn't count him out just yet, Okeanos," he said. "Timaeus has been in tough situations like this before and has always found a way to fight back. With everything we've seen over the past twelve years, he continually surprises us with something new." Master Byrne and Master Gorgias nodded in agreement with Master Phaedo's words.

In the centre of the Royal Court, while his body remained shapeshifted into water, Critias launched an offensive attack. Timaeus was forced onto the defensive, unable to protect himself against the relentless pressure of his opponent's strikes.

Although Critias was no match for Timaeus' speed, Timaeus still struggled to find a way to fight back. He decided to use his opponent's abilities against him. After dodging Critias' next attack, Timaeus raised his arm and shouted, "Pagoméno Neró!" This spell froze Critias in place.

While the strategy gave Timaeus a moment to catch his breath, it didn't work as effectively as he had hoped. He noticed that Critias was beginning to melt. Within seconds, Critias' body had dissolved into the surface they were on, but Timaeus could see no sign of Critias' Element Stone. Unsure of where his opponent would reappear, Timaeus stayed on high alert.

Less than ten seconds later, Critias suddenly reformed behind Timaeus and returned to normal. Without hesitation, he struck Timaeus' legs with his trident staff, knocking him onto his back. Critias looked down at Timaeus.

"That's payback for when you put me in this position twelve years ago," he said. "The Element Stone only appears when my body is dispersed after I've shapeshifted into water, not when I break myself down into a pool of water. So, by freezing me in place, you gave me the opportunity I needed to perform that sneak attack." Timaeus lay there with a smile on his face. "You got me," he admitted. "I won't make that mistake again."

Critias held his trident staff over Timaeus. "Yield," he commanded in a severe tone. "There's nothing else you can do against me; you have no hope of defeating me." Timaeus refused to be swayed by Critias' words. "It's not over yet," he replied. "I may be down, but I'm certainly not out."

Since his opponent would not yield, Critias declared, "Sóma Neroú," shapeshifting his body back into water once again.

Despite appearances, Timaeus remained emotionally calm, as tranquil as both the wind and the water. Circles of wind began to surround him, and the water he was soaked in started to turn into mist. Critias prepared to deliver the finishing blow, launching his attack toward Timaeus. In that moment, Timaeus shouted, "Anemomíchli!" As he did, he vanished, leaving behind only a cloud of mist. The entire Royal Court was astonished by what they had just witnessed; it seemed as if Timaeus' body had evaporated completely. Critias scanned the platform but could find no trace of him. Moments later, mist coalesced into a swirling twister of wind, and within seconds, Timaeus' body reformed. It was as if he had transformed into a mist of breezes.

Chapter Fifteen
For What Lies Ahead

King Okeanos was astonished by what he was witnessing. Master Byrne sat there with a smile on his face. "Hehe," he chuckled. "Don't worry, Okeanos, this isn't the first time this has happened."

Master Gorgias couldn't believe what was unfolding before him. "What the fuck has he done this time?" he asked. Master Phaedo, with an astounded expression, replied, "Despite the circumstances he was faced with, Timaeus managed to remain calm. He was as serene as both the wind and water, and that tranquillity has allowed him to unite his Wind and Water Magic. Now, like every time he combines his Element Magic, all we need to do is discover what this new combination is capable of."

Critias returned to his normal state and remarked, "I had a feeling this would happen with all the abilities you've used so far. Let's see if Windslash's new ability can level the playing field."

Timaeus stood there with a challenging expression on his face. "Bring it," he said confidently. Not backing down from the challenge, Critias declared, "Sóma Neroú," and transformed his body into water, aiming to strike Timaeus. However, Timaeus quickly evaporated into mist within a swirling twister of wind, vanishing just before Critias could land his blow. Moments later, Timaeus reformed at the edge of the platform.

As Timaeus began walking inward, Critias turned around, only to see Timaeus evaporate into mist once again, reappearing behind him. Critias swung his arm in an attempt to hit Timaeus, but his opponent vanished into mist yet again, re-forming somewhere else on the platform.

"It seems Timaeus has managed to even the odds," observed Master Gorgias. Despite this, Master Phaedo countered, "He's only managed to neutralise the threat, so neither of them can inflict damage on the other. Unless Timaeus finds a way to harm Critias, he hasn't improved his chances."

Master Byrne, Master Gorgias, and King Okeanos all agreed with Master Phaedo's words. In the centre of the Royal Court, Timaeus continued to evaporate into mist within a swirling vortex of winds, which was starting to annoy Critias. No matter how hard Critias tried, he could not land an attack on his opponent. Finally, overwhelmed by frustration, he launched a furious attack. Seizing the opportunity, Timaeus reverted back to his normal form, slamming his double-edged sword into the ground vertically. He shouted, "Astrapí Lepída!"

Using his Wind Magic, he manipulated the electrical currents in the air to charge the blades with electricity. When Critias' fist collided with Timaeus' electrically charged weapon while he was still in his water-shapeshifted form, Critias was electrocuted. The shock severely knocked him backwards, forcing him to revert back to his normal state.

While he was knocked down, Timaeus focused on the four wall fountains surrounding the Royal Court. Seizing the opportunity, he raised his left arm and spoke, "Metakiníste Ti Gi," using his Earth Magic to close off each of the fountains.

"I remember this from last time," said Master Gorgias. "Surely he can't be using the same strategy as before, can he?"

Master Phadeo, confused by Timaeus' actions, noted that Timaeus had just found a way to damage Critias. "What's he up to this time?" he asked. "Taking away the water won't do him any good because his opponent can turn into water."

As Critias got back up, he raised his left arm towards the water encircling the platform and proclaimed, "Éla Neró," summoning the water to himself. He pulled his arm inward, allowing the water to hit and soak his body. "Therapéfste To Neró," he said, healing himself in the process.

"He's already aware of that, Phaedo," said Master Byrne. "Timaeus knows that using the same strategy as last time won't be effective for him, but he needs to prevent Critias from healing himself. That's why he closed the wall fountains." King Okeanos listened with interest. "But I don't see how that makes any difference, Byrne," he replied. "Even with the fountains closed, Critias still has all the water around the platform to heal himself if he's injured." Master Byrne, wearing a confident smile, responded, "Just wait, Okeanos. Based on what we've just seen, I think I've figured out his plan."

Critias transformed his body into water and attacked again. "Anemomíchli," said Timaeus, allowing him to easily avoid Critias' strike by evaporating and reforming his body. Timaeus knew his opponent wouldn't attack in anger again because it would leave him vulnerable to the electrically charged blade.

After dodging several attacks from Critias, Timaeus counterattacked with his double-edged blade, cutting straight through Critias' body and sending splashes everywhere. The Element Stone landed in the centre of the platform. Without wasting any time, Timaeus evaporated and reformed in front of one of the four pillars. By the time Critias began to reassemble, Timaeus held his double-edged sword above his head.

After several seconds, Critias' body fully reformed but remained in a watery state. Seizing the moment, Timaeus charged his weapon with electricity using his Wind Magic. As Critias faced his opponent, Timaeus hurled his weapon at him, shouting, "Boulóni Krísis!" The sword shot toward Critias like a bolt of lightning.

Critias had no time to react, and Timaeus' weapon went straight through his body, electrocuting him in the process. The shock forced Critias to revert to his normal form, causing him to fall backwards to the ground.

Timaeus' weapon impaled the pillar on the opposite side of the platform. He quickly raised his right hand towards it and shouted, "Éla Neró!" Pulling his weapon back due to it being wet, he ran toward the centre of the platform. Once he reached the centre, he slammed his weapon into the floor horizontally, shouting, "Apólyto Midén!" This caused all the water around the platform to freeze.

"I fucking knew it!" Master Byrne exclaimed excitedly. Timaeus already knew how to defeat Critias, but he had to distract him long enough to get a clear shot with his electrically charged weapon. His plan was to freeze the water circling the platform to prevent Critias from summoning it to heal himself. Additionally, he had closed the fountains to prevent Critias from using them as backups.

The entire Royal Court could barely believe what they had just witnessed. With his opponent down, Timaeus raised his left arm towards the torch atop the pillar, where his weapon was impaled, and proclaimed,

"Éla Fotiá," summoning flames from the torch. He then walked around to Critias' left side, held the flame over him, and declared, "Flóga," which caused the temperature of the flame to rise, evaporating any water on and around Critias' body.

Timaeus placed his left foot on Critias' chest while holding his double-edged sword above him. He proclaimed, "Oi Flóges Svínoun," and extinguished the flames in his hand. With no access to water and having suffered heavy damage from Timaeus' electrically charged weapon, Critias was unable to continue. "Timaeus is the victor!" shouted King Okeanos. The entire Royal Court erupted in cheers and applause for Timaeus' victory.

He turned towards King Okeanos and the three Masters placing his right arm on his left shoulder. Critias lay on the floor, groaning in pain. Timaeus raised his left arm and said, "Metakiníste Ti Gi," which opened the wall fountains. He then lowered his left arm towards the ice and said, "Liósimo Tou Neroú," causing the ice to melt. Raising his left arm again, he commanded, "Ánodos Neroú," causing the water around the platform to rise. When he lowered his arm, the water fell onto the platform, soaking both him and Critias.

Then Timaeus said, "Therápefsé Mas To Neró," which healed both himself and Critias. However, in doing so, he also felt the pain he had inflicted on Critias by electrocuting him, bringing Timaeus to his knees. After being healed, Critias returned to his feet and looked down at Timaeus.

"Do you remember what my father said?" he asked, causing Timaeus to look at Critias with a confused expression.

He then offered to help him up. Taking Critias' hand to help him stand, the prince said to Timaeus, "You bow to no one." This brought a smile to Timaeus' face as the pain began to fade away, reminding him of King Okeanos saying those words to him.

"And do you remember what I said all those years ago?" Critias asked while extending his hand for a handshake. Timaeus smiled and accepted the gesture, recalling Critias' words.

"I do not fear defeat, but I'm prepared to accept it... But, fuck, Windslash is a powerful opponent." They both started laughing, and Timaeus replied, "Windslash still has a lot to learn about his abilities. I still don't know if there are more ways I could unite Element Magic. Last time, I stopped you from healing yourself with fire; this time, I stopped you with ice."

The two of them faced King Okeanos and the three Masters as the King stood up to address everyone in the Royal Court. He began, "What I witnessed for the first time twelve years ago was incredible. I stated on that day that, in due time, it would undoubtedly become something beyond incredible. Eventually, it became indescribable. What we have witnessed today is, without a doubt, indescribable. With his training now complete, as I mentioned last time, it's time for all of us to prepare for what lies ahead. But for now, let's give a round of applause for Critias and Timaeus!"

Everyone in the Royal Court stood up and cheered for both warriors. King Okeanos then dismissed the Royal Court. After a short while, most people had cleared out, leaving only a few who remained. King Okeanos and the three Masters approached Timaeus and Critias, who both placed their right hands over their left shoulders.

"I can explain what happened this time, Masters," said Timaeus. "Though I believe there's more potential in uniting my Wind and Water Magic." Master Phaedo looked intrigued by Timaeus' words. "How do you mean, Timaeus?" he asked curiously.

Timaeus continued, "It was similar to when I've combined Element Magic before; my emotions were different this time. I experienced the calmness of both wind and water, and this tranquillity allowed me to unite them effectively. However, as the battle progressed, I sensed I could achieve something even stronger with the help of my Green and Blue Element Stones, similar to what I did with my green and gold stones against Gorgas. It felt like a storm was raging inside me. Yet, since we are here in the Royal Court rather than the training arena, I didn't want to put anyone at risk."

Everyone was curious to see if Timaeus could achieve something even more powerful. "Let's all head to the training arena to find out," suggested King Okeanos. With a look of excitement on his face, Timaeus replied, "Please allow me, Your Majesty... Stratos, come on, boy!" Stratos let out a loud cry as he joined everyone in the centre of the Royal Court. Timaeus then placed a Teleport Rune on the floor and said, "Tilemetaforá," activating it. In an instant, Timaeus and his closest allies were teleported to the training arena in Western Atlantis. Everyone was eager to see if Timaeus could combine his Element Magic into something stronger.

"Before we begin," Timaeus said, "I have a request, Masters and Your Majesty." King Okeanos smiled and replied, "Of course, Timaeus. What is it?"

Timaeus placed his right arm over his left shoulder and asked, "May I request that Zephyr, Hermos, Gorgas, Roc, Ston, and Critias join me for this?" He continued, "Zephyr has never faced me before, Roc and Ston haven't gotten their rematch, and I haven't faced Hermos and Gorgas in years. I also don't want to leave Critias out."

King Okeanos and the three Masters exchanged excited glances. "Your request is granted, Timaeus," replied King Okeanos, which brought smiles to everyone's faces.

"Thank you, Your Majesty," Timaeus said. "I won't ask for the members of the Royal Guard to join me, as we don't know what we might encounter. Wouldn't you agree, Master Phaedo?"

Proud of his successor's words, Master Phaedo replied, "Indeed, Timaeus. Until we understand what we're dealing with, I agree."

Gale and the others understood Timaeus' perspective, so they decided to join King Okeanos and the three Masters in the seating area. Stratos chose to lie down at the edge of the arena in front of Master Byrne.

"Take your places," said King Okeanos. Timaeus positioned himself in the centre of the arena while the other participants formed a circle around him to increase the challenge. Everyone assumed a fighting stance, and Stratos let out a loud cry, prompting laughter from the group since they anticipated what would come next.

Then, King Okeanos and the three Masters shouted in unison, "BEGIN!"

Zephyr, Roc, and Ston all made their first moves, as one of them had never fought Timaeus before, while the other two hadn't faced him in years. The Green and Red Element Stones on Timaeus' right gauntlet began to glow, which confused the spectators a bit. He had mentioned that he could perform something stronger with his Green and Blue Element Stones.

"Dýnami Tou Foínika!" Timaeus shouted, causing flames in the shape of a bird to surround his body. Although Zephyr, Roc, and Ston landed their attacks on Timaeus, none of them were able to harm him, much to everyone's amazement. Wasting no time, Hermos, Gorgas, and Critias charged in to attack. The Green and Blue Element Stones on Timaeus' gauntlets started to glow, exciting the spectators because this was what he had promised to show them.

"Anemomíchli," Timaeus declared. Evaporating into mist within a whirlwind of breezes, evading all their attacks and reappearing in front of everyone.

With his Green and Blue Element Stones still glowing, Timaeus held his arms out diagonally and shouted, "Kataigída!" A powerful storm erupted, engulfing the entire training arena. Stratos flew into the storm while everyone else was caught in its fierce winds, knocking them all over. Fortunately, those in the seating area managed to protect themselves by hiding behind the walls separating it from the training arena.

"Kataigída Ptósi!" Timaeus cried, causing the storm to subside.

"Hey, Timaeus!" Master Byrne shouted. "As fucking amazing as that ability was, could you give us a little warning next time?"

Timaeus stood there, a horrified expression on his face. "Apologies, Master Byrne," he replied, "but we have a more urgent matter that needs our attention."

Master Byrne glanced at what Timaeus was focusing on, and a look of horror spread across his face. The same reaction followed from King Okeanos, Master Gorgias, and Master Phaedo as they saw the aftermath of the situation. Timaeus' ability had seriously injured everyone involved, and with no water source available in the training arena, healing them would be impossible. Filled with a mix of regret and rage, Timaeus managed to keep his composure, remaining as calm as a gentle breeze. His Green and Red Element Stones began to glow, and he shouted, "FLÓGES TIS ANAGÉNNISIS!!!" Flames in the shape of a bird materialised, but this time, instead of surrounding his body, the fire engulfed the entire training arena.

When the flames subsided, everyone was astonished to find that the fire had not harmed anyone; rather, it had healed them. "How is this possible?" Master Gorgias asked in disbelief.

Everyone began to stand up. "I'm sorry," said Timaeus. "This is why I didn't attempt that ability when we were in the Royal Court; I didn't realise it would be that powerful." No one was angry with Timaeus because, despite what had happened, he saved their lives. Just then, they heard Stratos cry out from the sky as he descended and landed back in the training arena. Master Phaedo approached them. "The flames taking the shape of a bird," he said, "that's no ordinary bird we saw; the flames are taking the shape of a phoenix."

Timaeus turned to Master Phaedo, placing his right arm on his left shoulder, and replied, "That's correct, Master Phaedo. When I faced Hermos in our rematch six years ago, I hadn't mastered my Green Element Stone, so I couldn't bring something stronger into the battle as I did against Gorgas because I had mastered my Green Element Stone at that time. I discovered the phoenix flames while practising how to unite Element Magic during my training here."

This brought a confused look to Critias' face. "If you discovered this during your training here," he asked, "why didn't you use it during our rematch?" Timaeus turned to Critias and replied, "The first ability I used against Zephyr, Roc, and Ston was strictly for defence; it can't be used offensively. The second ability I used to heal everyone, on the other hand, is too powerful to be used on just one person."

At that moment, King Okeanos approached, accompanied by Master Byrne and Master Gorgias. "You intended to demonstrate the defensive and healing capabilities of the phoenix flame abilities from the beginning," King Okeanos said. "You made the right decision by not having the members of the Royal Guard participate. From what you just told Critias, I assume six people is an adequate number for you to heal using the phoenix flame abilities safely. However, we all went in blindly because we didn't know how powerful the storm you created would be."

Timaeus placed his right hand on his left shoulder, feeling riddled with guilt. "You're right, Your Majesty, about everything," he replied. "We should have assessed the situation first, and if we had, I wouldn't have put anyone in danger, and I could have still surprised everyone with the phoenix flames abilities." Everyone agreed with Timaeus' words.

"The fault is not all yours, Timaeus," said Master Phaedo. "As Okeanos mentioned, we all went in blindly without understanding what we were facing." Slowly, Timaeus began to feel some of the guilt lift from his shoulders.

"Despite that, young Timaeus," Master Byrne added, "you never cease to amaze me." Although he still felt guilty about his actions, Timaeus stopped allowing the guilt to weigh him down.

"You have uncovered so much about your abilities in the last twelve years, Timaeus," said Master Gorgias. "It wouldn't surprise me if there are more secrets to be discovered later on."

No longer burdened by guilt, Timaeus stood strong once again. "Now that your training is complete," said King Okeanos, "it is time for you to return to Eastern Atlantis with Phaedo and stand by him until the moment comes for you to take his place as the guardian of the Dragon's Eye Crest."

After being away for nearly a decade, Timaeus finally returned home to Eastern Atlantis, where he worked with Master Phaedo, the Wind Elementals, and the Royal Guard to prepare for Darkslash's impending attack. He continued to train in order to refine his ability to unite his Element Magic.

Meanwhile, in the Atlas Mountains, Darkslash and the other Primordial Dark Elementals were biding their time, hoping to make Atlantis believe they would not see their attack coming. However, Atlantis was already preparing for them. Darkslash's strategy was delayed because, despite having obtained the blood of the beasts, his plan to create a Teleport Rune powerful enough to transport his entire army to Atlantis would take much longer than expected.

Three years later, disaster struck when Master Gorgias passed away. During his funeral ceremony, his body was united with the earth using Gorgas' Gold Element Stone. Following this event, Gorgas became the new guardian of The Dragon's Horn Crest. Meanwhile, Timaeus mastered his Gold Element Stone and refined his ability to combine Wind and Earth Magic. This breakthrough allowed him to bypass magical enhancements for extended periods.

Darkslash was facing delays with his Teleport Rune. While the blood of the beasts was enhancing its power, the process was slower than he had anticipated. Over the next three years, Dark Elementals were dispatched to Atlantis with two primary goals: to kidnap more recruits and to uncover any information that could jeopardise Darkslash's plans. However,

Atlantis fought back vigorously, protecting its Element Students from being taken and revealing nothing in the process. As a result, Darkslash remained unaware that they were preparing to confront him.

Three years later, disaster struck again with the death of King Okeanos. During his funeral ceremony, his body was buried at sea. Critias then became the new guardian of the Dragon's Fang Crest and was crowned King of Atlantis. Timaeus mastered his Blue Element Stone, refining his ability to combine Wind and Water Magic, allowing him to control the strength of the storms he created.

Darkslash's Teleport Rune had passed its halfway point a year earlier, and the blood of the beasts continuously increased its power. Over the next four years, Dark Elementals continued to sneak into Atlantis, but their efforts were in vain. Timaeus remained vigilant, searching for the Dark Fire Elemental who had attacked him as a boy, but there was no sign of him.

Two years later, another disaster struck when Master Byrne passed away. At his funeral ceremony, his body was burned on a funeral pyre, and Stratos let out a loud, sorrowful cry for his long-time friend.

Hermos became the new guardian of the Dragon's Claw Crest. Although Darkslash's Teleport Rune was nearing completion, it still had a long way to go. Two years later, disaster struck again when Master Phaedo passed away. During his funeral ceremony, his body was merged with the wind itself using Timaeus' Green Element Stone. Timaeus then became the new guardian of the Dragon's Eye Crest. After ten long years, Darkslash's Teleport Rune was finally completed.

Chapter Sixteeen
The War of Atlantis

Still mourning the loss of his master, Timaeus returned to his living quarters with Stratos when he heard a familiar sound. "Come to gloat, have you, Darkslash?" he asked.

"No, no, Windslash," replied Darkslash. "I merely came to offer my condolences. Phaedo was always a tough one, but the old bastard finally managed to fade away."

Furiously, Timaeus turned around, his Green and Red Element Stones glowing. "Emfanízontai Lepídes!" Darkslash shouted, summoning his blades in response.

"I did not come here to fight, Windslash," Darkslash said, but Timaeus was not listening. In his anger, he began walking towards Darkslash, his arms raised diagonally. Concerned about what Timaeus might do, Darkslash launched an attack in retaliation to Timaeus' rage.

"DÝNAMI TOU FOÍNIKA!" cried Timaeus as the phoenix flames enveloped his body.

When Darkslash's blades struck Timaeus' body, they did him no harm. Timaeus made no counterattack, but Darkslash could not believe what he was seeing. He quickly stepped back and withdrew his weapons as Stratos approached, angrily chirping at him.

"Apókrypsi Lepídon," said Darkslash, concealing his weapons. "As I mentioned, Windslash, I did not come here to fight, but it's clear you wanted to take your grief out on someone. I am curious to know what that ability was that prevented me from harming you."

Timaeus' Green and Red Element Stones stopped glowing, and he replied, "That's nothing you need to concern yourself with." An evil grin spread across Darkslash's face. "I should have expected you to say that," he said. "It doesn't matter anyway. I only came here to tell you that my plan is complete."

Timaeus looked at Darkslash with confusion, giving him the impression that he didn't understand what he was talking about.

"What do you mean?" he asked craftily. "I foiled your so-called 'plan' a decade ago." Timaeus' tactic paid off as Darkslash let his arrogance cloud his judgment.

"When you electrocuted and killed the Hydra a decade ago," he replied, "you caused the blood vessels in its nose to rupture, resulting in the left head's nose bleeding. This allowed me to obtain its blood after you left."

Timaeus continued his act, hoping to extract more information from Darkslash. "I find that a little hard to believe, Darkslash," he said. "If you had obtained the Hydra's blood, then why haven't you put your plan into action?"

Darkslash stood there with an evil grin on his face, his arrogance blinding him to Timaeus' ruse.

"Ordinarily, I'd say that's nothing you need to concern yourself with," he replied. "But at this point, who gives a fuck? The blood of the beasts provided me with what I needed to enhance that Teleport Rune, but what I didn't realize was how long it would take to make it potent enough to carry out my plan. Despite obtaining the blood of the beasts, it has taken ten years for that Teleport Rune to become powerful enough to execute my intentions."

Timaeus didn't have to feign surprise this time; what Darkslash just revealed was truly shocking. "So, as I mentioned, Windslash," Darkslash continued, "I came here to offer my condolences. However, I also wanted to warn you that the end is nigh. When the skies light up blood red, the Dark Elementals will descend upon Atlantis, and there's nothing you or anyone else can do to stop it or prevent us from claiming the Dragon Crests and Leviathan's Urn. Until we meet again… if we meet again."

In an instant, Darkslash vanished. Timaeus approached his loyal friend, Stratos, giving him an affectionate stroke on the forehead. "You played your part well," Timaeus joked. "Now, let's go inform His Majesty about what we've discovered."

Putting his grief behind him, Timaeus mounted Stratos, and the two set off for the palace in Central Atlantis. Their journey took less than an hour. Upon arriving, Timaeus and Stratos made their way to the palace and were escorted to the throne room.

"My Liege," announced a member of the Royal Guard. "The guardian of the Dragon's Eye Crest requests an audience with you, Your Majesty."

Critias rose from his throne and replied, "Send him in." The Royal Guard placed his right hand on his left shoulder and bowed his head. "Yes, Your Majesty," he said.

Timaeus and Stratos were then escorted into the throne room.

Critias approached the centre of the throne room to greet Timaeus. As he did, he saw Timaeus enter the room alongside Stratos. "Greetings, Your Majesty," said Timaeus. Stratos followed his words with a cheerful chirp. Critias raised his right hand, smiling. "Enough of that, you two," he replied. "I hear 'Your Majesty' enough every fucking day. You know you don't have to address me that way... So, to what do I owe the pleasure?"

Timaeus and Critias shook hands as Stratos settled down by the throne. "Darkslash came to see me," Timaeus said. "He didn't suspect that we had discovered he obtained the Hydra's blood, and he revealed his entire plan to me." A shocked expression crossed Critias' face. "Tell me everything," he urged. "What's he planning?"

Timaeus raised his right hand and replied, "Hold on, Critias. Before I say anything, let's get Hermos and Gorgas here because they need to know this as well."

Critias nodded in agreement, and the two of them set off to find Hermos and Gorgas. They brought them back to the palace, where Timaeus revealed Darkslash's plan.

"It turns out Darkslash's plan is exactly what we suspected when His Majesty and our Masters were still alive," he said. "The only downside is that, despite acquiring the blood of the beasts, it took ten years for the Teleport Rune to become powerful enough to execute his plan."

A look of terror spread across Hermos', Gorgas', and Critias' faces. "Did he tell you when he intends to carry out his plan?" Gorgas asked.

The answer to Gorgas' question brought the same look of fear to Timaeus' face. "He told me that when the skies light up blood red, the Dark Elementals will descend upon Atlantis," he replied. "However, he didn't specify when this would happen."

Despite the terrifying situation, Hermos maintained a brave facade. "How do we prepare for what's coming?" she asked. Timaeus also put on a brave face, refusing to let the frightening circumstances overwhelm him. "Now that we know what will happen when the time comes," he replied, "I have a plan for us to strike back. He thinks we won't see them coming when, in reality, we can ensure they won't see us approaching. For this plan to work, the first part requires help from the Earth and Water Elementals, while the second part relies on the abilities that come from uniting my Element Magic."

Gorgas and Critias also steeled themselves against the fear. "What do you need from the Earth Elementals?" Gorgas asked. Timaeus turned to Gorgas and replied, "Let's get to work. But first, I need to ask you something, Critias. Darkslash is after the Dragon Crests and Leviathan's Urn. Is there a way to seal the Urn so that the lid can't come off during a struggle and the Urn itself can't be broken?"

Critias looked at Timaeus with a confident smile. "It's already taken care of," he replied. "My father never mentioned it when he was alive, but centuries ago, to prevent what happened to the Primordial Dark Elementals from occurring again, a sealing spell was placed on the Urn. This spell ensures that the lid cannot be removed or knocked out of place, and it cannot be broken. The sealing spell can only be lifted if all four of the Dragon Crests are not bonded to a guardian. As for the matter at hand, what do you require from the Water Elementals?" Critias asked.

Timaeus then looked at Gorgas, Critias, and Hermos. "As I mentioned a few moments ago, let's get to work," he replied. The four of them began to prepare for the impending threat. With the little time they had, Timaeus' plan was put into action by spreading the forces of Atlantis across the entire island.

Wind, Fire, Earth, and Water Elementals guarded the four corners of Atlantis, while those stationed in Central Atlantis collaborated with members of the Royal Guard. Timaeus, Hermos, Gorgas, and Critias remained in Central Atlantis as they prepared for the impending battle. Timaeus utilized his magic training from North Atlantis to create a Magic Gem that emitted a blue light, signalling that an area was cleared of enemy threats.

Meanwhile, Darkslash was getting ready to implement his plan in the Atlas Mountains. He descended from his cliff and walked through the legion of Dark Elementals that comprised his army. Setting down his

Teleport Rune, which he had empowered to transport his entire army to Atlantis, he was approached by the Dark Fire Elemental, who had attacked Timaeus when he was a boy.

"Forgive me, my lord," he said, trembling in fear as Darkslash turned toward him. "With your permission, may I battle the one who can wield all four forms of Element Magic? I have been waiting for over twenty years to confront him, especially considering how he bested me by what I can only call dumb luck."

Darkslash glanced at the Dark Fire Elemental with an evil grin and replied, "If you find Windslash before I do, he's all yours... But don't expect an easy battle." A vengeful smile spread across the Dark Fire Elemental's face. "Thank you, my lord," he said, walking away, anticipating what he had been waiting for over twenty-two years.

Darkslash and the other Primordial Dark Elementals stood there with wicked grins, knowing that the Dark Fire Elemental would be no match for Timaeus. Darkslash placed his Teleport Rune down among his army and prepared to head to Atlantis.

Meanwhile, Timaeus, Hermos, Gorgas, and Critias were making some last-minute preparations back in Atlantis. "How many do you expect we will have to face?" Hermos asked. With an uncertain look on his face, Critias replied, "Who knows? The Dark Elementals have been finding and corrupting Element Students for years. We're definitely looking at an army's worth, but there's no telling how large that army might be."

Timaeus sat with Stratos, a worried look on his face. "I'll do what I can to slow them down or possibly even the odds," he said. "But I can't guarantee anything because there's no telling what we're up against."

Gorgas then approached Timaeus with a stern expression. "Don't worry. With this plan of yours, they won't see us coming. Plus, thanks to your insight into his plan all those years ago, they don't even know we've been preparing for them."

Gorgas' words brought Timaeus some encouragement and hope. He stood up, and all four friends embraced each other, with Stratos joining in. However, their smiles faded quickly when the sky suddenly turned blood red.

Timaeus rushed outside with Hermos, Gorgas, Critias, and Stratos close behind. Red lightning began to strike ominously from the sky.

Timaeus knew he didn't have long, so he wasted no time putting his plan into motion.

"Right, let's get started," he said. "I'll head to the top of the palace tower and signal the rest of Atlantis. You stay down here; use Earth or Water—either will work. You'll know when it's time to act."

Timaeus looked up at the palace tower and spoke, "Anemomíchli," causing his body to evaporate in a swirling gust of wind. He kept using this ability to evaporate and reform until he reached the top of the palace tower. Once there, he took a Magic Gem from his supply satchel and threw it into the sky, shouting, "EKTYFLOTIKÓ FOS!!!" A blinding green light erupted in the sky, signalling all of Atlantis to proceed.

A few moments later, the Dark Elementals arrived on Atlantis, only to find the island completely deserted, leaving them confused.

The Dark Fire Elemental, who was hunting Timaeus, was also annoyed because he believed he had been denied his chance for revenge. Unbeknownst to the others, he observed them from the top of the palace tower, satisfied that they had fallen for his plan.

Timaeus extended his arms outward diagonally, his Green and Blue Element Stones glowing brightly, and shouted, "KATAIGÍDA!" This unleashed a powerful and violent storm, even more intense than the one he had created a decade earlier, engulfing all of Atlantis and knocking down many Dark Elementals in the process.

Less than a moment later, Timaeus called out, "KATAIGÍDA PTÓSI!" The storm subsided within thirty seconds. While many Dark Elementals were left critically injured, a number of them managed to survive. The Dark Fire Elemental, seeing where the storm had originated, realized Timaeus was the one responsible and began making his way toward the palace to hunt down his prey.

As he began his journey, the Earth and Waters of Atlantis stirred as if they had come to life. The Earth and Waters transformed into the inhabitants of Atlantis, revealing Timaeus' plan. He instructed the Earth and Water Elementals to shapeshift themselves and those around them into their respective elements, allowing them not only to hide from the enemy but also to provide cover while Timaeus launched an attack on the Dark Elementals with a violent storm, which took down many of their forces in the process.

The battle for Atlantis commenced. Despite suffering significant losses due to Timaeus' strategy, the Dark Elementals remained a formidable force. However, with the four forms of Element Magic united across Atlantis, their defences were able to keep the enemy at bay. Once the storm had subsided, Timaeus returned to help guard the palace.

Hermos and Gorgas had hidden as a statue outside the palace, blending in with the stone surroundings, while Critias and Stratos concealed themselves in the water. When they re-emerged from the water, they took the enemy by surprise, quickly joined by Gorgas and Hermos. No Dark Elemental could match Stratos, and with the support of the Elementals, the Royal Guard successfully defended the palace.

After about an hour, Timaeus began to notice blue lights in the sky, indicating that those areas were clear of enemy forces. "How do we know when all the enemy forces have been defeated?" Hermos asked. Remaining vigilant against potential threats, Timaeus replied, "I planned for that when I created the blue Magic Gems. The light they emit will keep shining until one is activated from every area. Once that happens, the light will turn purple and then disappear."

Another blue light appeared in the sky, and the enemy forces attacking the palace were nearly defeated. Timaeus was about to throw a blue Magic Gem into the air when Gorgas interrupted him. "Timaeus, don't throw it yet," he warned. "We still have one more to deal with."

Another Dark Elemental was approaching along the palace walkway. "Long time, no see," he said in an eerie voice that sent chills down everyone's spines.

"Who is that, Timaeus?" Critias asked. "Is he one of the Primordial Dark Elementals?"

Timaeus didn't answer immediately; he had a furious look on his face. "No," he replied, his voice calm but laced with anger. "That's the fucking bastard who attacked me twenty-two years ago and almost cost my friend his life by unleashing a Chimera's Tail on our home."

The Dark Fire Elemental continued walking towards them along the palace walkway, an evil and vengeful smile on its face.

"Éla Fotiá," he called, summoning fire from a torch on the palace walkway. "Is that any way to greet an old friend?" Timaeus furiously began walking toward him.

"Do you want any help?" Gorgas offered.

Timaeus paused for a moment. "No," he replied. "I'm sorry, but this is personal. That bastard attacked me on the same day I found out I could use all four forms of Element Magic just hours after we met. I'd rather handle this alone. For twenty-two years, I've been waiting to get back at that bastard for what he did to me and my family. I'm not going to let him do it again."

Timaeus then continued onward toward the Dark Fire Elemental. "Finally, I can get my revenge on the little shit who defeated me out of sheer luck." Ignoring his words, Timaeus advanced, his Green and Red Element Stones glowing fiercely.

"KÓLASI!!!" cried the Dark Fire Elemental, sending violent flames toward Timaeus. "DÝNAMI TOU FOÍNIKA!!!" he shouted in retaliation, causing phoenix flames to surround his body. He faced the Dark Fire Elemental's attack head-on, which resulted in a massive cloud of smoke.

"You have no idea how powerful I am now," said the Dark Fire Elemental. "By the time I'm finished with you, your body will be nothing but ashes." He continued walking forward with an evil smile on his face, hoping to find Timaeus lying on the ground, severely injured from his attack. However, his grin quickly turned to astonishment as Timaeus emerged from the cloud of smoke, completely unharmed. "Emfanízetai I Lepída," Timaeus said, causing his weapon to materialize, having previously fought using only Magic and hand-to-hand combat. "I'm guessing your master never told you how powerful I've become... I must thank you for teaching me that spell all those years ago; I mastered it while training in North Atlantis."

The Dark Fire Elemental could not believe what he was seeing and was filled with fear. "Emfanízetai i Lepída," he said, causing his weapon to materialize. "This changes nothing... You're still the same little shit you were back then, and this time I'm gonna kill you."

The Dark Fire Elemental launched an attack on Timaeus, resulting in a furious sword duel. Timaeus, unlike twenty-two years ago, was able to handle his opponent without needing to separate his blade into two, which made the Dark Fire Elemental angry.

"I HATE YOU!!!" he cried.

"You hate the fact that you can't do what you did last time," Timaeus replied. "Last time, you went after a helpless young boy and tried to murder him. Now, it's you who's the helpless one. This is pointless; you can't defeat me."

His words infuriated his opponent. The Dark Fire Elemental continued to attack but to no avail. Timaeus countered by kicking him backwards. As the opponent charged in for another violent strike, Timaeus shouted, "Gíne Éna Me Ti Gi Kai Ti Vrontí!" This caused his body to transform into stone and emit sparks of electricity for a few seconds. When he reverted back, his clothes glowed with a lime-green colour, and his body still crackled with sparks of electricity.

The Dark Fire Elemental was too consumed with anger to hesitate; he continued his attack with no intention of stopping. Timaeus knocked the opponent's weapon from his hand and countered the Dark Elemental's strike by plunging his sword through its abdomen. "Your masters clearly didn't inform you that I possess the ability to unite Element Magic, particularly the power that allows me to bypass any enhancements created by magic."

The Dark Fire Elemental stood there with a blank expression and blood dripping from his mouth. "This battle was over before it even began," said Timaeus. "You had no hope of defeating me."

The Dark Fire Elemental did not respond to his words, and Timaeus' clothes stopped glowing. His Red Element Stone began to glow, igniting his body. "Nóva Kýrios," he proclaimed, creating a powerful burst of flames that incinerated his opponent.

Timaeus pulled his sword from the fallen Dark Fire Elemental, letting his scorched body drop to the ground. With his opponent now defeated, he felt a sense of relief wash over him. He reached into his supply satchel, took out a blue Magic Gem, and threw it into the sky, shouting, "EKTYFLOTIKÓ FOS!" This caused a brilliant blue light to erupt in the heavens.

All the blue lights in the sky turned purple and vanished, signalling that all enemy forces had been defeated. Everyone in Atlantis cheered for their victory over the invasion—everyone except Timaeus. He turned and walked toward the palace.

"What's wrong, Timaeus?" Hermos asked. "We stopped the enemy; shouldn't we be celebrating?" Timaeus approached with a worried look on his face. "I didn't expect all the blue lights to disappear so quickly," he said.

"All areas are clear of enemy forces, yet there hasn't been any sign of the Primordial Dark Elementals."

This revelation brought worried looks to the faces of Hermos, Gorgas, and Critias.

"What are you saying, Timaeus?" Gorgas asked. Timaeus looked at Gorgas and replied, "I'm saying I don't think this is over yet." Critias approached Timaeus and asked, "Did the Dark Elemental of Wind say anything else when he came to see you?"

As Timaeus was about to answer Critias' question, the skies turned blood red for a second time. "Oh fuck," he said worryingly. "We better get prepared. It looks like the enemy forces we just fought were only the vanguard, and the real battle is just beginning."

Timaeus' Green and Red Element Stones began to glow, and he cried, "FLÓGES TIS ANAGÉNNISIS!" This summoned phoenix flames that spread across Atlantis, restoring as many people's strength as he could. He then shouted, "Anemomíchli!" causing his body to evaporate and reform as he ascended back to the top of the palace tower.

Once he reached the top, he took a Magic Gem from his supply satchel and threw it into the sky, shouting, "EKTYFLOTIKÓ FOS!" A blinding green light shone in the sky, signalling all of Atlantis to prepare themselves once again. However, only a few were able to hide in time.

Timaeus looked down from the palace tower, gazing upon the legion of Dark Elementals that Darkslash commanded over the Atlas Mountains. What had initially been thought of as a simple invasion had now escalated into The War of Atlantis. Those who were unable to hide in time had already engaged in combat as the Primordial Dark Elementals arrived to claim the Dragon Crests and Leviathan's Urn. Noticing Timaeus atop the palace tower, Darkslash decided to pay him a visit. Staring into what could only be described as a living nightmare, Timaeus suddenly heard a sound he was all too familiar with.

"I see you've finally decided to make an appearance, Darkslash," he said.

The Dark Elemental of Wind stood inside the palace tower and replied, "Sorry I'm a little late to the party, Windslash. I thought I'd send you a warm-up vanguard first to wear down your forces. This has worked quite effectively; you hardly have any troops left."

Not letting Darkslash's words affect him, Timaeus stood tranquilly atop the palace tower, with his arms extended diagonally as his Green and Blue Element Stones glowed brightly. The winds began to pick up intensity as Timaeus prepared to make his move against the enemy forces. However, due to unforeseen circumstances, he decided to change his approach. His eyes started to glow with power.

"There's nothing you can do, Windslash, so you might as well hand over that Dragon Crest here and now," he declared.

"Not a chance, Darkslash," Timaeus retorted. "There are more of us out there than you think."

Confused by the response, Darkslash was about to answer, but before he could speak, Timaeus threw his arms upward diagonally and shouted, "THYELLÓDEIS ÁNEMOI!"

With that, he unleashed a raging tempest that engulfed all of Atlantis, knocking down the Dark Elemental forces with violent winds and crackling lightning, more powerful than ever before.

This situation gave some of Atlantis' forces the opportunity to hide from the enemy, but unfortunately, some were caught in the tempest. Darkslash could scarcely believe what he was witnessing, but the winds were too strong for him to do anything. As it was Timaeus' first time using this ability, he lost control of it. A bolt of lightning struck the palace tower, causing it to collapse and knocking Timaeus down with it. As Timaeus fell, his Green and Red Element Stones began to glow. Acting out of desperation, his eyes started to glow again, and he shouted, "LAMPERÍ DÝNAMI TOU FOÍNIKA!" This invoked the phoenix flames to surround his body, but this time, the flames shone white.

Chapter Seventeen
Duel on a Vanishing Island

Due to Timaeus being knocked from the palace tower, the tempest calmed down, but the rain and thunder continued. Emerging from the rubble of the collapsed tower, Darkslash furiously cried, "WINDSLASH!!!" Fortunately, Timaeus had survived the fall thanks to the protection of the phoenix flames. He then set out to confront his arch-nemesis once and for all.

The flames of the phoenix still surrounded his body as he followed Darkslash's voice. "WHERE ARE YOU, WINDSLASH?!!!" Darkslash cried furiously.

"WHEN I FIND YOU, I'M GONNA KILL YOU!!!" He then noticed a reflection in the water on the floor, illuminated by the glow of the shining phoenix flames. "I'm right here, you piece of shit," Timaeus said angrily. "This ends today." Darkslash then extended his arms outward diagonally and spoke, "Emfanízontai Lepídes," summoning his blades.

"Yes, it does, Windslash... We will finally fulfill the Archmage's prophecy. Leviathan will rise again, and Atlantis will fall." Standing his ground, Timaeus remained silent as Darkslash charged in for a powerful attack. However, the assault proved ineffective against the protective phoenix flames. Seizing the moment, Timaeus countered with a decisive punch, sending Darkslash hurtling down the palace walkway. Unbeknownst to them, the water on the walkway began to ripple.

"What is this power of yours, Windslash?!" Darkslash shouted, bewildered. Timaeus walked confidently along the palace walkway and responded, "I don't know... Usually, the phoenix flames can only be used defensively. But this new powerful upgrade allows me to use them offensively. They seem to have a significant effect on you and your Dark Magic. Even before I discovered my capabilities, I was always taught that light ultimately conquers darkness."

He attempted to punch his opponent again, but the shining phoenix flames vanished, allowing Darkslash to catch Timaeus' attack. "That useless old fool was always full of nonsense," Darkslash remarked as he held Timaeus firmly and rose from the ground. "I'm glad Phaedo finally faded away because there's one thing he never taught you: darkness can never be destroyed."

He then placed his hand in front of Timaeus' face and uttered, "Diachorismós Aéra," a form of Dark Magic that made those affected feel as if the air were being sucked from their bodies. Caught off guard, Timaeus was suffocating from the Dark Magic. His skin began to turn blue as he struggled to breathe, and he started losing consciousness. Just then, the water on the walkway began to ripple violently, and Stratos emerged from it, accompanied by Hermos, Gorgas, and Critias, all of whom had been hiding within the water.

Darkslash turned toward Stratos as the Griffin let out a loud, angry cry. He then slashed Darkslash with his right talon, releasing his hold on Timaeus and allowing him to catch his breath. "ARGH!!!" Cried Darkslash. "That does it you winged monstrosity, I will have your head!"

Despite coughing as he struggled to catch his breath, Timaeus was determined to protect his friend. His Green Element Stone began to glow. Just as Darkslash prepared to strike Stratos, Timaeus rushed to his friend's aid, shouting, "EMFANÍZETAI I LEPÍDA!!!" He summoned his weapon and blocked Darkslash from harming Stratos. The two stood locked in combat, their weapons clashing together. Timaeus' eyes started to glow. "There's something else you were never taught," he said as he pushed his opponent back. "Light can never be destroyed either."

Enraged and determined to get past his opponent, Darkslash launched another attack when Timaeus thrust his left hand forward and shouted, "Boulóni Krísis!" A powerful bolt of lightning shot from his hand, striking Darkslash and sending him tumbling off the palace walkway. As they all peered over the edge, they found that Darkslash had vanished.

"Where is he?" Hermos asked, looking concerned. Timaeus turned away from the edge and walked toward the centre of the palace walkway while Hermos, Gorgas, Critias, and Stratos watched him intently.

"He's gone," Timaeus replied. "I've seen him pull this disappearing act before. He's likely regrouping with the other Primordials. We need to act quickly. The tempest I created has already knocked down many of their forces, but our troops are unaware of the situation because the storm hasn't stopped. When I was knocked off the palace tower, it caused the tempest to diminish, but creating it has drained much of the Magic in my Green and Blue Element Stones. I don't have enough energy left to stop it. I'm afraid we'll have to let it subside on its own unless my Element Stones regain enough power."

Gorgas walked towards Timaeus and asked, "So, what do we do? Despite the damage you've inflicted on their forces, we don't have any of our own. How will we alert them to the situation?"

Timaeus turned to face Gorgas just before he reached him. "We have no choice," Timaeus replied. "We must stop the storm ourselves to signal the remaining forces to attack; otherwise, we won't stand a chance against the remaining Dark Elementals, let alone the Primordials."

Critias approached Timaeus, his face showing confusion. "How are we going to do that?" he asked. "We still have several of their forces to deal with here. How can we stop a storm?"

Timaeus looked at Critias with determination. "A fire needs fuel to burn," he explained. "That's where you and I come in. We need to dry out the air with cold temperatures. You will use all the Magic in your Blue Element Stone to freeze the island, which should be straightforward given the wet ground from the rain. This will stop the storm, but it will also trap our forces hiding in the earth and put them at risk if they emerge into the freezing temperatures. I will then use all the Magic in my Red Element Stone to create heat to free them. The downside is that this will cause the storm to return after a while, but by then, our forces will be back in combat."

Despite how crazy Timaeus' plan was, they had no other choice.

"How are you going to pull this off?" Hermos asked. "Freezing the island is one thing, but instantly warming us back up could be dangerous."

Timaeus approached Stratos before turning back to Hermos. "I will ride up with Stratos and signal Critias with fire," Timaeus replied. "It's like how you used to signal Stratos with the fire beacons. He will then freeze the island over. After that, I will generate heat to free our forces hiding in the earth, ensuring that those hidden in the water don't emerge and freeze to death. This is why you and Gorgas need to shelter in the palace with the Royal Guard. Use your Red Element Stone to keep yourselves and everyone in the palace protected from the cold. Our forces outside will be fine because they are concealed in earth or water. When they return to normal, their bodies won't be affected by the cold. This may give us an advantage against the enemy forces."

Gorgas approached Timaeus and placed his right hand on his friend's left shoulder. "You're still that same crazy fucking little shit I met all those years ago," he said, bringing a smile to both of their faces. "The only thing that puzzles me is how you plan to do this without harming Stratos or yourself, for that matter."

Timaeus turned away and mounted Stratos. "Don't worry, I've got that covered," he replied. "I have enough magic in my Green Element Stone for a little something I've been practising that I wasn't able to while training all over Atlantis."

Critias slammed the polearm of his trident staff to the ground. "You better head up there then," he said. "Signal me when you're ready."

Timaeus placed his right arm on his left shoulder and replied, "Very well. Gorgas, you need to get inside. I'll send Stratos back down so he isn't hurt in the process. Critias, after the storm dies down, you should also take shelter in the palace."

Gorgas, Hermos, and the Royal Guard took shelter inside the palace while Timaeus soared into the sky with Stratos, and Critias positioned himself on the palace walkway. After circling the area a few times, Timaeus' Red Element Stone began to glow.

"Right, Stratos," he said. "After I give Critias the signal, you need to go back down for your own safety." Stratos chirped, expressing concern for his friend.

"Don't worry about me, old friend. I'll be fine."

Using the Magic of his Red Element Stone, Timaeus ignited his right hand. Once Critias saw the signal he was waiting for, he raised his trident staff, causing his Blue Element Stone to glow as well. He then slammed the polearm into the ground and cried, "APÓLYTO MIDÉN!!!" This released all the Magic from his Blue Element Stone, causing the entire island to freeze over. The sudden drop in temperature not only stripped away the heat but also dried the air, removing the storm's fuel.

A moment later, the storm subsided, and Critias took shelter inside the palace. While still circling in the sky atop Stratos, Timaeus set the next part of his plan into motion. "As soon as I go higher into the sky, you need to head back down toward the palace," he instructed. Stratos responded with a cry of obedience. "Good boy, Stratos... I'll see you when I get back down there."

Timaeus then stood on top of Stratos and shouted, "Ánodos Anémou!" This action conjured a gust of wind that lifted him further upward. Halfway through his ascent, he called out, "NÓVA KÝRIOS!!!" This created a powerful burst of flames that resembled a rising star as Timaeus climbed higher into the sky. The heat generated by his flames melted the ice on the island and extracted as much moisture from the air as possible.

Now that Atlantis' forces had the signal they were waiting for, they revealed themselves and launched their attack on the Dark Elemental's forces.

As Atlantis' forces rejoined the battle, Timaeus' Green Element Stone began to glow brightly. He shouted, "Statikós!" and a strong charge of static electricity enveloped the cape of his robes, causing it to stick to his body. With his arms outstretched, the static cling allowed him to use the winds to glide back down to the surface. However, just before Timaeus reached the ground, his Green Element Stone ran out of Magic, and the static electricity dissipated, causing him to crash land. Fortunately, thanks to his Earth Magic, he barely felt the impact.

Meanwhile, with most of the island frozen over, nearly three-quarters of the enemy forces suffered from hypothermia. Timaeus used his Magic to rapidly reheat their bodies, leaving the Dark Wind, Dark Water, and Dark Earth Elementals with barely enough strength to fight back.

In contrast, the Dark Fire Elementals remained unaffected by the cold due to their mastery of Dark Magic. Dark Flare and several other Dark Fire Elementals utilized their Magic to gradually reheat members of their forces. This was not driven by compassion but rather a strategic decision to prevent losing most of their army to the frigid temperatures. However, the cold was the least of their concerns; now, they had to contend with the forces of Atlantis.

Meanwhile, the Dark Water Elementals sought out water sources to heal themselves and their allies. Although not all were successful, those who were able to tap into water sources enabled the war efforts of

Atlantis to continue. Timaeus regrouped with the others who had taken shelter in the palace. "Our forces have rejoined the battle," he said. "We need to get out there and help them."

Gorgas then approached Timaeus. "You fucking idiot," said Gorgas, shaking his head. "Despite nearly freezing us all to death, I can't believe that idiotic plan of yours actually worked." This brought smiles and laughter to everyone's faces.

"Now isn't the time for this," Critias interjected. "With this opportunity we've been given, we need to take down the enemy's forces and, in turn, stop the Primordials."

Hermos then began preparing herself. "We need to find the Primordials first," she said. "Any idea where we can find them, Timaeus?"

Despite his desire to stop the Primordials as much as anyone else, Timaeus had no idea how to respond to Hermos. "Unfortunately, no," he replied. "They could be anywhere on the island right now, and I've only met one of them, so I wouldn't even know who we'd be looking for among the other three."

Critias was able to provide Timaeus with valuable information. "My father told me something about the Primordials many years ago that could help us locate them," Critias said. "He mentioned that the four of them stay together and watch over the battle while their forces do all the work. So, if you've encountered one of them, you'll be able to locate all four at once. They only get involved if they're pursuing a specific target."

Critias' words sparked an idea in Timaeus. "I'll find them," he said. "Critias, you stay here and guard the Royal City along with the Royal Guard and the forces within the city. Gorgas and Hermos, you need to assist our forces outside the city. I will ride out on Stratos to search for the Primordials in the sky. If anyone encounters the Primordials, send up a Magic Gem. Do not attempt to confront them alone, especially if all of them are present."

Despite being intrigued by Timaeus' plan, Hermos raised an important concern. "Before we go out there," she said, "there's something we all need to consider. The Teleport Rune that allowed them to bring their entire army to the island also allows them to travel anywhere on the island. So even if we find them, there's nothing stopping them from moving to another location."

Taking Hermos' words to heart, Gorgas replied, "If you locate them, don't engage." He continued, "Timaeus and I can hide ourselves if we find them, but you can't. We'll go out and search for them, regroup in an hour, and then discuss where to go from there if we do find them."

Agreeing with Gorgas' suggestion, the four of them set out to assist Atlantis' forces with the Royal Guard. Gorgas and Hermos fought their way through the Royal City to support the forces outside, while Timaeus took to the skies on Stratos to search for the Primordials.

The battle and bloodshed continued across the island, escalating to the point where the Primordials themselves became involved. A platoon of Atlantis' forces fought bravely against the Dark Elementals and launched an attack on the Primordials. Dark Gaia retaliated with a powerful form of Dark Magic, shouting, "Aposynthéto!" This incantation caused the entire platoon to disintegrate into dust.

As the four Primordials advanced, they encountered their forces engaged in fierce combat with the Atlantean troops, watching as both sides tore each other apart. Dark Tide, growing increasingly impatient, unleashed a formidable wave of Dark Magic, crying out, "AFYDATÓNO!!!" This unleashed power dehydrated the bodies of all the Atlantean and Dark Elemental forces in the vicinity, killing them all in the process.

After nearly an hour of searching, Timaeus spotted the Primordials from the sky as they approached Central Atlantis from the east. Instead of engaging with them, he decided to return to the palace and regroup with Hermos, Gorgas, and Critias to warn them. As he began his journey back, the storm started to intensify.

Hermos noticed Stratos flying back to the Royal City. Despite her efforts to locate the Primordials, she chose to return and regroup as well. Unfortunately, just as she was about to head back, the Primordials caught up with her.

"You must be Burnout's successor," said Darkslash. "Hand over that Dragon Crest, or the successor will be burned out."

Hermos stood her ground, refusing to surrender the Dragon's Claw Crest. "I'm not giving you Primordial's shit," she declared.

"Now fuck off unless you want to see what I'm capable of," Hermos warned. Darkslash, not feeling threatened in the slightest, stepped forward, ready to confront Hermos. However, Dark Flare quickly intervened, blocking his path. "Oh no, you fucking don't," she said firmly. "If memory serves me correctly, the saying goes, 'you fight fire with fucking fire'."

Darkslash flashed her an evil grin. "Very well, Dark Flare," he said. "I won't spoil your fun... But don't take too long; we have more excitement waiting for us in the Royal City."

Knowing that their Fire Magic would not affect each other, both drew their weapons and prepared for armed combat. They matched each other blow for blow, and even when their weapons locked together, neither could push the other off balance. As the battle continued, Hermos and Dark Flare occasionally got past each other's guard, but this only increased Dark Tide's impatience.

He was on the verge of unleashing Dark Magic once more, frustrated by the lengthy wait. However, Dark Gaia intervened, concerned about his reckless use of power. In the end, Hermos gained the upper hand over Dark Flare, holding her sword firmly to her throat.

Although she managed to gain the upper hand over one of the Primordials, her victory was short-lived. Dark Gaia intervened, not wanting to tolerate Dark Tide's impatience. He seized Hermos by the throat and declared, "Aposynthéto," which caused her body to disintegrate.

"I can't believe you, you fucking idiot!" Dark Flare shouted. "I could have handled that myself." Dark Gaia simply stood there, a grin on his face. "Hehe," he chuckled. "That's not how I saw it. Besides, you had your fun, and you got the prize you were after. Plus, someone was getting impatient, and we didn't want him dehydrating us all."

Standing over Hermos' ashes, Dark Flare picked up the Dragon's Claw Crest with her sword. Although she understood Dark Gaia's reasons for intervening, Dark Flare remained angered by it. "I'll let you off this time because of Dark Tide's impatience, but in the future, don't interfere." The bickering was starting to annoy Darkslash. "That's enough, you two!" he shouted. "Now come on, as I mentioned earlier, we've got more fun waiting for us in the Royal City." The Primordials then continued onward toward their destination.

Back in Central Atlantis, Timaeus and Stratos landed outside the palace and regrouped with Gorgas, Critias, and the Royal Guard. "The

Primordials are approaching the city from the east," said Timaeus. "Where's Hermos?" A worried expression appeared on Gorgas and Critias' faces. "We were hoping you could tell us," Gorgas replied.

"Has she not returned yet?" Timaeus asked, worry creeping into his voice. Not wanting anything bad to happen to her, he was about to head back out to look for Hermos. "Which way did she go out of the city?" His question struck fear into both Gorgas and Critias. "She went out through the east side of the city," Gorgas replied. Without wasting any time, Timaeus hurried outside to search for her.

Once outside, he heard painful screams coming from the east. Dark Tide had lost his patience again and dehydrated everyone standing in the Primordial's way. The four of them marched through the city, slaying anyone who dared to try to stop them.

"Windslash has noticed us," said Darkslash. "Let us split up and meet at the palace. Ordinarily, I wouldn't have us do this, but he can bypass enhancements created by magic. Earlier, he conjured an ability to which our Dark Magic is vulnerable."

His words agitated Dark Tide. "I told you; you should have killed with him years ago." Darkslash, annoyed more by the words than the attitude, replied, "Yes, Dark Tide, you keep reminding me. However, I took a gamble to obtain the blood of the beasts and create a way to bring our army to Atlantis all at once. Despite how powerful Windslash has become, this is only a distraction for the time being so we can get into the palace and obtain Leviathan's Urn. Once we unleash the Sea Serpent, he won't be able to stop us. And please, Dark Tide, while Windslash is distracted, dehydrate your victims one at a time instead of in large groups; otherwise, he'll find you easily."

With the Magic in his Element Stones restored, Timaeus decided to approach stealthily rather than head-on. "You stay here, Stratos," he said, stroking his friend on the forehead.

"I'll signal you if I need you." Using the storm as cover, Timaeus spoke the incantation "Anemomíchli," evaporating his body within a swirling twister of wind. He reformed on top of a building in the Royal City. Sticking to the rooftops, he tracked the Primordials by continually evaporating and reforming his body. In doing so, he located Dark Tide and Dark Gaia, but he didn't intervene; he wanted to see what they looked like first.

A little while later, he spotted Dark Flare holding the Dragon's Claw Crest, which devastated him as this meant one of his best friends was dead. Despite the emotional blow, he decided not to take action just yet. Then, he heard a familiar voice. "*Zephyr*," he thought to himself. Following the sound of Zephyr's voice, he found him being attacked by Darkslash. "Diachorismós Aéra," Darkslash said, using his Dark Magic to suck the air out of Zephyr's body.

Having already lost one friend, Timaeus was determined not to lose another, so he went on the offensive. "EMFANÍZETAI I LEPÍDA!" he cried, summoning his weapon as he leapt from the rooftop and knocked Darkslash down before his Dark Magic could deal with Zephyr.

"Found me at last, did you, Windslash?" he said with an air of arrogance. "I'm surprised it took you this long to catch up." Timaeus held his weapon firmly, standing his ground. "I've been tracking you and the other Primordials for a while now," he continued. "I wanted to see what the other three looked like."

This revelation annoyed Darkslash, as he realized he was the one being outsmarted. "Emfanízontai Lepídes!" he shouted angrily, summoning his weapons and launching an attack on Timaeus. His Green and Red Element Stones began to glow, and his eyes shone white with intensity.

In retaliation, he shouted, "Lamperí Dýnami Tou Foínika!" causing the shining phoenix flames to appear once again. Timaeus absorbed Darkslash's attack without taking any harm, then countered with a powerful punch to the face, sending his opponent flying through the street. To conserve Magic within his Element Stones, Timaeus stopped using the shining phoenix flames.

"Want some help?" Zephyr asked, and Timaeus turned around, relieved to see his friend was okay. "Cover me," he replied, and the two of them began making their way toward Darkslash. "This ends today."

Just before they reached Darkslash, he vanished. "Shit," Timaeus exclaimed. "The bastard must have used that Teleport Rune to make a quick escape. I need to warn the others." As Timaeus was about to return to the palace to inform Gorgas and Critias, he heard a familiar sound.

"You were right about one thing, Windslash," said a familiar voice. Timaeus and Zephyr quickly turned around to see Darkslash. He swung the blade in his left hand horizontally, cutting Zephyr's throat and killing him instantly. "Not a quick escape," Darkslash remarked. "More like... a stealth attack." He then activated his Teleport Rune to move to another location, where he joined the other Primordials on the palace walkway.

Mortified that his best friend had just been murdered before his very eyes, Timaeus knelt beside Zephyr and turned him onto his back. He gently closed his friend's eyes with his hand. Before departing to avenge Zephyr's death, Timaeus used his Green Element Stone to merge Zephyr's body with the wind. "Anemomíchli," he uttered, causing his body to evaporate within a swirling gust and reappear on a rooftop.

He made his way back across the rooftops by evaporating and reforming his body. Meanwhile, the Primordials had reached the palace walkway and encountered Stratos, who was guarding the entrance. Determined not to let them pass, the Griffin let out a loud, threatening cry. Darkslash then shouted, "Aerofotografía!" unleashing a powerful blast of wind that knocked Stratos aside.

"As much as I'd like to deal with that winged monstrosity," he said, "we have more important matters at hand. Once we're finished here, then I'll take care of him."

The Primordials entered the palace, where they found Critias, Gorgas, and the Royal Guard waiting for them. "Tríaina Emfanízontai," said Dark Tide, summoning his Trident Staff. Dark Gaia cracked his knuckles, a wicked smile spreading across his face. "Hehe," he chuckled. "There's no point in resisting, and by the time Windslash gets back here, it will be too late."

Everyone stood their ground as Gorgas and Dark Gaia assumed fighting positions, preparing for a face-off. Darkslash decided to let Dark Gaia enjoy this battle while making sure Dark Tide behaved. Meanwhile, Dark Flare was still pissed off because Dark Gaia had finished her fight for her.

The two combatants launched their opening attacks simultaneously. From that moment on, they fought hand-to-hand, utilizing their fighting skills for offence and Magic for defence. Dark Gaia struggled to land hits on Gorgas, who was much faster due to his extensive training with Timaeus. At the same time, Gorgas found it difficult to penetrate Dark Gaia's defences, which were bolstered by his Dark Magic.

After some time, both fighters began to tire. They simultaneously landed punches to each other's faces, causing both of them to fall to the ground.

Gorgas and Dark Gaia both struggled to rise. Gorgas nearly got back to his feet ahead of Dark Gaia but fell down again. He refused to stay down. Despite Dark Gaia also struggling, Gorgas was gaining on him. The Primordial managed to rise almost completely but then fell to his knees, lacking the strength to get back up. Gorgas finally stood up again, but his victory over Dark Gaia was short-lived. Dark Tide stood behind him and said, "Afydatóno," causing Gorgas' body to dehydrate and kill him. The Dark Elemental of Water then ripped the Dragon's Horn Crest from around Gorgas' neck before his body fell to the ground. Dark Tide then spoke, "Therapéfste To Neró," healing Dark Gaia in the process as his body was drenched in sweat. "Get up, you pathetic excuse for a warrior," said Dark Tide.

Dark Gaia stood up and walked toward Dark Tide, both exchanging menacing glances as he handed Dark Gaia the Dragon's Horn Crest. "I should have expected nothing less," Critias said with a tone of disgust. "I see you also possess the Dragon's Claw Crest, which means you've also killed Hermos. However, you've confirmed that Timaeus is still alive; otherwise, you would have the Dragon's Eye Crest. I swear on my duty as King that you fuckers will not obtain all of the Dragon Crests or Leviathan's Urn."

Darkslash clapped his hands while standing in the background. "A very touching speech, Your Majesty," he remarked. "Unfortunately, it makes no difference. It will take more than your duties as King to stop us from obtaining what we came for and releasing Leviathan." The Royal Guard positioned themselves defensively to protect their King.

Dark Tide stepped forward and shouted, "Afydatóno!" He intended to dehydrate the entire Royal Guard, but their armour protected them from the full force of his Dark Magic. However, his spell still had an effect on them. Instead of fully dehydrating the Royal Guard, it made them appear as if they had aged rapidly. While this didn't kill them immediately, it left them unable to defend themselves or fight back.

With the Royal Guard no longer posing a threat, Dark Tide violently slaughtered them all. He then turned his attention to Critias, pointing his trident staff at him. "The Dragon Crest," Dark Tide said, "NOW!!!"

Critias rose from his throne, determined not to hand over the Dragon's Fang Crest. "I've already stopped one storm today," he replied. "There's no reason why I can't stop another."

With his Blue Element Stone glowing, Critias slammed the polearm of his trident staff to the ground and shouted, "APÓLYTO MIDÉN!" This time, he only froze the area inside the Royal Court instead of the entire island, trapping the Primordials in the process. He then lifted his trident staff into the air vertically and exclaimed, "Diamantoskóni!" The ice shattered, causing the four of them considerable pain, though not as much as usual due to their Dark Magic providing some protection.

Critias charged towards Dark Tide and swung his trident staff at his legs, knocking him to the floor. "ARGH!" he cried out. While Dark Magic shielded him from Element Magic, it did not guard him against physical pain. Critias had also cooled his body down, which allowed him to amplify the pain his opponent felt.

Meanwhile, Timaeus was racing back to the palace as quickly as he could, leaping across rooftops. To conserve the Magic in his Element Stones for use against the Primordials, he evaporated and reformed his body across certain distances.

He sent up a Magic Gem, creating a red light to signal Stratos, unaware that his friend had been injured. Back at the palace, Critias was holding his own and gaining the upper hand over Dark Tide by physically impairing him with cold temperatures. This made it difficult for Dark Tide to speak or concentrate, which hindered his ability to use Magic against Critias; Critias prevented him from speaking the incantations and broke his concentration. Soon, Dark Tide found himself in a position where he couldn't fight back. Critias stood over his opponent, ready to deliver the final strike.

"Éla Fotiá!" shouted Dark Flare as she charged toward Critias. Summoning fire from one of the four torches in the Royal Court, she pulled her arm toward her, allowing the flames to strike her. This didn't harm her; instead, it raised her body temperature, enabling her to move faster.

Before Critias had time to react, Dark Flare plunged her sword through his shoulder, preventing him from killing Dark Tide. "ARGH!!!" cried Critias as he dropped his trident staff in the process. Dark Flare then pulled her sword from his shoulder, causing him to fall to his knees in pain. She placed her hands on both sides of his shoulder and said, "Kafstikó Ángigma," which caused the touch of her hands to burn Critias' shoulder and close the wound, ensuring he didn't bleed to death. The Primordials needed him alive to obtain Leviathan's Urn.

Dark Tide, still in pain and feeling cold, spoke slowly, "Therapéfste... To... Neró." Drawing upon the water from the partially melted ice, he began to heal himself. Dark Flare, however, struck Critias on the back of the neck with the hilt of her blade, knocking him out. "Éla Fotiá," she commanded, summoning fire from one of the four torches.

She then shouted, "Kólasi!" The flames swirled around the Royal Court violently, warming the other Primordials without burning them with her touch.

"Come, let us proceed to the Royal Vault," said Darkslash. "We need to bring His Majesty along with us. After what happened centuries ago, we can't be sure how much Magic is being used to keep the Royal Vault secure. There's no doubt that there are spells preventing Dark Tide from unlocking the magic seal, and it likely requires a living member of the Royal Family."

Seeing the logic in Darkslash's words, Dark Gaia picked up Critias, and the Primordials proceeded to the Royal Vault. Inside, they placed Critias' hand on the magic seal to unlock it. The four of them then entered to obtain Leviathan's Urn. Darkslash attempted to remove the lid of the Urn, but he was unsuccessful.

He then attempted to break the Urn, but it was futile. Although he had anticipated the possibility of more Magic being employed to secure the Royal Vault, he felt frustrated that he hadn't considered that Magic might also be used to keep Leviathan's Urn from being opened.

"Good thing you decided to bring along His Majesty," said Dark Flare. Timaeus was almost back at the palace, opting to take the walkway so he wouldn't have to expend any more magic.

As Critias regained consciousness, the Primordials emerged from the Royal Vault with Leviathan's Urn in their possession. Clenching his injured shoulder and feeling too weak to fight back, he simply stood there with a smile on his face.

"You can't open it, can you?" he asked. Dark Flare angrily pressed her blade against Critias' neck.

"How do we open it?" she demanded. Despite how dire the situation appeared, Critias did not fear what might happen to him but was prepared to accept his fate.

"You can't," he replied. "As long as the Dragon Crests are bound to a guardian, you can't open or destroy the Urn." Dark Flare then violently slashed his throat, killing him in an instant. She took the Dragon's Fang Crest from around Critias' neck and handed it to Dark Tide.

Meanwhile, the ground began to rumble all over the island. Timaeus felt the tremors as he reached the entrance to the palace, where he found an injured Stratos. Wasting no time, he spoke the words, "Therapéfste To Neró," healing his loyal friend with minimal effort, thanks to the storm providing the water he needed.

"You fool!" cried Dark Tide. "Atlantis is connected to the king. If he dies, then Atlantis will die with him! We still need to find one more Dragon Crest before we can open the Urn, and if that little shit dies because the island has already started sinking, the Dragon Crest will be lost with him!"

With the ground shaking beneath their feet and a storm raging overhead, Timaeus knew he had to act quickly. He held up his Enchanted Chalice, filling it with rainwater, and then drank from it to gain foresight. The vision that unfolded before him left him horrified.

"From what I just saw, old friend," he said, "it seems we're headed for the underworld. On the plus side, we're taking Leviathan with us."

Stratos chirped fiercely, determined to stand by Timaeus' side.

"You stay out here for now, Stratos," Timaeus replied. "I want to see what the Primordials are up to first."

Entering the palace, Timaeus found himself in the Royal Court, and he could hardly believe his eyes. The entire Royal Guard was dead, including Gale, along with everyone he had lived with on the abandoned farmland all those years ago.

"KATAIGÍDA!!!" he cried out in despair.

A powerful storm erupted within the Royal Court, devastating both it and the palace. "Kataigída Ptósi," he commanded, causing the storm he had created to subside so it wouldn't escalate further due to the natural storm raging outside. The ground continued to rumble as Atlantis sank into the ocean.

The Primordials emerged from the Royal Vault to find the Royal Court in ruins, rain pouring down on the remnants of the palace, with Timaeus waiting for them.

"Well... well... well," said Darkslash. "Finally decided to join us, have you, Windslash?" The other Primordials were taken aback, as it was the first time they had ever seen Timaeus.

"This is him?" Dark Flare asked, stepping forward cautiously. "This is the one who can wield all four forms of Element Magic and has been causing you so much fucking trouble over the years?"

She continued forward, not feeling threatened at all. "Be careful, Dark Flare," said Darkslash. "He's more powerful than he looks." Timaeus stood his ground and spoke, "Emfanízetai I Lepída," causing his weapon to appear.

"Because of you fuckers," he said. "All the people who I've ever known as family are dead... Now, you four will join them in death, but I will make sure you are denied an afterlife. By my hand, I will send you all straight into the fucking pits of Tartarus." Dark Flare just ignored his words. "Éla Fotiá," she said, summoning flames from the torch on the pillar that survived the storm that Timaeus created. "If anyone will be experiencing the pits of Tartarus, you fucking piece of shit, it will be you." Not seeing Timaeus as a threat, Dark Flare shouted, "Kólasi!" Sending violent flames towards Timaeus, which struck him and knocked him into the pillar.

This surprised the others, especially considering the amount of trouble Timaeus had given Darkslash over the years. "This little fucker gave you all that trouble, and I just took him down with one hit," Dark Flare said arrogantly. "I think you might be losing your touch, Darkslash." She then walked toward Timaeus to claim the Dragon's Eye Crest.

Darkslash couldn't believe that Dark Flare had knocked Timaeus down so easily, but soon he began to understand why. He noticed water rippling around Timaeus' hand. "Dark Flare, don't! It's a trap!" Darkslash shouted, but it was too late. Having not been hurt by Dark Flare's attack,

Timaeus raised his hand and shouted, "Págoma Neroú!" The water in front of him froze into icicles. He then shouted, "Ríxte Neró!" causing all the icicles to fire straight toward Dark Flare, skewering her.

Blood poured from her mouth and body as Timaeus got up and walked over to her. "I think you might be losing your touch, Dark Flare," he said angrily and sarcastically. He then gave her a small push, and she fell backwards to the floor, lifeless. Timaeus had just accomplished what no Elemental had ever managed to do—kill a Primordial. As he looked down, he noticed the Dragon's Claw Crest in Dark Flare's hand and took it from her corpse. "I'm sorry, Hermos," he said softly, gazing at the Dragon's Claw Crest in his palm.

The three remaining Primordials were in disbelief over what Timaeus had just done and were determined to make him pay for it. "You're mine, Windslash," said Dark Gaia, approaching Timaeus with vengeance in his eyes for what had happened to Dark Flare. "Hold on, Dark Gaia," warned Darkslash. "He's likely set a trap for you as well."

Timaeus stood his ground, splitting his weapon into twin blades before merging them at the hilts to create a double-edged sword. He then placed the weapon into the ground. "Don't worry, Darkslash," said Dark Gaia. "He won't outsmart me like he did Dark Flare. By the time I'm finished with him, he'll be a pile of dust." He then extended his hand toward Timaeus and shouted, "Aposynthéto!" In a swift response, Timaeus shouted, "Anemomíchli!" He evaporated his body within a swirling gust of wind, preventing Dark Gaia from disintegrating him. A few seconds later, he reformed and struck his opponent. Whenever Dark Gaia attempted to counterattack—whether with physical blows or Dark Magic—Timaeus would evaporate again and reform, skilfully outmanoeuvring his foe and launching sneak attacks. Despite hitting Dark Gaia in open and vulnerable spots, Timaeus' efforts only served to irritate his opponent.

Changing his strategy, Timaeus waited until the next time he evaporated and reformed. As his Gold Element Stone began to glow, he shouted, "I Orgí Tis Gaías!" and punched his opponent in the abdomen, causing immense pain. His opponent dropped the Dragon's Horn Crest in the process.

"Éla Neró," Timaeus commanded, summoning the Dragon's Horn Crest to himself as it was soaked in water.

As he held the Dragon's Horn Crest in his hand, he said, "I'm sorry, Gorgas." He then shifted his focus back to Dark Gaia. "Your moniker suits you, don't get me wrong," Timaeus remarked, "but you don't deserve to bear the name of a titan; you only deserve to feel the wrath of one." Irritated by Timaeus' words, Dark Gaia charged at him. With his Gold Element Stone glowing, Timaeus countered with full force, shouting, "I ORGÍ TIS GAÍAS!"

His counterattack sent Dark Gaia flying out of Central Atlantis and into an area that had been swallowed by the ocean. If the pressure of the water hadn't killed him, he would've drowned anyway because Dark Gaia was no swimmer. Timaeus then picked up his double-edged sword, ready to take on his next opponent.

"All the centuries we've survived against every Elemental we've fought," said Dark Tide, "and he's just killed Dark Flare and Dark Gaia as if they were nothing... THIS ISN'T FUCKING POSSIBLE!!!"

Darkslash noticed that Dark Tide was reaching his breaking point. "Dark Tide, calm down," he urged. "All we have to do is deal with Windslash, and Leviathan will be freed."

Seeing an opportunity to use this to his advantage, Timaeus added, "That's right, Dark Tide... All you have to do is kill me, and you can unleash that malevolent catastrophe. It all depends on whether you can kill me. Dark Flare and Dark Gaia weren't very successful, were they? It was as if they were nothing."

Seeing through Timaeus' game, Darkslash shouted, "That's enough, Windslash!" Dark Tide, however, did not heed his comrade's warning. Upon hearing Timaeus' words, Dark Tide reached his breaking point. He exclaimed, "URGH!!! THIS IS ALL YOUR FUCKING FAULT!!! WHAT I WARNED YOU ABOUT HAS FUCKING HAPPENED!!! NOW, I'M GOING TO DO WHAT YOU SHOULD HAVE FUCKING DONE YEARS AGO AND KILL THIS FUCKING LITTLE SHIT!!!"

Before Darkslash could talk some sense into him, Dark Tide lunged to attack Timaeus in a fit of madness, dropping the Dragon's Fang Crest in the process. Timaeus noticed the crest on the floor and thought to himself, "*I'm sorry, Critias.*" Having successfully manipulated his opponent's mental stability to his advantage, Timaeus' Green Element Stone began to glow.

Using his Wind Magic, Timaeus electrically charged his weapon by manipulating the electrical currents in the air. Despite witnessing what was happening, Dark Tide had no intention of stopping and charged forward in a fit of rage. Timaeus then threw his weapon and shouted, "Boulóni Krísis!" causing it to shoot towards his opponent like a bolt of lightning. Still caught in his blind rage, Dark Tide did nothing to evade the attack. Because his body was wet from the rain, the weapon impaled him and delivered a powerful electrocution, knocking him backwards to the ground, killing him.

"Éla Neró," Timaeus said, summoning his weapon back to him since it was soaked in water, while Darkslash picked up the Dragon's Fang Crest. The two of them locked eyes and prepared to face each other in combat once again.

"You have just killed the only friends I've ever had, Windslash," Darkslash said. "Despite the Dark Magic of Leviathan coursing through me, my friendship with them is the one thing I managed to keep. I will ensure that their deaths are avenged, and you will fucking pay for this, slowly and fucking painfully."

Timaeus split his double-edged sword back into twin blades, showing no shame or remorse at Darkslash's words. "I already have," he replied. "Today, I have lost all the people who were not only my friends but were also like family to me. I watched you slowly and fucking painfully kill each and every fucking one of them... So, it's their deaths that will be avenged, and if anyone will be fucking paying for it, it will be you, Darkslash." As the rain poured and thunder roared from the heavens, Darkslash said, "Emfanízontai Lepídes."

As his blades materialized in his hands, Timaeus faced off against Darkslash. Both had lost those closest to them, and with the island sinking beneath them, they charged toward each other with an unwavering determination to achieve their goals. A fierce sword duel erupted between the two arch-rivals. Having fought one another numerous times over the years, they were equally matched, countering each other's offence, defence, style, and skill. Neither was able to inflict damage on the other.

Realizing they were making no progress and with the island continuing to descend into the ocean, Timaeus decided to change his strategy, merging his blades back into one. Darkslash lunged forward to attack, but Timaeus shouted, "Lamperí Dýnami Tou Foínika!" Instantly, the shining phoenix flames enveloped him, rendering him invulnerable to Darkslash's strike. With one hand free, Timaeus delivered a powerful punch to Darkslash's abdomen, leaving him stunned. Seizing the opportunity, Timaeus then slashed across Darkslash's chest with his blade and, with a sudden move, grabbed his opponent's black robes and threw him over his shoulder.

When he landed, the impact caused the Teleport Rune that Darkslash had created to fall from his robes. Timaeus walked over to it and plunged his blade into the rune, destroying it.

"What have you done, Windslash?" Darkslash asked as he got up.

"With Atlantis sinking into the ocean, that was my only way off the island." Timaeus lifted his sword out of the remnants of the Teleport Rune.

"You are not leaving this island," he replied. "The threat of the Dark Elementals ends today, and it goes down with Atlantis."

Darkslash's expression shifted to worry and confusion. "You're a fucking idiot, Windslash," he countered. "If you go down with Atlantis, you'll die. Once that happens, your Dragon Crest will no longer be bound to you, meaning Leviathan's Urn will be able to open—whether it's the lid falling off due to the water currents or it's broken by something in the ocean."

Timaeus was unfazed by Darkslash's words. "Don't you think I already know that?" he said. "Thanks to Water Magic, I can breathe underwater. I don't care what happens to me as long as I make sure Leviathan's Urn is securely hidden at the bottom of the ocean where nobody can find or open it. Now, who's the fucking idiot? And just so we're clear, my name is Timaeus!"

Darkslash seethed with anger—not only because he was trapped on Atlantis but also because Timaeus had already devised a way to keep Leviathan locked away, meaning he had been outsmarted once again. However, to thwart his arch-nemesis' plan, he needed to kill Timaeus before the island sank, which left him little time.

"AEROFOTOGRAFÍA!!!" he shouted, unleashing a powerful blast of wind in an attempt to knock Timaeus down. Timaeus held out his left arm, successfully blocking Darkslash's Wind Magic, and simultaneously caused the blast of wind to subside.

Timaeus had pulled his arm back while bracing against the blast of wind. To his opponent's surprise, he suddenly threw his arm forward, sending the wind blast back at him and knocking Darkslash to the ground. Darkslash quickly got back up and locked eyes with Timaeus. Without hesitation, both fighters charged at each other, determined to fight to the finish before the island sank completely.

A fierce sword duel began, but this time, Timaeus didn't split his weapon into twin blades. Instead, he fought Darkslash with a single sword, leveraging his knowledge of his opponent's fighting style, as well as his own speed and reflexes. Neither could penetrate the other's defence, so Timaeus decided to step up his game. By carefully observing Darkslash's attacks and timing his moves perfectly, Timaeus managed to slash Darkslash's left arm, causing him to drop his left-handed sword.

With his opponent's left side exposed, Timaeus prepared to deliver a clean strike. However, Darkslash countered with Dark Magic. "Diachorismós Aéra!" he shouted. Holding his left hand in front of Timaeus, Darkslash's Magic made it feel as though the air was being sucked out of him, suffocating him. Despite being put in this predicament once again, Timaeus remained focused. He looked Darkslash in the eye, and although his rage was building, he maintained a calmness as steady as the wind.

His Green and Red Element Stones began to glow, and his eyes shimmered brightly as well. In that moment, the radiant flames of the phoenix erupted, breaking Darkslash's concentration and freeing Timaeus. Timaeus then plunged his sword through his opponent's abdomen, and blood started pouring from Darkslash's mouth. Afterwards, Timaeus pulled his sword out of Darkslash's body and fell to his knees, coughing as he struggled to catch his breath after escaping the Dark Magic used against him.

Despite Timaeus having just stabbed him through the abdomen, Darkslash was determined not to go down without a fight. He grabbed his sword and advanced towards his opponent. After catching his breath, Timaeus' Green and Red Element Stones began to glow again, as did his eyes. Just as Darkslash was about to deliver a fatal blow, Timaeus shouted, "ASTRAFTERÓS ÁNEMOS FOTOVOLÍDAS!!!" This unleashed a shining whirlwind of flames that knocked Darkslash backwards, inflicting severe damage.

With his opponent down, Timaeus hurriedly picked up Leviathan's Urn. Knowing he had little time, he used his Earth Magic to encase the Urn in stone, ensuring it could not be opened after his death. He then cast the stone containing the Urn into the ocean. Unfortunately, things were far from over.

Timaeus turned around to find Darkslash alive and well, getting back up. "How are you still alive?" Timaeus asked. "And don't give me that 'nothing you need to concern yourself with' shit, especially after I killed the other three Primordials."

Darkslash stood there, an evil smile on his face. "Very well, Windslash. Since you don't have much time left anyway," he replied. "As you would have undoubtedly been informed by your masters and the former King, Dark Elementals are immortal and cannot die from ageing. However, what your masters and the former King failed to understand is that the Primordials, as you call us, are Avatars of Leviathan. The Dark Magic we were exposed to centuries ago was divided among us. When one Primordial is killed, the Dark Magic within them is distributed among the remaining Primordials."

"When three of the Primordials have been killed, the last one is granted true immortality by Leviathan, ensuring that the Sea Serpent always has an avatar." Timaeus could not believe what he was hearing. "So, despite everything you've put Atlantis through today," he said, "you or one of the other Primordials would have survived no matter what happened. This makes all of our efforts in vain."

Darkslash simply stood there, retrieving something from his robes. "As I mentioned earlier, Windslash," he replied, "darkness can never be destroyed. Though I didn't expect you to destroy my only way off the island, fortunately, I brought this as a contingency plan." With that, Darkslash held a large, brilliant-cut black crystal in his hand.

"Good thing I brought someone along as a contingency plan too," he added. Darkslash felt no threat from Timaeus' words at all.

"Nice try, Windslash," he replied. "You already told me that you've lost everyone who was once your friend and like family to you. This crystal isn't meant for escaping the island; I intend to seal myself inside it. Once Atlantis sinks, it will be found who knows how many years from now, and I will be released to fulfil the archmage's prophecy and resurrect Leviathan."

Unbeknownst to Darkslash, Stratos had just walked in. He held up the black crystal and spoke: "Sfragíste To Fýlaka Mésa," causing the crystal to begin glowing. "I never said my contingency was a human," Timaeus added, bringing a worried look to Darkslash's face.

He turned around to find Stratos rearing up on his back legs and letting out a slow and angry cry. In that moment, Timaeus ran towards Darkslash and tackled him to the ground. During their struggle, Timaeus managed to restrain Darkslash beneath Stratos and grabbed hold of the Griffin's talon. Once the crystal was fully activated, the three of them were sealed inside it because Timaeus had contact with both Darkslash and Stratos. The crystal lay on the ground in the remains of the Royal Court. Moments later, the palace was underwater, and Atlantis was lost to the seas forever.

Chapter Eighteen
10,000 Years Later

With Atlantis now lost to the seas forever, the Elementals were all but extinct, except for the last Elemental, who was trapped inside a magic crystal along with his loyal friend and his arch-nemesis. They were accompanied by the four Dragon Crests, while Leviathan's Urn remained encased in stone at the bottom of the ocean. Any Atlanteans who survived the invasion and managed to escape the island, those who managed to brave the storm, reached the mainland to the east, close to the Atlas Mountains. Continuing on foot, they eventually found a place they could call home, which is known today as Greece. When the Atlanteans arrived, it was during a time of developing primitive human proto-communities. With the assistance of the Atlanteans and the knowledge and resources they brought from their homeland, these communities were able to improve significantly over the course of nearly a millennium.

For nearly four thousand years, with the assistance of the Atlantean Descendants and the knowledge of their ancestors, agricultural societies were established. This led to the development of the first organized communities and advancements in basic art, culminating in a period known as the Bronze Age. The Atlantean Descendants played a crucial role in this transition to a metal-based economy by sharing their ancestors' blacksmithing skills and introducing Greece to bronze tools. This exchange facilitated the creation of complex urban societies, enabling cultures and civilizations to thrive for over two thousand years.

Unfortunately, this prosperous period came to an abrupt end due to a sudden, violent, and culturally disruptive societal collapse. However, with the continued support of the Atlantean Descendants and their shared ancestral knowledge, Greece managed to recover. After five hundred years, a new era known as the Iron Age began, introducing Greece not only to iron tools but also to iron weapons, thanks to the blacksmithing secrets of Atlantis.

One hundred years later, the philosophy introduced by the Atlantean Descendants was used to make sense of the world through reason, continuing to do so for over seven thousand years into the present day.

The only mistake the Atlanteans and their descendants made was sharing their secrets of Magic and the knowledge of magical creatures. Although Magic brought great benefits to Greece for over seven thousand years, it came at a significant cost. While some used Magic to build and improve communities, others resorted to Dark Magic, believing they were protecting these communities. Unfortunately, this often led to disastrous consequences, prompting divine intervention—some as retribution, some as forgiveness, and some as support. When the Atlanteans first arrived in Greece, they discovered magical creatures not native to Atlantis, such as the winged horse known as Pegasus, the half-man, half-horse known as the Centaur, the half-man, half-beast known as the Satyr, the winged lion with a scorpion's tail known as the Manticore, and the one-eyed giant known as the Cyclops.

Many of the creatures known to Atlantis were also found elsewhere, and the Atlanteans, along with their descendants, attempted to tame these creatures as Timaeus successfully did with a Griffin, hoping they would help protect Greece. However, they never encountered a Minotaur. This changed due to an Atlantean Descendant named Daedalus, who was both a skilled architect and craftsman.

Utilizing Magic, Daedalus discovered a way to use feathers from a Pegasus' wings to create a pair of wings that he attached to his son Icarus, allowing him to fly. Additionally, Daedalus found a method for a Minotaur to be born. Through the use of Dark Magic, he engineered a way for a magical bull to mate with Pasiphaë, the Sorceress Goddess.

Although a Minotaur was successfully born, it could not be controlled and was imprisoned in a labyrinth that Daedalus constructed for this very purpose.

An Atlantean Descendant, whose name has been lost to history, attempted to tame a Chimera using Dark Magic. This risky endeavour resulted in the Chimera giving birth to two equally deadly creatures. In response to this threat, Poseidon, the God of the Seas, and Zeus, the King of the Gods, intervened.

Eurynome, another Atlantean Descendant and the Queen of Corinth, had an affair with the God of the Seas, which led to the birth of the demigod Bellerophon. Meanwhile, Danae, also an Atlantean Descendant and part of the Argive Royal Family, had a liaison with the King of the Gods, resulting in the birth of the demigod Perseus.

However, Poseidon's actions did not go unnoticed. His lover, the Gorgon known as Medusa, discovered his infidelity and sought vengeance against the Atlantean Descendants and anyone who obstructed her path, transforming them into stone with her gaze.

Both Perseus and Bellerophon grew up to be celebrated Greek heroes and slayers of monsters. Bellerophon defeated the Chimera, putting an end to its reign of terror and preventing it from giving birth to more deadly creatures. Meanwhile, Perseus slayed Medusa, stopping her vengeful attacks on the Atlantean Descendants. Although these two monsters were vanquished, many more remained to be dealt with. One of the Chimera's offspring, known as the Sphinx, was defeated by an Atlantean Descendant named Oedipus, who solved the Sphinx's riddle. Aethra, another Atlantean Descendant and a member of the Troezenian Royal Family, had an affair with the God of the Seas, resulting in the birth of the demigod Theseus. He also became a Greek hero by slaying the Minotaur. The last Atlantean Descendant to have an affair with a God was Alcmene, who was also the granddaughter of Perseus.

She had an affair with the King of the Gods, which resulted in the birth of the demigod Heracles, who would become known as the greatest of all Greek heroes, but at a significant cost. Driven mad by Zeus' wife, Hera, Heracles tragically murdered his own family. To atone for his actions, Heracles was required to complete twelve impossible tasks, known as the Labors of Heracles. Most of these tasks involved slaying deadly creatures.

The first labour was to defeat the Nemean Lion, a monstrous offspring of the Chimera. His second labour required him to kill a Hydra that had been subjected to Dark Magic by the descendants of Atlantis in order to control it, which came to be known as the Lernaean Hydra. Other creatures that he encountered during his twelve labours included the Ceryneian Hind, the Erymanthian Boar, the Stymphalian Birds, the Cretan Bull, the Mares of Diomedes, and Cerberus.

It remains uncertain how many of the creatures were offspring of the Chimera that had been attempted to be controlled with Dark Magic. The only creatures confirmed to be unrelated to the Chimera were the Cretan Bull, as it was the father of the Minotaur, and Cerberus, which served as the guard dog of the underworld and existed long before the

Chimera. After Heracles dealt with these threats, a group of magical practitioners of Atlantean descent took it upon themselves to ensure that Magic would never be misused or fall into the wrong hands again. This effort led Greece into a dark age, resulting in a decline in both population and literacy. Traditionally, the Greeks have blamed this decline on the Greek citizens of Atlantean descent. As Magic was kept hidden away, the Greek Dark Ages lasted for three hundred years, eventually giving way to a period known as the Archaic Period, which lasted for three hundred and eighty years.

During this time, the Greek alphabet and early Greek literature emerged alongside the development of the city-states in Ancient Greece. The Greeks also expanded to the shores of the Black Sea, Southern Italy, and Asia Minor. Toward the end of this period, the Persian Empire invaded the Greek territories twice, seeking the secrets of Magic. This conflict led to the Greco-Persian Wars. However, the Greeks managed to defend themselves using their knowledge of Magic, which helped them overcome the Persian Empire on both occasions. After the second invasion, the Archaic period came to an end, giving way to the Classical period, which lasted for one hundred and fifty-seven years. This era was crucial for the foundations of mathematics, science, artistic thought, theatre, literature, philosophy, and politics that shaped Western civilization.

During the Greco-Persian Wars, the use of Magic played a significant role in overcoming the Persian Empire. This led to a prolonged conflict between Athens and Sparta, known as the Peloponnesian War, which lasted almost thirty years and remained unresolved until the Persian Empire intervened in support of Sparta. This intervention altered the balance of power in the ancient Greek world, making Sparta the leading power in Greece. Despite this shift, the Greek city-states ensured that the Persian Empire would not gain access to Magic, keeping it hidden away.

The Classical period came to an end with the death of Alexander the Great, a king of Atlantean descent. Following this, the Hellenistic period began, lasting for one hundred and seventy-seven years. During this time, the significance of "Greek proper" within the Greek-speaking world sharply declined.

The Hellenistic civilization expanded Greek culture beyond Greece. Two of the major centres of Hellenistic culture were Antioch in Seleucid Syria and Alexandria in Ptolemaic Egypt. Alexandria was founded by Alexander the Great just eight years before his death and became the second-largest city in Egypt.

Twenty-two years before the end of the Hellenistic period, Macedonia came under Roman control following the defeat of King Perseus at the Battle of Pydna. This was followed by the Achaean War, which was fought between the Greek Achaean League and the Roman Empire. At this time, only a few descendants of Atlanteans had access to Magic. Since one Empire sought to control Magic and was unwilling to let it fall into the hands of another, they opted not to resist with Magic.

After the defeat of the Greeks at the Battle of Corinth, Greece was conquered by the Roman Republic, marking the end of the Hellenistic period. This led to the establishment of a new era known as Roman Greece, which lasted for four hundred and seventy years.

Greek culture continued to thrive during this period, and Roman society adopted many aspects of it. Poets often retold and incorporated Greek myths, blending them into Roman culture. Romans even claimed a cultural lineage with Greece, especially highlighted in their founding myth that depicted the Roman people as descendants of the Trojan Aeneas. This connection allowed Atlantean Descendants to conceal themselves and their Magic in plain sight.

With the aid of foresight, it was revealed that Greece would not remain under the control of the Roman Republic indefinitely and that it would one day be reclaimed by the Greeks. Unfortunately, after four hundred and seventy years, this prediction did not come to fruition. Although the Roman conquest eventually ended, it transitioned into a period known as Byzantine Greece, marking the beginning of Medieval Greece.

During this time, Greece came under the control of the Byzantine Empire, which lasted for over eleven hundred years. Almost nine hundred years into this period, a new era known as Frankish/Latin Greece began, marked by the establishment of several primarily French and Italian states on Byzantine territory. This period came to an end as Byzantium experienced a gradual weakening of its internal structures and a reduction of its territories due to invasions by the Ottoman Empire, ultimately culminating in the fall of Constantinople. The Ottoman conquest of Constantinople marked the official end of both the Eastern Roman Empire and the Byzantine period of Greek history, leading to the Ottoman Greece period, which lasted almost three hundred and seventy years. When the Ottomans arrived, two significant Greek migrations occurred.

During the first wave of migration, the Greek intelligentsia moved to Western Europe. In the second wave, Greeks of Atlantean descent left the plains of the Greek peninsula and resettled in the mountains. There, they concealed any magical practices so that these abilities could be used when necessary without falling into the wrong hands.

During the Ottoman period of Greek history, the Greeks enjoyed some privileges and freedoms granted by the Empire, but they were also subjected to tyranny due to the malpractices of regional administrators. Eventually, after nearly two thousand years, a prophecy made by a Seer at the beginning of the Roman conquest of Greece came to fruition. This led to the official end of the Ottoman period and Medieval Greece, paving the way for Modern Greece, which continues to exist today.

The Greeks declared their independence, which sparked the Greek War of Independence. For the first eight years of Modern Greece, they revolted against the Ottoman Empire.

No magic was used against the Ottoman Empire due to the assistance from the British Empire, the Kingdom of France, and the Russian Empire. After eight years of conflict, Greece gained its independence from the Ottoman Empire. At the height of its cultural and geographical influence, Greek civilization and its emigrants assimilated into various societies around the world.

Nearly two and a half thousand years ago, a philosopher named Plato wrote about Atlantis in his works. Today, he is recognized as a Greek philosopher, but what many do not realize is that he was a descendant of Atlanteans. His writings mention 'Timaeus' and 'Critias,' but unfortunately, his accounts of 'Hermos' and 'Gorgas' have been lost to history.

Descendants of the Atlanteans still exist today, both in Greece and in other cultures. However, after Greece gained its independence, knowledge of their ancestors began to fade away, leading to Magic and the concept of Atlantis itself becoming little more than a myth.

For ten thousand years, the black crystal containing Timaeus and Darkslash drifted within the ocean's waters until it eventually washed up on a beach in a country known as the United Kingdom. On a hot summer evening, with a beautiful sunset painting the sky, a young red-haired woman was walking along the beach with her dog, a female black Labrador. The dog was running around playfully along the shore.

"Lola!" the young woman called out, wanting to make sure her dog didn't wander too far. Lola raced past her, caught up in her playful mood, and headed toward the shoreline where the black crystal lay. After sniffing around it, Lola picked it up in her mouth.

"Lola!" the young woman shouted again, urging her to come back. This time, Lola walked quickly back to her owner, the crystal still in her grasp.

As she approached the young woman, Lola sat down and began to whimper. "What do you have there, Lola?" the young woman asked, kneeling down to get a closer look. She gently took the black crystal from Lola, who continued to whimper quietly. As she held the crystal in her hands, Greek words—Απελευθερώστε τα από μέσα—began to glow on its surface. Unbeknownst to the young woman, these glowing words represented a spell to release those trapped within the black crystal.

Timaeus' Vision:

Before Timaeus entered the palace to confront the Primordials, he drank from his Enchanted Chalice to gain foresight and determine if Atlantis had a chance of survival. However, he was horrified by the vision he experienced.

In the vision, Timaeus saw himself in a town with architecture completely different from that of Atlantis—unfamiliar and strange. Moments later, the vision shifted, and he found himself battling an assassin who was his equal in ordinary combat but was no match for his Magic.

Shortly after that, the vision changed again, revealing Timaeus walking through the rain. However, instead of ordinary raindrops, he saw that they burst into flames upon hitting the ground.

The next vision shows Timaeus facing a Chimera, but this one possesses different animal heads. He also witnessed people drowning in sorrow, yet something seemed to keep their hope alive.

Afterwards, Timaeus experienced visions of poisonous substances unknown to Atlantis—substances that could kill more quickly than the venom of a Chimera's Tail. He then saw images of people being exploited through their suffering. Another vision depicted people providing various services. In each of these changes, a rose of a different colour appeared.

Finally, Timaeus soon found himself back in the town he had seen at the beginning of the vision. This time, however, there was a giant sea serpent in the background. On the ground in front of him lay a black rose and a white rose. He also heard a male voice proclaiming, "This is how things work in the criminal underworld."

When Timaeus emerged from the vision, only a few seconds had passed, but he felt as if he had witnessed the underworld and that there was no hope for survival. Yet, he understood that the world would be protected from Leviathan because it would be sent there. However, the true meaning of these visions remained unclear to Timaeus; what was he really seeing? It seems he has yet to find out...